DATE DUE

JA 2 '92			
JA 14'93			
AG 23'95			
SEP 8 2000			
AUG 0 2 2001			
AUG 0 5 2016			

DEMCO

MURDER ON MARTHA'S VINEYARD

DAVID OSBORN

BOOKS
York

For Robin, Raphaella and Sebastian, with love

This book is published by Lynx Books, a division of Lynx Communications, Inc., 41 Madison Avenue, New York, New York, 10010. The name "Lynx" together with the logotype consisting of a stylized head of a lynx is a trademark of Lynx Communications, Inc.

Printed in the United States of America

PROLOGUE

That innocent night eight years ago was, I suspect, the point at which my life took a turn that eventually culminated seven years later in the awful horror of last summer. Out of sheer loneliness, I attended a lecture at New York University on Washington Square. The subject was "Retirement Options for the Single Woman." I remember the hall as though yesterday; it was a large schoolroom, really, with uncomfortable wooden chairs in uneven rows and, in spite of the bitter chill of a New York City early-March night, stuffily hot and uncomfortable with the heat turned up much too high.

I remember the lecturer even better—a sexless, boring, and balding little man of fifty-odd years with a doctorate and other smug letters after his name. He was totally depressing about his subject. The one option he never mentioned, as his voice droned on and on and on, was living; he regarded the retired woman, in fact any retired person, as over the hill and finished.

He showed a lot of slides and when he paused to

change cartridges, turning up the lights a moment, I looked around at the audience; every person was taking copious notes. They were all women approaching or past the age of fifty: widows, late-life divorcées, career-women spinsters. Although clearly from a variety of backgrounds, their expressions were identical. Each face reflected lost hope of ever again enjoying either romance or adventure. I suddenly could see them all on vacation; a clubby group of gray-haired ladies packed into a tour bus and being guided around Williamsburg, or attending all together, in a block booking, a summer concert at Tanglewood. Worse, I could see myself as one of them.

My name is Margaret Barlow. I am a widow and admit to being in my mid- to late fifties only if forced to—what woman wouldn't stop short of fifty itself if she thought she could get away with it? I was once naturally light blond, although recently an element of gray, I regret to say, has made me indulge in a certain amount of streaking at my hairdresser's when I go to get it cut. I am average height, perhaps a little taller, and was once quite slender—willowy, I believe the expression used to be—with a full bosom and good legs. I still don't look too bad; vestiges of more carefree days cling to me, thank heaven, although time has brought about a slight broadening of the hips and a little lower bust silhouette, to say nothing of the indignity of a few wrinkles, especially around my eyes. I do my best with all of it—with clothes that are as fashionable as my budget will bear, with Jane Fonda workouts, good hand care, and low-key makeup. I skip lipstick, always have.

On the night of the lecture, my husband, George, had been dead a year, and I had already discovered that besides grief, if a woman has had a successful and happy marriage, as I had for twenty-five years, widowhood at any age brings other problems. She not only has to cope with a frightening scarcity of eligible men—they all seem to be either married, gay, chasing after pretty young things, permanently sunk into bachelorhood, or total rejects—but also she has to struggle with the fixed notions society has about her status. If a widow is serious and calm, the automatic assumption by most seems to be "hands off," because to approach her in her time of grief is to insult her, and, needless to say, the time of grief seems to go on forever. If, on the other hand, a widow is outgoing and cheerful, the opposite holds true. She is summarily regarded as frivolous and disrespectful of the sanctimony of marriage as well as the gaunt tragedy of death.

She can't win and she ends up in perpetual struggle; fighting to keep so busy she is too exhausted at night to feel alone; fighting to keep up old friendships from her marriage and having them slowly erode away—couples prefer couples; fighting not to be viewed as superfluous and in the way.

She also ends up desperately trying to disassociate herself as long as possible from the living death of the all-female sort of group I had joined that night. I still could not get used to being on my own, but staring around at my peers, I determined, if nothing else, to maintain an independent identity and vowed never to let myself be classified as someone for whom life was over.

I didn't sit through the whole lecture. I couldn't. Unable to look another moment at all those heads bent studiously and obediently over pencil and notepaper, I got up and walked out.

I had no plan, no thought. I was very tired and luckily caught a taxi immediately to take me back to my East Side apartment. It was a nice apartment; I'd lived in it for more than fifteen years, but every room emphasized "two," when now there was only "one." I planned to sell it as soon as possible. I took a shower, brushed my teeth, defiantly put on my prettiest nightgown, and went to bed, very much aware of my oneness.

I was reading a book, something by Proust if I remember correctly, and waiting for the eleven o'clock news when the phone rang.

"Mom?"

It was my married daughter, an overworked corporate lawyer in New York. She had children aged three and five, and she wasn't going to have enough time off from her job to get them out of the city for the summer. She wanted me to take them to the house George and I had bought years before at Edgartown on Martha's Vineyard, the loveliest of New England villages on that lovely magical island three miles off southern Cape Cod. The house, built in 1803, was a big, old, four-bedroom, white-clapboarded thing with green shutters. It had a large garden out back and a widow's walk with a view of all of Edgartown's inner harbor with its scores of moored yachts and sailboats. I planned, however, to sell it along with the apartment. I had got it into my head to travel, to see the whole world if possible, as a sort of aggressive antidote to my new social status.

But then minutes after I'd picked up the phone, my instincts as a mother had prevailed over my rebellion and I had very reluctantly surrendered to my daughter's request, with the strictest condition, however, that she order the children never to call me "Grandma," a title and role that didn't at all fit into my plans.

Yes, that was the beginning. What it all ultimately led to, you will see when I have finished my story. It was the beginning because, feeling fairly trapped, I went that year to Martha's Vineyard with an attitude, by way of compensation, that made me want to put myself at risk and never play anything safe before my time had come to do so.

Do I wish I had not? There is little point in regretting past actions. What's done is done. But with any insight into the future and confronted again with setting myself up for what ultimately was to become horror upon horror, I most certainly would have chosen otherwise.

ONE

Murder, I was to learn during last summer's terrible events, is a most sordid and unpleasant business; the reality of unwanted and brutal death is a far cry from the romanticized and impersonal corpse of a mystery story and nothing at all like dispassionately reading about it in the morning newspaper. The gray-white pallor of features often contorted into horrible ugliness, the unnatural position of the limbs, the stiff coldness of the flesh, the sickly browning color of congealed or half-congealed blood, and, above all, the very smell of violent death, are all terrifying, especially if the deceased is someone you know.

But at Woods Hole on New England's Cape Cod that lovely morning early last June, while I waited for the car ferry to Martha's Vineyard, murder was the furthest thing from my mind, although I was soon to find myself embroiled in more murder of a more ghastly nature than I could ever have thought possible.

I was not alone; I had with me my grandchildren.

Seven years had passed since that first summer when I agreed to take them to the Vineyard, and Christopher was now a normally rambunctious ten and Nancy a quiet and speculative young lady of twelve. The aging-grandmother trap I had feared had surprisingly turned out not to be a trap at all. In fact, from day one the situation had turned out just the opposite. Everyone except old friends who knew better soon came to regard the children as mine, produced by me late in life; supermarket clerks, new summer neighbors, the local police, and beach lifeguards all made the same assumption. Even old friends after a while began to refer to Nancy and Christopher as "your two little ones."

Unbelievably, I found myself reliving the early years of my marriage as I arranged playtimes for "my children" with the children of "other mothers" and found myself talking of the P.T.A., television rules, tooth fairies, and everything else included in the vocabulary and life-style of the youthful parent. To my surprise, the first summer, years ago, initiated a second at the end of which I found myself in tears returning the children to their real mother and eagerly looking forward to a third.

The subsequent years began to fly by. Soon I had a part-time job helping out in Doris Ketteridge's Edgartown Craft Shop. The children no longer went to play-school mornings; now they attended sailing classes. There were beach parties for their friends. I lived.

Perhaps the greatest boost I got, however, had nothing to do with the children themselves. It happened that miraculous day the first summer with the children when I met Essie Peck, a lifelong year-round Martha's Vineyard resident, and we embarked together on the incredible adventure of becoming balloonists. Yes, balloonists! Can you imagine? Two independent ladies, young in spirit only, soaring at ten thousand feet! Well, that's Essie and I, and so much for lectures on retirement options. But more later about dear Essie, how we met and discovered ballooning, and how during the intervening years it changed our lives so drastically.

At the ferry dock, I had left Christopher and Nancy guarding my heavily ladened station wagon and had gone to buy some doughnuts and orange juice from a bakery just up the road from the ticket office. It was eight-thirty, and we hadn't had breakfast yet.

I was only halfway back when I heard them calling excitedly, "Margaret! Margaret! The ferry's here. Hurry up!"

They were right. Where ten minutes before there had been only water between the two high walls of weathered-gray pilings that made up the ferry slip, there was now a sizable steamer, the *Islander*, already disgorging from its bow a veritable stream of trucks and cars returning from Martha's Vineyard to the mainland.

The children dragged me back to where we were wedged between lines of other cars simmering in the early-June heat as they waited to take the place of those leaving the boat. Motors had started, doors slammed, anxious mothers rounded up their little ones, fathers whistled for family dogs, vacationing couples glowed as they began momentary freedom. A few minutes later, we drove into the ferry's cool cavernous interior, a clean shipshape world of white pillars and bulkheads and a red deck of hard solid iron, and made our way upstairs to the top. There, ignoring scores of waiting chairs soon to be filled by other drivers and those many passengers who came aboard on foot, we went to the rail to look out on the small harbor of Woods Hole; at a famous Oceanographic Institute ship recently come home from probing the deep; at the rocky little islets that marked the harbor's entrance; at the red "nuns" and black "cans," and buoys that indicated the channel.

A slight early breeze had come up, here and there darkening with fresh ruffles of "cats' paws" the smooth mirrored surface of the blue-gray water. Over the deep rumbling vibration of the ferry's big engines far below us I could hear the familiar "chug-chug-chug" of a small lobster boat as it made its way in from collecting traps out in the sound. The sun was warm and promising, the sea air sheer perfume.

I hugged the children to me, hearing but not listening to their chatter. I wasn't thinking at all, really, not even of the pleasant hour's voyage ahead of us before we'd dock at Vineyard Haven on the north side of the island and then drive fifteen minutes east to Edgartown. This was one of those moments when the spirit soars and you only *feel*; when it seems nothing in the world will ever change. Moments like that should be cherished and put away somewhere in one's mind and never forgotten.

The trip across Vineyard Sound was uneventful except for Christopher's spilling an entire plastic cup of Coca-Cola down the back of Nancy's freshly laundered blouse with all the subsequent brother–sister havoc that ensued. The *Islander* arrived at Vineyard Haven a little after ten. The children and I drove directly to Edgartown, taking the shore road that runs from the old summer spa of Oak Bluffs with its fine array of Victorian architecture and along the east coast past Senegekontucket Pond, a mile-long body of shallow salt water separated from Nantucket Sound only by a beach and a causeway. The full summer season had not yet started, and traffic was light.

Martha's Vineyard, if you haven't had the good fortune ever to go there, is a sizable island some eighteen miles long and ten miles wide at its widest point. Together with its rival sister island, Nantucket, to the east, it forms a sort of last bastion against the vast reaches of the Atlantic beyond.

The Vineyard was settled by Englishmen in 1602. Thanks to friendly Indians, the area thrived and in the nineteenth century sent out an important whaling fleet to join other intrepid globe-circling Yankees from neighboring New England seaports such as New Bedford, Fall

River, Gloucester, and Nantucket. Now it is an enormously popular summer resort with excellent small-craft facilities at the fishing port of Menemsha up-island to the west, at the busy town of Vineyard Haven, and at Edgartown, where a quaint little three-car open ferry shuttles endlessly back and forth all summer long across the narrow harbor entrance to Chappaquiddick. This famous almost-island is connected only by a thread of dunes to the rest of Martha's Vineyard. A relatively unsettled area, its mostly deserted eastern beaches, several miles off across a cover of pine and scrub oak and the occasional farm, are wild and breathtakingly beautiful.

The Vineyard, or "Island" as it is called by locals, is flat in some parts, hilly in others. At Chilmark, a large rural township to the west, its highest point is about three hundred feet, and at Gay Head, its westernmost tip, a famous lighthouse above high multicolored clay cliffs warns continent-bound navigators of dangerous shoals. Its southerly beaches, like those of Chappaquiddick, are spectacular; mile after long straight mile of empty white sand shoulder the full sweep of the Atlantic. Between the beaches and higher ground, rolling dunes and saltwater marshes are a haven for birds of all kinds from land-bound hawks to seagoing cormorants. The interior, mostly rural with occasional small villages, is shared by woodlands, farms, and open land, once sheep pastures, and is crisscrossed by ancient hoary stone walls. Here among scattered thicket, wild grapes, blueberry and huckleberry bushes abound, while Queen Anne's lace, goldenrod, blueflower, bittersweet, black-eyed Susan, and pasture rose mingle their soft scents with the fresh smell of salt air, kelp, and sand to create an unforgettable fragrance.

It all adds up to indefinable magic, an atmosphere of sky and space and refuge from the rest of the world and to a sense of intimacy that is seductively unique.

My home was on South Water Street, well away

from the bustle of Edgartown's Main Street, which, during the full summer season, is more often than not jammed with people and traffic. Amos Samuel, a whaling captain, built the house, and George jokingly used to call it "Sam's Place," a title I am not certain would have set well with the wealthy originator, reported in town records to have been a God-fearing churchgoer of great moral righteousness who sired seventeen children by three wives, all of whom suffered him widowerhood for his pains.

I had called Essie from New York to say when I'd be arriving, and she had come down from her little saltbox cottage near Menemsha the day before to open the house for me, as she did every year, and put some basic groceries in the refrigerator. I was disappointed on entering the front hall to find her note saying she would be tied up until after lunch with the sale of some property, one of two small fields she owned up in Chilmark and adjacent to the home of Grace Chadwick, around whom much of my story centers. I knew only too well where the money from the sale would end up and that I would have to match it with an equivalent sum of my own, probably from an increase on the mortgage I had taken on my house last year.

I felt guilty about that mortgage, almost as though I'd stolen something. Ballooning was becoming more and more expensive and more addicting. Essie and I, both usually thrifty, were spending far too much. The previous year we had finally saved enough money to buy our own rig: a beautiful seventy-seven-thousand-cubic-foot lime-green, azure-blue, and pale yellow sleeve with a two-person willow-wicker gondola and a heat-generating propane burner unit to be fed by sixty-liter bottles pressurized at a hundred pounds per square inch. That coming autumn, we planned a trip down the Loire River in France, stopping off whenever we felt like it at French country inns to sample the best food in France.

With some difficulty, I dismissed ballooning from my mind and turned to getting the children settled in. As usual, it took a while. It never ceases to amaze me how a place you leave in perfect order in the fall can become, all on its own during the winter, something you have to straighten up again in the spring. The children, reneging on the help they were supposed to be giving me, rushed about rediscovering things and places they'd almost forgotten during the winter: the attic with its old toys, skateboards and fishing rods in the downstairs hall closet, a badly weathered soccer ball that had been left on the back lawn at the end of last summer and miraculously was still there, beach equipment, paddling boards, and lastly, of course, the television set.

"You come away from that thing at once, both of you. There's still a great deal to be done."

"Aw, Margaret."

"At once! And put your suitcases away in the attic."

"Aw . . ."

After I'd made the beds and fixed them a sandwich lunch, I dashed to the A&P on Upper Main Street to stock up for dinner and tomorrow's breakfast and then went on to the Harbor Bookstore to order my daily and Sunday *New York Times*. I was suddenly tired and depressed. Changing residence always does that to me, even when I go to a familiar place. I have a disorienting sense of being uprooted. In the past three years as the children got older, I'd found the summer migration to Martha's Vineyard more and more exhausting. It was never until I was fully settled in that I began to feel myself again.

Peter deBord was back behind the cash register as the Harbor Bookstore summer manager. I think I just stood and stared at him a moment. I couldn't believe how he'd changed during his last year at college. Always handsome, he was suddenly no longer a college boy but a very beautiful young man with a mane of dark curly hair, rugged features, piercing blue eyes, and the tall, powerful, long-muscled body of a swimmer. The local girls couldn't take their eyes away from him, I noticed. What female could? In his shorts and polo shirt, with his slender bronzed legs, he was every woman's secret fantasy.

"I'm all finished at Michigan, Mrs. Barlow. Next January I go to Yale for a master's degree in fine arts. How are your children?"

"They're fine, Peter." I congratulated him on finishing school and told him to start calling me Margaret. He grinned and said that suited him fine and told me I looked sixteen as usual and complimented me on my dress. "The color suits you perfectly." I blushed—can you imagine?— like one of the town girls who really was sixteen, and I came out of the bookstore floating on air. My depression had completely disappeared.

Back home, I had hardly begun to put things away when the doorbell rang. I could hear the children somewhere upstairs; in the attic, I guessed. I had my arms full of oranges and shouted, "Could one of you get the door?"

There wasn't any answer. *Oh, damn*, I thought, and hurried to free my hands, wipe them off on a kitchen towel, and head for the hallway and the front door.

But I never got there. Heather Mikele, tired of waiting, had let herself in and there she stood in the kitchen doorway, looking her usual wide-eyed waiflike self, her dark eyes shining warmth and welcome to me, her twin daughters behind her looking fresh and lovely in their summer dresses and smiling delightedly.

I threw open my arms, and all three rushed into my embrace.

TWO

I had met Heather four years previous at an exhibition of her husband's paintings. Algar, who had been a psychologist before turning painter, was a tall, dark-bearded, and brooding Upper West Side New Yorker, which is where the Mikeles live in the wintertime. I was never surprised that his work was not particularly successful. His canvases always looked to me as though someone had done nothing more than indiscriminately squeeze tubes of paint on them. I didn't care that much for Algar personally, either. There was too much ego there for my liking. Although Heather and his daughters clearly adored him, I found him repressively uncommunicative and I suspected him of having a vicious temper.

I took an immediate liking to Heather, however. Always thin and pale and tired-looking, she had dark eyes and long dark hair that she usually wore down her back in a braid that reached below her waist. She had slender hands, delicate wrists and ankles, and a lovely slender figure, too, but she wore very plain tent dresses and most of the summer went barefoot. There was something of the hippie about Heather, which I rather enjoyed. Her twins, Angela and Judith, who looked just like their mother, were midway between Christopher and Nancy in age, and all four became friends.

I suppose Heather more than anyone represented young motherhood to me, but that's not what made me like her so much. It was her character I found attractive. There was something very strong and loyal and good about her. And plucky. She had stood by Algar Mikele through thick and thin and with a smile while their lot, as each year passed, grew harder and harder.

Their trouble—disaster is really the only way to describe it—began the first year I came to the Vineyard. They had already spent several summers there and loved it so much that they wanted to move from New York and live there all year round. Then one day, wandering about, Algar came across a huge old Victorian house we all knew well on Tea Lane, a backcountry dirt road in Chilmark. It was called March House (although nobody knew why) and belonged to the Grace Chadwick I have mentioned, who was an elderly spinster and recluse from an old Boston family of some social standing. With the house there were some dozen acres, mostly woods, part of which backed onto Essie Peck's two fields and most of the rest onto the run-down farm of Owen Fuller, a local bad character. Algar fell in love with the place immediately.

Grace, seventy at that time, was very ill and rumored to be dying of cancer, although old Dr. Meyrick—now dead—would never confirm it for certain. To everyone's astonishment, and ignoring the protests of Arthur Heston, her financial advisor and Boston bank trustee of her inherited income, she sold March House to Algar for forty-five thousand dollars—a good price then—while retaining the right to live in it for the rest of her days. I at first suspected she might have had a soft spot for Heather and the twins, but most people disagreed and

DAVID OSBORN

Essie, who had once known her well, said that Grace more likely wanted some money unencumbered by Heston's "sensible" guiding hand with which to enjoy, unrestricted, her last year or so of life, and who could ever blame her?

Then, incredibly, as if in warning to all who would presume to read the future, Grace did not die. Instead she recovered, or at least enjoyed remission. She went away late in November that year, as always, to a small house in Sarasota, Florida, and came back at Easter looking infinitely better. As each year that she continued to live went by, however, the value of her property rose in an unparalleled Martha's Vineyard land boom that put even the smallest property beyond the reach of most average families. And as property values went up, so did the rents demanded from Algar for whatever he and his family could find to occupy each summer.

Algar's earnings as a painter obviously were not enough to cope with this, and the fees he'd saved from his practice as a therapist had run out. The summer previous to my story, he had been close to going broke. His and his family's clothes were in rags, and their car was the same rusted-out Ford they'd had now for six years. Trapped, the Mikeles waited helplessly for fate to resolve their problem.

People asked why Algar didn't sell out his ownership to someone who'd have less pressure on him for Grace to die. The property was now worth nearly ten times what he'd paid for it, a small fortune.

"It isn't that easy," Heather had explained to me. "When we bought it from Grace, she wanted a sixty-day option to buy it back for twice what we paid her for it if we should ever decide to sell it. That was Arthur Heston finally getting his oar in and covering every possibility, with plans, I guess, as her trustee, to use her inheritance to do it with if the opportunity ever arose. We agreed because we hardly expected her to live, and that was that.

"But now, any time we get an offer, no matter from whom, Grace threatens to exercise her option. So word's got around the property can't be sold until she dies and nobody even asks anymore. It's terrible, Margaret. We can't afford mortgage payments, and lots of times we've thought of giving up and selling the damned house back to her no matter what it will be worth when she finally goes. She's told us she'll buy it back any time. But with everything now costing so much more, we'd hardly have enough after taxes to buy even some slum shack."

I hadn't bothered to ask why they didn't move to a place on the mainland where it was less expensive than on the Vineyard. I knew that there was pride involved, as well as monetary consideration. Any place other than the Vineyard would have seemed second-rate and a total defeat.

When I arrived last year, the Mikeles had already been there about ten days, and seeing the dark shadows under Heather's eyes, I was almost fearful to hear her news. I had to wait for a few minutes to ask, however. Nancy and Christopher had heard the twins—even though they couldn't hear *me*, naturally—and came racing downstairs, and the kitchen was instant bedlam.

When the noise finally died down a little and I got in my question, Heather shook her head sadly and managed a wry smile. "Grace is still alive, Margaret. The old woman's incredible! What is she now? Eighty? We saw her in Vineyard Haven yesterday, and she looked nearly as well as she did last year. There she was with all that powder and lipstick—can you imagine, a woman of her age? And the hat and scarf. You couldn't miss her."

I thought of Grace. She'd begun putting on makeup the moment her father died—her mother had died earlier—and going about as though trying to hide from the world. That was fifteen years before she'd contracted cancer. It was then that she also began to shut herself off from everyone, eventually even chasing old friends from her property and rarely being seen in town or at the local post office until finally most people had forgotten who she was.

"Some young guy was helping her cross Main Street," Heather said. "And even with two canes she was very nearly pulling him. I thought for a moment Algar was going to run her down. We were in our old car."

"Oh, dear," I said noncommittally, more for the children's benefit than for anything else.

I could have saved the tact. Christopher, never known for subtlety, at once burst out, "Jeepers! When's the old witch going to kick off, anyway?"

I snapped at him. "Christopher! Don't talk like that and don't use that expression."

"What expression?"

"You know perfectly well which one. Either of them, as long as you ask."

"But she's living in their house, Margaret," Nancy protested, "and not even all year round. She's away every winter."

"*Her* house, Nancy." Heather said it gently and with a smile. "Until she dies."

"*Not* 'kicks off,' Christopher," I said.

"Jeeps! Can't I even talk?"

"Not in that fashion about a poor sick old woman, who is, incidentally," I added, "not a witch, either."

"Well, she *is* a witch."

"Nonsense."

"She is, too, Margaret," Nancy insisted. "Last summer Angela said they saw her flying around at night, didn't you, Angela? They drove by once after dark, and she came tearing across the lawn in the moonlight and ran up onto the front porch." She turned to Angela again. "You said she had to be flying because she can hardly walk, remember?"

"I think Angela was exaggerating a little," Heather said.

"But, Mom, Judith saw her, too," Angela said.

"And so did you, Mom," Judith added.

"I never said I did," Heather replied. "I was busy driving. And it was probably just Owen Fuller."

I didn't doubt the children had seen somebody, but I also thought Heather was probably right. Very old women don't run, especially at night. I pictured Owen, Grace Chadwick's small, mean neighbor who always wore a strangely menacing black hat low over his forehead and who had fought for years with Grace over a livestock right-of-way he claimed he had across her lawn. He was forever hanging around her place just to annoy her, and in the dark from a moving car he could easily have been mistaken for a woman.

I decided we'd had enough of Grace. I shooed all the children outside and poured myself and Heather a cup of coffee and found out where she was living that summer. There was a run-down garage not very far away belonging to Ed Rupert, a bullying beer-drinker who kept company with the very bottom rung of Martha's Vineyard social life. The place was a mess and a graveyard, too, for burned-out cars and pickups cannibalized for still usable parts. At the rear of the garage where Rupert kept extra oil drums there was a small cement-block slum apartment, its exterior unpainted. What a terrible contrast to the lovely tree-lined streets and old colonial houses of the rest of Edgartown. I was shocked.

"Oh, no, Heather," I said. "You're not living there?"

"I'm afraid so."

"Does it have a bath?"

"The toilet is the one the garage uses. There's a cold shower outside." She was suddenly close to tears. "We almost stayed in New York this summer, but Rupert said he'd cut down the rent if Algar gave him a couple of days of work a week."

I thought of Algar. Regardless of how I personally felt about him, I thought how much lost pride he'd have to suffer for the horrible indignity of doing menial labor for a pig like Rupert, who would certainly take out on Algar all his resentment of any intelligence and education.

I said, "Last summer you told me you were going to talk to Grace to see if she wouldn't let you stay in the barn at March House, in the chauffeur's old apartment."

"Oh, but we did! Algar asked her two days ago. He drove by. She wouldn't come out and she wouldn't let him in, so he had to talk to her through a crack in the kitchen door and he talked himself blue and begged her."

"And?"

"And she said no. She said the children would make too much noise."

"But they wouldn't," I protested. "Not yours. They'd make far less than most children of their age. And the apartment is at the very back of the barn. For her to hear them in the house, they'd have to be screaming their lungs out or playing Angela's 'ghetto-blaster' full volume. Besides, Grace is away nearly half the year."

Heather shrugged helplessly. "What can we do? That's the way she is. And she said that even if she agreed, Arthur Heston wouldn't let her because of the old Lincoln."

I exploded. "Oh, for God's sake!"

The Lincoln she referred to was a magnificent vintage limousine, bought, I believe, in the early twenties, and a sad reminder of better times in the Chadwick family. A properly liveried chauffeur once conveyed Grace's mother around in it. Now it was driven only once a year by Arthur Heston, who every summer vacationed on the island, staying at the exclusive Charlotte's Inn in Edgartown. The car was kept on blocks in the main part of the barn, and Heston would come to brush the winter's accumulation of dust from its lusterless black surface, switch its tires around and pump them up, fuel and oil it, and then take it for a brief spin down-island to Vineyard Haven and Edgartown before he put it away for another year.

I heard Heather say, "Grace said Arthur would be afraid the children might play with the car and hurt themselves somehow. And finally she said she wasn't dead yet anyway and slammed the door."

"Heather, did Algar tell her what this was costing you both? And the girls? And I don't just mean money."

A look of stubborn pride came over her. Her jaw tightened, and her eyes lit with a kind of proud defiance. "Algar isn't ever going to ask for mercy from anyone, leastways that woman. Nor am I."

I felt sick. I think it was right then that I resolved to try to talk to Grace myself and see if I couldn't persuade her to relent. What better thing for her than to have someone living close at hand to help her if she got into trouble and to let a little light into the old place? I was certain I could persuade Algar to clean up the grounds, which were badly neglected, perhaps even to paint March House itself. But I didn't get the chance to tell Heather that. The phone rang. It was Essie, sounding mildly indignant.

"What are you doing? Are you coming up?"

I started to tell her I couldn't possibly when Heather, guessing who it was, interrupted to say she'd love to take the kids to the beach for the afternoon if I wanted to run up-island to Menemsha. Heather had none of the jealousy problem where I was concerned that Essie had. From the first day I met Heather, Essie regarded her as a threat to our ballooning, although I think the real reason she had it in for Heather was a sort of sublimated envy of both Heather's and my virtually shared motherhood. Essie was an old maid and had little use for men, babies, runny-nosed toddlers, or young mothers gossiping at the supermarket. She had also taken an instant dislike to Algar the moment she met him.

"That man is bad news," she said. "Be careful, Margaret. Be very careful. I wouldn't trust him around the corner."

I told Essie I'd be over in an hour, and when I'd hung up I gave Heather a thank-you kiss. "You really are an angel," I said.

She laughed. "No. I just think your ballooning is the most marvelous thing in the world, and you deserve the afternoon of planning with Essie I'm sure you must have been looking forward to all spring."

Neither Christopher nor Nancy thought so when we told them. They were as jealous of Essie as Essie was of Heather.

"Aw, gee. I knew it. Stupid balloons."

Before I could feel guilty, Nancy chimed in. "Christopher!" she exclaimed with her best attempt at adolescent sarcasm. "If Margaret wants to fall out of a balloon a hundred miles up and get squashed, that's her business."

"Thank you, Nancy," I said. "But I shan't do either. Nobody balloons from here, as you well know. One switch of wind and I'd end up in the mid-Atlantic."

"Fish food." Christopher's ghoulish smile showed a row of newly placed braces.

Ten minutes later, I was on my way to Menemsha.

THREE

The Vineyard is divided into six large areas, mostly rural and known as "towns." I drove through the lovely rolling farmlands of West Tisbury, well up-island and on the way to Chilmark, which I've already mentioned, to a crossroads in its middle, a village of the same name consisting of not much more than a church, a library, a town hall, a store, and a school.

From there, I headed via the shortest route to Menemsha, taking the narrow macadam Middle Road, which passed through the town center of Chilmark at Beetlebung Corners and which, like West Tisbury, is nothing more than a handful of community buildings.

Naturally I was thinking of Essie, and my mind went back to our first rather enchanted meeting seven years previous and my first summer with the children, then to all the marvelous times we'd had ever since. Whether fighting or laughing, there hadn't been a dull moment in years.

It started with a dreadfully boring Garden Club

party at The Rookery, Rose Perkins's Chilmark summer home. Rose, then in her mid-fifties and long divorced and single, was the archetypal social snob with a spoiled teenaged daughter, Estelle, just entering college. She had sold part of her lovely property, situated in high fields with a view of the distant sea, to Ann Alfreda, the now slightly fading movie star recently separated from the governor of California, and Miss Alfreda planned to build on it.

Rose could talk of nothing but "darling Ann," and, thoroughly bored, I had escaped for a few minutes to wander down to the end of the lawn beyond the pool.

There, staring through a nest of purple lupins bordering an old lichen-covered wall that held back a half-grown-up field scattered with less-exotic wildflowers, I suddenly became aware of an elfin face nearly nut-brown from years of sun and capped with short straight gray-black hair. Amused dark brown eyes stared back at me. Then a cultured voice spoke. "Impossible, isn't she? Rose, I mean, with her ridiculous celebrity fixation." And Essie, all five-foot-two of her, climbed back over the wall from the field.

"I followed this little miss into the nest of a lace spider," she said. "A female spring azure, I believe." She uncupped a garden-worn hand, releasing its fragile pale-blue prisoner. "There you are, my darling. Freedom!"

The butterfly flitted lightly off into the warm afternoon sunshine. "I am most grateful to it," Essie continued matter-of-factly. "It led me to a splendid bed of wild rosemary, see?"

She dropped an uprooted rosemary plant into her shoulder bag, a wicker fisherman's creel as out of keeping with the party we'd both fled as her plain brown oxford shoes and her faded country gingham dress; indeed as Essie herself was, all bones and tendons and stringy muscles from a life of country householding and hard work outdoors as well, digging and turning soil, and lobstering, too.

Keys had fallen through a large hole in the creel and were lying in the grass. I picked them up for her and began talking when Essie suddenly interrupted, staring at the sky.

"Oh, look! Do!" she cried. "Oh, how splendid!" Her eyes were as wide and wondering as a child's. "Oh, oh, oh!"

High in the sky to the north, across Vineyard Sound, Cape Cod way, there was a blot of color, a slowly drifting hot-air balloon. We could just make out the gondola hanging below it. Someone on the mainland had made a mistake, misjudged the wind, or perhaps whimsically the wind had simply changed direction, as it does sometimes on the Cape, and the balloon was drifting out to sea with only Martha's Vineyard between it and an eventual watery grave. Of course, the pilot released air a half hour later and landed harmlessly on a farm in Chilmark not far from Rose's.

With that, the two of us spontaneously made the decision to embark on the miraculous adventure of ballooning. We left the party for Pebbles, Essie's weathered little saltbox cottage that stood just up from a narrow half-moon beach at the head of that large shallow tidal basin known as Nashaquitsa Pond. Across even larger Menemsha Pond beyond it was the lovely old fishing port of Menemsha itself, with its wharves and trawling fleet, Essie's view of them only partially blocked by the rotting forty-foot hulk of the *Janet B*, a once hardworking fellow boat beached by a hurricane some years previous.

We had herbal tea—Essie was an herbologist extraordinaire—in her low-ceilinged kitchen with its old coal stove and its shelves crowded with detective stories by the score with which she passed long winter evenings and with herbs and jars of "put-by" vegetables, jams, and jellies. We drank our tea from cup after old blue cup that Essie kept filling from a matching teapot seamed with ancient cracks and as faded as her country dress.

We'd hardly mentioned ballooning when suddenly neither of us could contain ourselves any longer. We both burst out at once, "Let's do it," and "Why not?", and "It can't be that difficult. Why, the pilot of that thing must have been seventy."

"My daughter tried it on her honeymoon," I ventured. "In England. She said it was like a dream. The earth just unrolls beneath you, she said, like a toy world, and you can hear every sound, dogs barking and people talking, hundreds of feet below."

We drank yet another cup of tea, laced this time at Essie's insistence with a shot of elderberry brandy, and clinched our decision. We took our first flight that autumn, a pair of single ladies slightly out of their youth who within a year became bolder and bolder. Whenever we got the chance we ballooned anywhere we could. At first we stayed close to home but later traveled farther afield to Arizona in a stiff wind with the desert racing beneath us and Wyoming on a calm crystalline morning. Can you imagine the beauty of skimming slowly above treetops and low over snow-capped peaks reddened by sunrise?

And finally with our own balloon we planned romantic flights even farther afield—the French trip would be first, and then Essie started talking about even grander expeditions. "Serengeti, Margaret. All those great herds of zebra and wildebeest moving like the sea. Can you imagine?"

I could very well. It was thrilling. "We'll have to rob a bank," I said as humorously as possible, but I think I almost meant it.

Musing like that on Essie and ballooning, I suddenly saw the flashing blue and white lights of a police car in my rearview mirror and heard the wail of a siren. I thought for a moment I'd be stopped since I was ten miles an hour over the limit, but the lights weren't for me, and in a blast of air and sound the police cruiser rushed past. It was going like the devil, but I recognized the driver. It was Otis Cramm, one of Chilmark's local police officers, usually found hiding on side roads zapping motorists with the much-too-expensive radar gun he'd talked the town selectmen into buying for him.

Otis didn't do much else except endlessly read hunting and fishing magazines and send them semi-illiterate attempts at personal-experience stories they always rejected. He wasn't very bright. And when you saw him out of his uniform in overalls that were too short, leaving a gap of inches between their bottoms and the tops of his farm boots, and you looked at his always vacant face of which his little cookie-duster mustache was the sole indicator of mature masculinity, you wondered how he ever got to be a law officer. I suppose nobody else wanted the job. I knew his parents, respectable, first-rate fisherfolk who ran a deep-water trawler out of Menemsha. The son could never hope to match the grizzled old father in brains or in personality, or the mother, an expert sailmaker and fine seafood cook.

Almost more surprising than Otis was the continuing scream of another siren that came in his wake, and I'd hardly glanced in my mirror a second time when the Chilmark volunteer ambulance whooshed by, right on his tail. Wondering what had happened and to what poor person, I automatically eased my station wagon back to the legal speed limit. There was a long slow bend coming up. As I rounded it, I saw both ambulance and police car turn up Tea Lane, the country road that led past March House. It ran through my mind immediately that perhaps the trouble concerned Grace Chadwick—someone her age is always a worry. I wondered if she'd fallen or perhaps had suffered a heart attack, and I thought to follow along to see if I could help. But then I thought, *No, it's none of your business, Margaret. It could be any of a dozen people who live up there, or it could be that Otis and ambulance are taking a shortcut up to North Road and thus to a new development around Spring Pond.* I continued on toward the high open fields and downs of Chilmark with their glorious glimpses of the sea.

Ten minutes later, I had gone through Beetlebung Corners. Then, a mile farther on, I had turned off at a faded old sign that read THE PEBBLES, and was driving down the narrowest of dirt lanes flanked on each side by high dense growths of privet and hydrangea. A few rough potholes and a scurrying rabbit, and finally there was the old saltbox itself, more weathered than ever, its shingles more gray, its shutters more faded blue, and, beyond it, the rotting hulk of the *Janet B* with the *Pot-Pourri*, Essie's own little ancient one-stroke motor lobster boat trailing from its stern on an ebbing tide.

Essie's vintage Chevy pickup was parked on the dirt strip before the front door. The last time I had seen it, it carried the huge lime-green, lavender, and pale yellow nylon balloon sleeve of our very own rig, carefully folded to no bigger than the average couch, the heavy wicker basket that was the gondola, and the big padded canvas bag containing the butane tanks and burner to provide the hot air the balloon needed to ascend.

I'd hardly got out of my station wagon when Essie appeared through the summertime screen door and stepped down onto the wide granite slab that was the saltbox's welcoming door stone.

"Hurrah!" she said, and the smile she gave me dispelled any trace of discomfort I might have felt because of her jealousy of Heather. We embraced and went inside. It was as though five minutes had gone by since our last meeting, not a month and a half.

"Well, how did it go?" I asked. On the telephone we hadn't discussed the sale that morning of one of her fields. Rich with herbs and wildflowers, the fields were all that was left of a much larger acreage her father, the Reverend Peck, had owned. Essie would spend hours there, parking her pickup at Owen Fuller's, from whom she bought eggs, corn, and the occasional pieces of useful junk from a pile of old farm, household, and boating equipment he kept in a cobwebby shed behind his barn. Essie lived on a tiny inheritance, and the herbs and wild-flowers she'd select and pick earned her a small supplementary income from an herbal distribution company in Boston. Lobstering was another way she'd scrape money together.

"It's gone," she said with a wry smile. "The south field is the one that I sold since it had the least-interesting herbs. They don't take possession until mid-November, so I'll have time to get almost everything out of the ground either into the north field or down here. I saw their plans for the house. Ghastly-looking modern thing with a 'cathedral' living room, whatever that means. But they're planting trees close around it, so in a few years perhaps I shan't even have to see it."

She was wearing a familiar farm-wife dress of a nondescript rust-brown and wearing her low oxfords, practical shoes as she always called them and excellent for ballooning. Her hair was combed straight down as usual and she looked as tan and lean and sinewy and part of the soil as ever. I knew how much the fields meant to her and how selling one must have pained her, but when I looked at the stacks of ballooning magazines and technical manuals lying about her kitchen where there had once been only literature on gardening and herbology, I also knew she felt more than compensated.

I thought, then, of the first time I met her, how she had freed the little azure-blue butterfly. Both of us had felt trapped; I by widowhood and the conventions of society; Essie, orphaned young by repressive parents—her father was the strictest sort of Presbyterian minister—and rarely able to leave the Vineyard, by a lifetime of lonely nights crowded with frustrated visions of something better, and by days coping with the narrowness of country people with no other horizons than the shores of the island that bound them. When it came to money, we might have been crazy, she and I—outside her kitchen window I could see that her little *Pot-Pourri* badly needed paint, and her kitchen garden clearly wanted weeding—but ballooning had given us both a new lease on life. Up in the heavens, we lived.

Essie had put on a kettle, and as she poured tea, we started a delightful reminiscence of our last flight late in April, when we'd tried out our new balloon over Pennsylvania's Brandywine Valley, gliding gently over the rolling countryside, fresh green with spring, its beautiful farms awakening from the winter, its trees blossoming. Essie had brought a bottle of Krug Brut and kept it ice cold in a cooler. By the time we landed we were both singing and giggling like schoolgirls. Totally unprofessional of us, I'm sure—our volunteer ground crew, following in a Jeep, looked disapproving—but we didn't care. It was the most glorious of days. Our very own beloved balloon was now neatly stowed away along with its gondola and hot-air equipment in Essie's little garage-barn, which lay beyond the house close to the end of the pebbly beach.

Time flew, and the strike of five on Essie's old cuckoo clock came almost as a shock. I took hurried and reluctant leave, and Essie, knowing that I was rushing back to relieve Heather, for once took it like a soldier and let me go without a barbed comment. I started up my station wagon, waved to her where she stood on the granite threshold stone waving cheerfully back at me, and drove up the narrow lane between the privet and hydrangea. At the top, I turned onto South Road and stepped on the gas. With luck, and if Otis Cramm didn't zap me with his radar, I'd be back in Edgartown by a quarter to six, time enough to stop Heather from cooking a meal. I decided I would take her and her children out to dinner, and Algar, too, if he condescended to come.

I had no way of knowing I wouldn't reach Edgartown until nearly eight o'clock.

FOUR

It happened after I had gone back through Beetlebung Corners and regained Middle Road. As I approached Tea Lane in West Tisbury, I remembered the police car and ambulance turning into it and was just wondering again what might have happened when, almost at the junction of the two roads, I saw a familiar convertible coming toward me, roof down and slowing.

I recognized the car at once. It belonged to Glenn Rothenberg, a young pathologist from Boston who came every summer in exchange for a small cottage for himself, to assist the local medical examiner and to help out at Vineyard Hospital. For the last three years he was usually to be seen in the company of Samantha Sanderson, the determined and very feminist young actress who five years before had established the Clam Shell Theater, a summer-stock company located in an old barn near Vineyard Haven.

Something told me that Rothenberg was probably going to see Grace Chadwick. Perhaps it was because in the past few years I had occasionally noted him driving Grace into town or picking her up to bring her home. I still hadn't connected him to the ambulance. I glanced in my rearview mirror; the road behind me was empty. I slowed opposite him as he began to turn down Tea Lane and I leaned out my window.

"Hello, Dr. Rothenberg."

"Margaret! How are you?"

"Better than the day before yesterday, when I was still trapped in New York." Inane, I agree, but how else do you renew the most casual of friendships after a nine-month separation? I then got to the point. "What brings you down here?"

His warm smile faded. "March House," he said. "They pulled a woman from Grace Chadwick's fish pond just after lunch."

I found my heart in my mouth. "Grace?"

"Must be. They called me because this week I'm medical examiner. They also want me to identify her. She's being kept there until a forensic expert from Falmouth gets through whatever he has to do."

A horn suddenly blared. A car had come up behind me. Rothenberg somberly waved his hand and made his turn. The horn blared again, angrily. I had either to go on or follow the doctor. I confess the choice was not difficult. I am not a busybody, but I have almost never been able to control my curiosity. Besides, I knew Essie would never forgive me if I missed a chance to give her firsthand information.

March House was perhaps a quarter of a mile distant, the dirt road potholed and dusty. I kept well behind Glenn Rothenberg, wild thoughts in my head. If it wasn't Grace who had drowned, who could it have been? Nobody ever went on her property anymore, except Owen Fuller, and either he or Otis Cramm could easily have identified her. And why a forensic expert? Didn't that always mean foul play? And Falmouth meant the state police, surely. The expert would have had to fly over to be there in so short a time. All extraordinary for an ordinary drowning, usually only of local interest.

Before I knew it, March House had appeared, and Glenn Rothenberg, ahead of me, had turned into its narrow overgrown driveway, crowded with other vehicles. There were two more police cars besides Otis Cramm's cruiser, one belonging to the state police. Two other cars were unmarked, and I didn't recognize them. But I did recognize a sixth vehicle, a black utility wagon from the Bache-Turner Funeral Home in Vineyard Haven, which usually doubled as a county morgue.

I hadn't been by the house in a year, and I was at once struck by how it had become even more run-down than I remembered its having been last June. It looked now half a ruin and haunted. It was three stories in some places, plus attic, and there was a two-story servants' wing out back. Some of its brick exterior was mossy, its gabled roofs sagged, shutters hung half off their hinges, paint peeled, the gardens were grown up into weed, and the once-raked gravel driveway could hardly be seen for crabgrass and leaf mold and for twigs and branches fallen from trees that had never been pruned or thinned and had grown so big and overcrowded as to almost completely shut out the sun from both house and grounds. Beyond March House I could see the barn, home of the old Lincoln limousine. Its few windows were filled with cobwebs, and weeds grew against its sides. It also appeared to be deserted.

When I pulled up behind the doctor, my heart was thudding. Anything that hints of accident and injury always frightens me. Glenn got out of his convertible without seeing me and went directly around the side of the house toward the back lawn. There was a small crowd around an ornamental fish pond at the lawn's end, and I saw Owen Fuller standing at a gate in the old stone wall that separated his property from Grace's, his customary black hat low over his forehead and his darkly malevolent eyes glowering at everyone.

I left my station wagon and followed Rothenberg. Halfway across the lawn to the fish pond we were intercepted by none other than Otis Cramm himself, who in the face of drama had shoved his hunting magazine in his hip pocket and was attempting to look important, while succeeding only in appearing even more like the unsure-of-himself hick he really was.

He let Glenn Rothenberg proceed, but he stopped me. Now that I was this close, however, nothing could prevent me from seeing the rest. I immediately pulled sex, rank, and age—all three. I stood to my full height and haughtily told him to behave himself and stand to one side. Conditioned from childhood to regard me as authority, he did, all red-faced and stammering. "But, gee, Mrs. Barlow, the trooper told me not to let anyone back here. . . ." He then dogged my steps like an anxious little boy. I would have felt sorry for him if I hadn't seen my behavior as just revenge for at least a few of the times he'd nailed unfortunates with his cursed radar.

The fish pond was oval-shaped and not much bigger than a fair-sized room. It wasn't very deep, either, perhaps four to five feet. There had once been goldfish in it, lovely ones given to Grace Chadwick's mother by someone important from old Imperial China. As the years went by, their descendants' numbers slowly diminished, many turning nearly white with only a touch of red remaining. Correspondingly, the once-exotic appearance of the pond, originally surrounded by rare shrubs, lilies, and some flamboyant Chinese water flowers, had also changed. An invading and less exotic undergrowth of huckleberry, shadbush, and swamp azalea, along with frequent skeins of ugly catbrier, had choked out both shrubs and lilies. The water flowers had been replaced by thick pond weed, and the water, once clear with a white sandy bottom, where children, including my own, used to sail their little boats and dangle their feet, was now ominously dark and covered with slimy green scum.

By last summer, the year of my story, children never came to March House anymore, of course, and there were no more goldfish either. That was not just because Grace had turned into the sort of recluse who would appear like a ghost in the darkness of a suddenly opened door to shake her cane at people and order them away. There was another reason. Four or five years before, someone with a sick sense of humor, or perhaps just to spite Grace, brought a pair of snapping turtles over from the mainland, big Jersey meadow ones. Snappers are not native to Martha's Vineyard. Their nasty parrot-like beaks made short shrift of the poor goldfish, and after they took a slice out of some child's foot, a few attempts were made to net them. They always managed, however, either to hide in the pond weed or dash off through the surrounding undergrowth until the danger to them was over. Eventually, children were simply warned to stay away.

It was the turtles that now made the death so extraordinarily gruesome. As I came across the lawn, the knot of men blocking my view of the pond shifted enough for me to see the body of a white-haired woman lying on the weedy grass by the pond's edge and clothed in a flower-print dress that still looked wet. She was clearly dead; her bare arms and legs had that awful pallor. Poor Grace, I thought. She must have slipped and fallen in. I tried not to think of her weak struggles to get out again and slowly sinking back down into the water, or perhaps because of her advanced age, just standing helplessly neck-deep in its dark slimy coldness and calling vainly until mercifully she passed out.

Someone was measuring, somebody else taking pictures. Dr. Rothenberg had bent over her. I strained but for a moment couldn't see much.

Behind me, Otis Cramm said, "I guess I ought to get hold of Arthur."

I half turned. "Is he here?" Arthur Heston usually didn't come down until July.

"Came two days ago. Staying at Charlotte's Inn."

I let Otis savor his little triumph of superior knowledge and moved closer to the body. Nobody paid any attention to me. Then, as the state trooper and the Bache-Turner undertaker, Len Turner himself, a big florid man who looked like a car salesman, got hold of her arms and legs to shift her body onto the body bag, I finally saw her face.

I didn't expect what I saw. I expected death. But not anything else. My stomach turned, and something gagged in my throat. There was a roaring in my ears and a sudden grayness before my eyes. I guess I nearly fainted.

But I didn't. I held on and slowly looked away from the flesh-shredded, eyeless, tongue-torn-out, lipless mess the snapping turtles had made of their helpless victim.

Glenn Rothenberg happened to see me. I must have been chalk-white. He stood up. "Margaret! You shouldn't be here. Are you all right?" He gently took my arm to steady me, then led me a few yards away to the shade of two giant maples that dominated the lawn's center.

I said, "It's awful, Glenn. How did she get there?"

His eyes darkened. "In the pond? She had her neck broken and then was pushed in," he said, "and, if I am right, held under until she drowned."

I found I couldn't speak again. I simply stared at him. I guess I'd already known something terrible was involved; the amount of police present and Glenn's having said something about a forensic expert were proof enough. But suspicion is one thing, fact is another. I had trouble fitting the cold-blooded murder of someone I knew into my vision of things, especially a murder so ghastly. You read about these things—they didn't ever happen to you; they happened to other people.

I finally found my voice. It sounded thick to me, not my own. "It's not Grace Chadwick," I said.

"Oh?" Rothenberg glanced sharply at a man in a business suit who had come over with the uniformed trooper. He was an ugly bullying sort of person who looked like a frog and obviously was in charge. Coldly authoritative and hardly mindful of the state I was in, he brushed aside Glenn Rothenberg's introduction—he was a Lieutenant Fisher from the State Police Homicide Division at mainland New Bedford—and snapped a question at me.

"Not Miss Chadwick? Who is it, then? Do you know?"

I knew. I'd seen the expensive gold bracelet and the rings: the engagement one of two large rubies set on each side of a four-carat diamond and the wide diamond-studded wedding band. I'd seen the hands, younger by far than Grace Chadwick's, and the talonlike fingers with their long curving nails.

I nodded. "Yes," I said. "I do. It's Rose. Rose Perkins."

FIVE

"But what was Rose doing there?" Heather asked.

"Who knows?" I said. "Came to call, I suppose, and found Grace already in bed."

"Late at night like that?" There was doubt all over Heather's face. Glenn Rothenberg had said Rose died about midnight.

I had to admit it seemed very odd.

I had come home to find that Heather had already prepared dinner, set the table in the dining room, and even mixed me my favorite drink, a frothy daiquiri on the rocks. I should have called Essie at once, of course. I knew she'd want to hear what had happened and would be furious with me if she wasn't the first person to be told. Essie's parents and Grace's had been close friends, and as a child, Essie had frequently played at March House. When older, she had remained friendly with Grace, parking her car in Grace's drive to walk through the woods beyond the fish pond to her own property, which no longer had a road leading to it. When Grace began her reclusive retreat, Essie had philosophically accepted being shut out along with everyone else, although I think she was hurt more than she even cared to admit to herself.

It would have been completely tactless to arrive and sit right down at the telephone, however, so I joined the others for a first course of clam chowder. Algar was there, too. He looked gray and exhausted, I supposed because of all the desperate money worries I knew he had. But he put on a pleasant smile for a change instead of his usual brooding frown and even apologized when he left the table before dessert to go look at a ballgame on the library television. At least that was the excuse. I think the reason was that he had a phone call to make to someone. Over the children's chatter and Heather's questions, I heard him talking, although I couldn't catch any of what he said.

We grown-ups had tried not to discuss the awful business of Rose in front of the children, but I'm afraid we just couldn't help ourselves. Heather soon could no longer control her curiosity, and I could not bring myself to refrain from answering her questions. So bit by bit, it had all come out: how Rose had died, who had discovered her—Owen Fuller had—and, finally, how the police had no real clues and no immediate idea of a motive, which clearly was not robbery.

"Margaret." I looked across the table at Nancy, who characteristically had been more thoughtful and less pestering than the others. "Where was Miss Chadwick this afternoon?" she asked. "I mean, when the police came."

"Shopping, I guess," I answered. "Dr. Rothenberg telephoned Samantha just before I left, and she told him she'd seen Grace around noon on Main Street in Vineyard Haven. Apparently she'd gone in early." I shook my head. "When I left, the police were going to pick her up, unless she showed up soon in one of Bert's taxis, which is how she usually gets home if Glenn or Samantha doesn't bring her."

Heather interjected with an incredulous note. "I can't understand why Grace didn't see Rose in her pond before she left. She almost always uses the back kitchen door, and you can see the pond quite clearly from it."

"I know," I said, "but her eyesight can't be the best anymore, can it?"

"Maybe she did see Rose and was glad," put in Judith. She was the more daring of the twins.

"Judith!"

Judith retreated back into her cheesecake dessert with sidelong glances at her sister, Angela.

"The thing that I find more surprising," I said, "is that Glenn Rothenberg didn't know right away that it was Rose—I mean, the way I did from all her jewelry. After all, she was hardly a stranger to him, was she? He and Samantha went to several of her parties last summer, and I think he even treated her when she got that allergic rash or poison ivy or whatever it was last Labor Day."

Heather's laugh had a touch of acerbity. "Margaret, I would have thought by now you'd know that most men have no idea what a woman is wearing unless it's so décolleté she risks being arrested."

I thought of how young Peter deBord had complimented me that morning and thought what she said didn't necessarily apply to all men, but I decided not to press the point.

"What does décolleté mean, Mom?" Angela wanted to know.

"It means showing too much boob, silly!" Judith exclaimed, and Christopher and Nancy and Angela went off into a thoroughly obnoxious fit of tittering. For a moment, all that could be seen around the table were mouths full of cheesecake framed by cheesecake-jammed braces. I honestly think Heather blushed.

"Judith!"

Judith was unchastened. "I bet whoever pushed her in thought she was Grace."

That was exactly what the police *did* think. Both women, Grace and Rose, were about the same height, and they both had nearly white hair. On a moonless night, their age difference wouldn't have been obvious, and mistaken identity would have been understandable. Then, too, for whatever their reasons, perhaps because Rose's jewelry hadn't been taken, the police seemed to have discounted a wandering maniac or a burglar caught in the act. The state trooper had said quite clearly, "They got the wrong woman, that's my bet." And it turned out that the unpleasant frog-faced Lieutenant Fisher from Homicide thought the same. Clearly, the police considered the murder premeditated.

If they were right, I thought, it somehow made Rose's death even worse. It meant someone we probably all knew was the killer. I shivered at the thought and decided the children had heard enough. I rapped my glass for silence—they were having one of those meaningless arguments children have—and said, "All right, you four, you can go get brainwashed by television now."

Christopher pushed back his chair at once, then stood up and said, "Which eye did the snappers eat, Margaret?"

"Both," Judith answered before I could draw breath. "And her tongue, too, I bet. That's supposed to be the juiciest part."

"Judith! Angela! Leave the table at once." Heather's voice was sharp. The twins hadn't budged.

"Daddy's watching a ballgame," Angela protested.

"You can watch it, too," Heather said firmly.

The twins reluctantly obeyed, although they obviously wanted to hear more about Rose Perkins. Judith, as she left the table, had to have a parting shot. "I bet Daddy was the one."

"Judith!" Heather's dark eyes blazed. "One more

word from you and you'll clean the garage bathroom for a week."

Judith fought back, regardless. "Well, if he didn't, he should have. Then we could live in our own house instead of—"

She broke off. Her father was standing in the doorway. His mouth was smiling. His eyes were not.

If Judith hadn't got the message from her mother, she got it now. She sidled carefully past Algar and ran for the comparative safety of the library. I turned from watching her and from Nancy, Christopher, and Angela, who followed, to catch Algar's eyes meeting Heather's in silent and fleeting communication. Then he disappeared after the children.

Heather and I began to clear the dishes and she tried to cover up a certain awkwardness. "Did someone tell Estelle? I mean, before the police went there?"

"Dr. Rothenberg said he would," I replied.

Estelle, Rose's daughter, had by now graduated from college and, except for Rose's sister, who lived in California, was Rose's only family. Rose's husband, a useless alcoholic, had abandoned Rose shortly after Estelle's birth, eventually to die of cirrhosis of the liver. Estelle had always spent her summer holidays on the Vineyard.

It was difficult to have sympathy for her, however. She was the antithesis of a modern hardworking girl like, say, Samantha Sanderson. Although attractive as a child, even sometimes quite winning, she had always appeared to me in the last few years as lazy, insolent, spoiled rotten, and totally selfish. I'd had the impression the most work she had ever done during any summer since she'd reached sixteen was to rise to get another joint or to have sex. For the last two years she'd had a fiancé who was totally worthless, a fortune hunter, and God knows what else. I think he smuggled drugs. I knew he smoked endless pot right in front of everyone and used far more cocaine than could be good for anyone. He was a young Frenchman from a noble family dating back to the year 900, and in spite of a name as long as your arm with several titles to go with it, reduced fortunately by everyone simply to François, his entire bank account usually could be spent in less than a minute at any grocery store.

In my imagination, I could see no tears at all in Rose's household. Estelle, whom I had rarely seen demonstrate much affection for her mother, stood to inherit all of Rose's estate, including the jewelry the snapping turtles had left intact. As for François, his future was now obviously assured.

Coming back from the kitchen to fetch more dishes, I saw Heather wearing a frown. She hadn't moved from where I'd left her standing. "Margaret, do you think anyone will actually think that?"

"Think what?"

"That Algar pushed—well . . . wanted Grace dead?"

"Heather, what on earth are you talking about?" I put a dish back on the table, sat down, and stared at her.

"Well, they might, mightn't they? I mean, claim he pushed Grace in the pond so we could move into our house?"

"Oh, do stop!" I exclaimed. "Nobody murders for a house."

She stared back at me a moment, expressionless, then laughed slightly and shrugged. "Of course not. I'm just tired, I guess." There was a sharp edge to her voice.

"I should think you would be," I said sympathetically. "The garage must be hell."

"It is."

I rose to give her shoulders a hug. "Never mind. Nothing lasts forever. Grace Chadwick is eighty and she *is* in remission, don't forget, and it may sound awful to say it, but she could become ill again at any moment, poor old thing. Or simply die from something else. Heart trouble, for example."

I thought of my own mother, who at ninety, when seemingly on top of the world, had suddenly in six months gone downhill like lightning.

I said, "You've stuck it out ten years, Heather. Don't despair now."

We finished cleaning up. But when she and Algar and the twins had gone home and my own two young devils were safely tucked away for the night in the guest room with the yellow-flowered wallpaper they'd decided on for the summer, Judith's remark about her father's pushing Rose in the pond lingered insistently. Presuming the police were right and there had been a case of late-at-night mistaken identity, Rose for Grace, and then supposing it had actually been Grace who'd been murdered, not Rose, Algar would have been immediately relieved of all the economic anxiety and misery he suffered. Many murders had been committed for far less.

With Algar basically a failure with no future and the kind who broods on misfortune rather than setting out to overcome it, and knowing as I did how island tongues could wag, I thought perhaps poor Heather had reasons for being apprehensive.

Essie certainly thought so, too. When I went upstairs, I dialed her number the moment I reached my bedside extension. My little Tiffany traveling clock said ten-thirty. Essie rarely went to bed before midnight, and I think sometimes not at all. She never seemed to need sleep, whereas I needed lots. She answered on the third ring, and I thanked my stars she hadn't heard the news yet. The first thing she said when I told her what the police thought was, "Oh, dear. I shouldn't like to be in Algar Mikele's shoes. They'll have him in for questioning before you can say 'Paul Revere.' I do hope he has a solid alibi."

"Nonsense, Essie. He may be difficult, but he's hardly a murderer."

"Oh, I made no accusation, Margaret, dear." Essie sounded especially spinsterish. "But he's always seemed very deep to me, that one. And you know, he's constantly over there at March House, as bad as Owen Fuller in his own way, sneaking about punishing himself with envy. I saw him a dozen times last summer and twice already this year, standing right out in the driveway, staring at the house like a hungry dog. Others might have seen him, mightn't they? And let's be realistic, word does get around."

I didn't argue, and Essie—to my relief—went on to ask what the police had asked me and I recited as many of their questions as I could remember: how I'd come to know Rose and for how long; how long I'd known Grace and if I saw much of her; if I knew anyone who would want to kill her and why; or kill Rose; and what I thought Rose was doing over there at that hour.

"That's the thing I can't understand!" Essie exclaimed. It was virtually what Heather had said.

"Nobody can," I replied.

"Do you have to see the police again?"

"Probably."

Essie sniffed. "I'm surprised they haven't come knocking on my door. They must have talked to Owen and he surely would have told them I had the fields back of the pond."

I nearly laughed. Essie couldn't bear to be left out of things.

A note of distinct amusement crept into her voice. "Perhaps I shall call them. Yes, I think I shall. Do you know how Grace is taking all this?"

I told her what I'd told Heather.

"Poor Grace." Essie's voice softened sympathetically. "I wouldn't wish what's happened on anyone, leastways her. I must call her, and if she won't see me, I'm sure Glenn Rothenberg can tell me how I can be helpful.

And, Margaret, we must send flowers to Estelle. Regardless."

I said I thought I'd take some over in the morning and offered to give them from both of us. I had known Rose better than Essie had.

Essie thanked me, and we chatted on for a while like two schoolgirls—how could one not endlessly discuss the murder of a friend?—until finally we both had to admit we were falling asleep and finished our talk with my promise to Essie to give her a full report on Estelle and to pick up some detective stories she'd loaned Rose, if at all possible. "Really excellent ones," she said.

In spite of her feelings about Algar, our talk had made me feel a million times better. I loved Heather, but Essie always gave me a lift the way nobody else could. She somehow could make the darkest cloud look far less menacing. I undressed, took off my makeup, and brushed my hair with her last words ringing in my ears. "Now mind, Margaret, dear, if you have any trouble at all with that loathsome police lieutenant, let me know. I'll bring him down a peg in a thrice. You will, won't you?"

In my shower and while brushing my teeth, I pictured Essie standing up to Fisher and laughed joyfully.

When I finally got to bed, however, my momentary lift ebbed and I lay awake a long time staring up at the ceiling of my bedroom and the ghostly pale reflections of lights around the calm, dark harbor. I couldn't help remembering the odd look that had passed between Heather and Algar, and I began to feel uneasy. Essie might sometimes be unfairly judgmental, but far too often she was right. For a man of Algar's strength, pounding his fist into the back of an old woman's head in a sudden uncontrolled fit of temper, then pushing her into a pond would be the simplest matter in the world. And solve a host of problems for him at the same time.

Unless, of course, he got caught. Then his wife and

children would suffer undeservedly and for the death of a woman who perhaps wasn't even supposed to be the victim.

What indeed had Rose Perkins been doing on Grace Chadwick's back lawn in the middle of the night?

It was a long time before I finally fell asleep.

SIX

I hadn't really planned to go straight to Rose's the next morning with flowers and condolences; but when I'd driven the children to their Vineyard Haven sailing class and put them in the hands of the competent young woman who ran it, and when I had picked up my morning paper from young Peter deBord and had my ego boosted again by his seemingly quite sincere flattery, I found myself once more heading west up-island, stopping only a few moments at a roadside flower stand.

I could never stand unsolved puzzles, but there was much more than curiosity motivating me into wanting to see Estelle first thing. Heather's frightened eyes last night, the sight of her shepherding her two girls when they all left and went toward their pathetic old wreck of a vehicle, which to me represented completely what their life had become, aroused protective instincts I didn't know I had. If there was to be trouble—and a sinking feeling told me there would be—Algar wasn't going to be the one to help his wife and children, for Algar was far more likely to be the cause of their disaster.

The first thing I'd thought when I opened my eyes that bright cloudless day was that the police would indeed soon be all over Algar. For if Grace really had been the intended victim, Algar, of all people, had a motive for urgently wanting her dead. Intuition, if you wish, told me he had no way of proving his whereabouts at the time of the murder. When I'd gone to bed the night before, I guess my thinking hadn't progressed that far. But now, lying in bed listening to Christopher and Nancy getting themselves up, I remembered how he loved surf fishing, especially at night. If he'd gone off alone to some lonely beach, he was going to have a hard time convincing the police of it. But, rising myself, I suddenly had the idea that if I could find out why Rose had been at March House, I might discover that the police were wrong and that she was the intended victim after all. It was a wild hope, I realized, but if true it would remove suspicion from Algar. He could hardly be accused of having a motive for murdering Rose Perkins.

The Rookery was on Ridge Hill just off Middle Road in Chilmark, not very far from Tea Lane and March House. Once the home of a prosperous sheep farmer, its fields and pastures were squared by old lichen-covered granite walls and it commanded a fine sweeping view of the distant Atlantic across mostly open countryside. Half hidden, fortunately, in a lower field was a very large and abysmally ugly three-story modern mansion just built by Rose's friend, the film star Ann Alfreda, to whom Rose had sold the land.

Rose's own house, built like mine in the early nineteenth century, was low and sprawling and had weathered-gray shingles and dark green shutters. Two wings gave it a U-shape at the back side and protected its enclosed flowered terrace and swimming pool from all but direct easterly winds. It was flanked by old, thick-trunked oak, linden, and beech trees and approached by a long gravel driveway coming straight off Middle Road and running up through an avenue of lovely maples to end in a circle before the front door. A second narrower driveway branched off about halfway to Rose's house and led down a shallow valley to Miss Alfreda's.

I drove up, parked, knocked, and waited. In spite of my armful of gladiolus, delphiniums, and some early summer hydrangea, I admit I felt an intruder. It did no good to tell myself that I was Estelle's senior by too many years to think about and if for no other reason than that, she had to be polite to me.

Then suddenly the door opened, and I found myself confronted by Estelle herself. She was wearing one of those new Mediterranean string bikinis that is nothing more than three of the scantiest of triangles, and her perfectly proportioned body, muscular-lean and hardened by gym work, was deeply bronzed and glistened with sun oil. Together with the chiseled lines of her slender young face, her dark green eyes, and her straight dark brown hair, which reached the middle of her back, she made quite an impression. It flitted through my mind that she was every bit as lovely as Rose had always claimed, and it was a shame that she didn't have a character to match.

"Good morning." I was suddenly tongue-tied and could think of nothing else to say. "I've brought you some flowers." And then: "I'm so dreadfully sorry about what's happened." What can one say, anyway, to someone whose mother had recently been murdered and who doesn't seem to care?

Estelle didn't speak for a moment. She smiled briefly, almost tauntingly, then took the flowers and finally asked me to come in. I did and she said, "We're at the pool." Before I could answer, she walked across the hall to the living room with an insolent catlike grace, which, if body language meant anything, indicated I had better understand right away that Rose's death was not going to have a negative effect on her own life.

I followed, aware even as I did that Estelle probably wanted to shock me simply to assert her independence. That was childish, and I chastised myself for going along with it—but I couldn't just stand there in the doorway.

We crossed the luxurious living room with its expensive modern furnishings loaned texture by the occasional antique, then went outside to the terrace and the pool, where I found Estelle's young French title lounging back on a pool chaise longue in a short terry-cloth robe open to his waist. He was about twenty-six, with narrow shoulders, a weak chin, and a petulant face in need of a shave. He had dark straight hair that was already receding, too prominent a nose, and decidedly unmuscular legs. He didn't speak and he didn't rise. He simply stared at us and then drew heavily on a joint he'd just rolled. When he exhaled, I recognized the pungent smell of marijuana at once. I thought, *What a difference between this fop and young Peter deBord.*

Estelle skipped all formalities. She waved at a chair for me to sit on and abruptly said, "The police were here most of yesterday and last night going through Rose's things and asking a lot of stupid questions. We really don't feel like talking to anyone today. Essie Peck loaned Rose a couple of books. I'll get them and you can drop them off."

She dumped the flowers I'd brought on a wrought-iron glass-topped table, where they were bound to wither at once from heat, took the joint from Francois's fingers, dragged on it deeply, handed it back, then glided across the terrace to open French doors that I knew led to Rose's bedroom. I was beginning to get very angry. Certainly I wished I'd never come. Then, glancing around the pool, I realized François was not the only person there. There was a young couple lying on mats on the far side. The man had on a pair of those Italian jockless trunks that show everything and force you to look twice even though you don't want to, and she, lying on her stomach with one arm dangling in the pool, seemed to be wearing nothing.

Estelle reappeared almost immediately with Essie's books, four well-thumbed paperbacks, and held them out dismissingly. I took them, and she said, "We're not going to have any service here for Rose. There'll be one in Boston. She's being cremated. I think her sister plans to dispose of the ashes someplace. She's flying in from the Coast."

It was too much for me. I couldn't bring myself to ask any questions about Rose's presence at Grace's. I said inanely, "Of course. If there's anything I can do—"

"Thank you."

Estelle took the joint from François's fingers again, put it between her lips, and turned her back. I was obviously dismissed.

I left, defeated. All I could think of was what a miserable mess Estelle had become. If she was so far gone her mother's murder wouldn't straighten her out, whatever would? Just inside the living room door, I turned. The girl across the pool had risen. I was right—she wore nothing. She had an almost androgynous body, and for a moment I thought she was a boy. Then she faced my direction and walked slowly around the edge of the pool, and I could see all of her. She disappeared into Rose's bedroom. Ignoring her, Italian Trunks slipped into the water. François rose, took off his robe, and stood by the edge of the pool watching him. He also wore nothing. Estelle lay down on the chaise longue François had been occupying, put dark glasses on, and, still dragging on the joint, turned her face to the sun.

I fled, but there was a last straw yet to come. Going down the maple-lined driveway, I saw Ann Alfreda coming up the branch driveway from her house in her open-topped mini beach buggy. She had two young men with her. They looked like beautiful golden-maned stallions, which instinct at once told me was precisely what she had them for. She sat between them with an arm around the bare shoulders of each. They waited for me to go by, then turned up toward Rose's.

I thought of my own youth. Before I met George, when I was in my early twenties, I had a body perhaps as beautiful as Estelle's and a real zest for life. Men found me attractive and pursued me. Sometimes, naturally, I'd find one fascinating and pursue him back, and we'd end up in bed, where if not love there was at least passion. We certainly weren't the prudes we are sometimes made out to be today, but we had a sense of privacy about sex and a kind of respect for it that demanded a selectivity most of today's youth doesn't seem to have. For all their liberation, I don't think they have the excitement we had. To us, nakedness, sexuality, and sleeping with someone had a mystery, an aura of the forbidden that spelled romance without which carnality eventually palls.

I went straight to Essie's, cursing my failure to gather any helpful information about Rose. Essie's old Chevy pickup was parked in the driveway, but there was no response to my knock on the door. I went inside, calling out. My only answer was the hollow metallic ticking of the big old-fashioned alarm clock atop the refrigerator.

Eventually I found her—or, more accurately, Essie found me. Standing out on the little lawn that separated the old saltbox cottage from the pebbly Nashaquitsa beach, I heard a shout.

"Margaret!"

I looked around and there she was, up on the bow of the half-beached trawler *Janet B.* Windburned and sinewy and dressed in old work pants and a checked shirt, she was pulling lobster traps from where she'd stored them in the forward hull. Thinking what a contrast the scene was to the one I'd just left, I joined her, climbing up a permanent ladder she'd fixed to the bow of the old hulk.

"I use the forward hold to store traps in," she explained. "Keeps them out of the sun, which wrecks the wood worse than water." She nodded at the hulk's stern, half sunk in the pond. "The after hold's no good. It floods right up to the hatch with high tide, and if there's a wind, they rattle around in there and break up."

She sat down on a trap, a big slatted box with a funneled entrance from which her lobsters could not escape, and pushed one over for me. "Well, tell me all. How is the prodigal daughter taking it, and did you manage to collect my books?"

I said, "What makes you think I've been there yet?"

"Because I know you. Ten lobsters to one you got up this morning and wasted no time."

I confessed she was right. "And I have your books," I said.

"I also bet that dreadful child produced them out of pure defiance to show you she doesn't care that her mother met a miserable end."

"Your lobsters are safe," I said.

Then I told her all. More or less. I told her how I'd failed to find out anything about Rose's being at Grace's in the middle of the night. I blamed it on Estelle's and François's appalling callousness and left out the sex-and-nudity part. No matter what my own opinion was of the degenerate goings-on at The Rookery, I felt vaguely guilty at the thought of betraying someone else's secrets, or perhaps it was just that this morning I didn't feel like listening to Essie's disapproval of any form of sexual expression, including my own relatively mundane yearnings. The spinster side of Essie was an area from which I had gradually learned to stay away. The Essie I loved was the adventuress, the Essie who reached out so joyously to be free from earthbound troubles and restrictions.

When I'd finished, Essie was silent a moment, thinking. Then she said, "If the police should for some reason be wrong about our murderer making a mistake in the dark and getting the wrong woman—Rose instead of Grace—and Rose actually *was* the intended victim, then François and Estelle definitely would be prime suspects."

I should have realized from her faintly facetious tone that Essie was laying some sort of trap for me. She'd done so frequently enough in the past, especially when she wanted to get her own way about something.

"Estelle and Francois?" I repeated. To my chagrin, I had to admit the suspicion had never entered my mind. And of course it should have if I thought Rose herself had really been the murderer's target.

Before I could absorb the thought, I heard Essie ask, "Just one of Rose's diamond rings would keep them both in drugs for years, wouldn't it? I wouldn't know myself, but from what I read I should think so. To say nothing of what her whole estate might do for them."

I found myself protesting. "But if that were true, why get her over to Grace's to do it?"

"Instead of disposing of her with some sort of convenient accident at home?" She smiled. "All right, try this. Home accidents can always be suspect. So get Rose over to Grace's—one contrived middle-of-the-night phone call would do it—kill her there, and a false trail has been laid for the police, who would then be almost certain to think just what they do think—that Rose was mistaken for Grace."

I wondered whether François or Estelle was capable of such a thing. Perhaps one of them could come up with the plot, but the actual killing? Somehow I couldn't attribute the violent death Rose had suffered to either. I shook my head slowly. There would have to be a stronger motive than a need for drugs, which they already seemed to have an endless supply of, and for the life of me I couldn't think of one.

I said so and Essie shrugged. "But Margaret, who else could have killed Rose if she was the intended victim? Ann Alfreda? Hardly. Grace herself?"

My reply was a smile that belied how discouraged I was beginning to feel.

Essie began to close her trap. "Look, Margaret," she said quietly, "I understand what you are trying to do and I respect your loyalty. But for your own sake, do try to be objective. The police don't think Rose was murdered by a maniac or a burglar, probably because, as you say, there was no robbery. Nobody we know of would benefit from Rose's death except François and Estelle, and it doesn't look as if even they had sufficient motive. So suppose for a moment the police happen to be right and the murderer did intend to kill Grace. Who has a motive, then? Owen Fuller? Arthur Heston? Isn't that stretching things a little?"

She was right, of course. Owen Fuller was a cruel abomination who was reported to be the father of his daughter's mongoloid child and who had once thrown a sack of screaming cats onto the town's Halloween bonfire. Arthur Heston was a weak, devious, insufferably patronizing Boston banker only a mother could love. Neither man, however, had any motive I could think of for wanting to kill either Grace Chadwick or Rose Perkins.

Nobody, in fact, had a motive. Nobody except Algar Mikele.

I felt stricken, the more so because I knew Essie's trap was kindly meant. For once she wasn't goading me about Heather. Her attitude was pure concern and affection. A sea gull screamed someplace, and two dark loons scuttered low over the glassy surface of Nashaquitsa Pond, their long slender necks outstretched like arrows. Far off I heard the sound of someone raising a sail. Essie stood up from her lobster-trap seat and turned to haul a last trap out of the hold.

I said, a little bitterly because the truth often is bitter, and resentfully, too, because I felt Essie had outmaneuvered me with a lot of superior knowledge picked up from the many detective stories she'd read, "For all your realism, you still haven't explained Rose's presence at March House at that hour. And don't tell me she was paying a social call. I'll never believe it."

Essie finished stacking the trap along with the two we'd been seated on and then replied, "No, I certainly won't tell you that. Why she was there is a puzzle, all right. But if Grace and Estelle don't offer the police a reason, and unless Rose kept a diary, do you think they will ever find out why? I very much doubt it."

She put her hand on my shoulder and said gently, "I'm sorry, Margaret. I think you're in a perfectly horrid position and I don't think this is the time for delusions. They could only make things far worse later on."

I didn't reply. Chagrin had momentarily got the better of me. As we left the *Janet B* for the house and tea, I remember thinking what a turnabout in our personalities we were both experiencing. My optimism and dauntless hope, perhaps even recklessness, had been checked by her realism when usually where we two were concerned, especially in ballooning, it was exactly the opposite. Essie was the reckless one, and I was always the sobering influence.

At that moment I think we both decided not to discuss murder again that day. Neither wanted to risk in any way upsetting or causing pain to the other, which is what any discussion of Algar Mikele might well have done. After a brief awkwardness, we lost ourselves for the next couple of hours in studying up on France. Essie spread out maps and then served a delicious light lunch with a cold bottle of white wine, and for a time we escaped.

But for me escape would be short-lived. I have a stubborn streak a mile wide, and something had happened to me as we came down the ladder at the *Janet B*'s bow to the beach. Essie was right, without question, but even if Algar were guilty, what about Heather and the twins? I kept seeing them again as I had last night going to their car: Heather's arms around her girls' thin shoulders, her own hunched with anxiety, and worse—from some new kind of fear far more debilitating than desperate money worries. Something awful had happened. I had seen it in her eyes. I was sure of it.

In one of those not-so-rare instances in my life when my emotions overruled my head, I rebelled against logic, against every rule of society, and against all common sense. I decided I didn't give a damn if Algar had murdered Rose Perkins by mistake or not. I decided Grace probably needed what apparently was intended for her and nobody would really miss Rose Perkins, who was a spoiled wealthy bore. I decided Heather was the one who counted, and her twins even more so. The girls deserved something better in life than the back of Ed Rupert's garage. They needed a home for a start—March House—and I decided I had valid arguments that might persuade Grace to let them at least move into the chauffeur's apartment. Nobody had arrested Algar for murder or even brought him in for questioning. Not yet, anyway. A man can't be arrested just because he has a motive. There has to be concrete evidence connecting him to the crime. There was an outside chance Grace Chadwick wouldn't have heard the gossip and speculation that was bound by now to be flying around and might not think Algar killed Rose. Grace could hardly know the state of desperation Algar was in. Both Heather and he—especially Heather—were too proud to let her know.

Grace would be frightened, however, and possibly for the first time she'd be receptive to having people live close by whose very presence could offer protection. Conversely, if Grace allowed the Mikeles to move in, it might make Algar appear far less guilty and take a lot of tension out of the situation.

I resolved to say nothing to anyone, neither to Heather nor to Essie, and somehow get in touch with Grace Chadwick as soon as possible.

To me, at that moment, it seemed impossible that she would not at least let me talk to her.

SEVEN

I called her at nine the following morning, thinking that although she was probably an early riser, as so many elderly people are, she would need time to adjust herself to a new day. She would want to bathe and get dressed before she felt ready to speak to anyone and, in her case, to rouge and powder her face far too much for any woman past the age of forty-five.

As the telephone rang, I tried to imagine her answering. There were two phones in the house, I remembered. One was upstairs in her bedroom, where I'd never been; the other was in the formal front parlor. I pictured her at the latter, small and frail, her white hair tucked up under her ever-present hat, and high around her neck the scarf she always wore to keep out damaging air—cold air in the winter and hot air in the summer.

I saw her surrounded by ancient frayed furniture; by tassel-shaded bronze Victorian lamps, fringed antimacassars, overstuffed chairs, dark bronze imitation-Grecian statuary, a potted palm—all barely discernible in the faint light that filtered through heavy shutters barring the room from the front driveway made equally gloomy by its overcrowded trees.

I felt guilty the moment she spoke because she sounded so old and quavery.

"Miss Chadwick? This is Margaret Barlow."

There was a moment's silence. I thought perhaps she hadn't heard.

Then: "Barlow?"

"George Barlow's wife." I started to say "widow," but thought she wouldn't remember George had died and that she'd only be confused. When younger, she had liked George very much.

"Who?"

"Barlow. George Barlow."

"Oh, yes. George Barlow. That excellent young lawyer. How is he?"

"He's fine, Miss Chadwick, thank you." I almost automatically said, "He sends you his best," but stopped just in time. It would have been too lugubrious for words.

I told her then that I wanted to pay a call on her to discuss a most urgent matter and refused to tell her what it was all about. I knew if I said one word on the telephone I'd risk never getting in a second one. But I ran into a stone wall just the same.

"I'm very tired," she said. "I don't really want to see anyone."

"It would only be for a few moments, but at your convenience, of course."

"Perhaps next week," she said. "Yes, call next week." The phone rattled. I was scared she'd hung up.

"Miss Chadwick? Hello?"

But she was still there. "No, I'm sorry. I really don't feel like seeing anyone, especially if there's a problem. Was it about Miss Perkins? I told the police everything I knew. Awful people! They were here for hours. Poking about everywhere. And all their silly questions! How should I know what she was doing in my pond? Shocking, I think. But then, Rose was always a little peculiar. And why should I have heard anything? I was asleep."

Against my better judgment, I surrendered. I said, "Miss Chadwick, actually I'm calling about your house." And I launched into my plea for Heather and the twins. When I finished, there was another long silence, and I would have thought that this time she had indeed put down the receiver if I had not heard her breathing.

"Miss Chadwick?"

She said it then, the one thing I'd taken a chance I wouldn't hear. She said, and with a kind of terrible indignation, "Algar Mikele tried to kill me."

My heart sank, and for a moment I couldn't find an answer. I had been so hopeful that I hadn't prepared any options.

"Miss Chadwick, I assure you he didn't."

"He killed that silly Rose instead. That's what the police think."

Suddenly I knew what to do. I knew I had to lie, and I did. "No, Miss Chadwick, he couldn't have. He was with me. All evening. He and his wife. Helping me settle in for the summer." I rushed on. There was no possible way she could know that two nights ago I was still in New York. "We didn't stop until past two in the morning, and he went straight home. I know because he left his wallet and I called him to let him know it was safe with me. That was at two-thirty. Rose died between ten and midnight, Doctor Rothenberg said."

My story sounded convincing to me, but it had no effect whatsoever on Grace. It was as though I had not spoken at all.

"If I let him in here, the next time he perhaps wouldn't get the wrong person. Good day to you . . . Mrs. Barlow, was it? My regards to George. Yes, George. Dear man."

This time, the sound of the receiver's being put

down was unmistakable. I dialed her number again. Frantically. The phone rang and rang. There was no answer. I wanted to scream with fury at myself. Why had I ever thought she'd want to speak to me in the first place, let alone speak about Algar? Where was my common sense? Had I completely forgotten what sort of a person I was dealing with? This wasn't Heather or Essie. This was a secretive old recluse who was probably half senile.

I managed to swallow total frustration and pulled myself together. In a funny way I did the equivalent of having a good cry: I put on a new bathing suit I'd bought in New York—one of those new bare-hip styles that no one over the age of forty-five should ever wear—concealed it temporarily with a wraparound skirt, armed myself with suntan lotion and a beach mat, took the children to sailing class at Vineyard Haven, then drove back to South Beach.

Since the summer season had barely got under way, there were very few people around, and I spent a heavenly hour with the beach mostly to myself. I lay in the sun enjoying the daringness of my suit, the loveliness of the sea and sky, and the rustling pounding sound of the ocean striking the shore and retreating again before it struck once more. I say "heavenly" because I forcibly put everything out of my mind and surrendered myself, mind and body, to the delicious warmth of the sun. For that one hour I was just me, the sensual nonthinking Margaret.

On the way back home, I detoured off the main road to a run-down area on the outskirts of Edgartown and stopped by Ed Rupert's garage. I tried to see neither the gas pumps out front, even though they were not so badly kept, nor Ed Rupert himself, drinking beer with some friends who'd stopped by in a derelict van. He needed a shave, as usual, and his shirt was open enough to reveal the sallow gray of his flabby pectorals. As I drove toward the back he gave me a look from his close-set eyes that made me wish I'd put my skirt around my bare shoulders and low-cut bathing suit top instead of my waist and legs.

I kept going past the score of rusted-out cars, most half stripped for parts, and had no trouble identifying the apartment by its four ugly, steel-framed, shutterless windows. Paint was peeling from the "front door." I knocked, and when there was no answer I tried to open the door and found it locked. I was almost glad. I didn't think I could have faced what I knew the interior to be like, though through one window I could see a gorgeous blue-and-gold Japanese paper fish hanging from the ceiling, and there was a vase of lovely wildflowers on a windowsill, both obviously Heather's attempt to turn a concrete cell-block into a home. My escape on the beach was over. This was reality, and my heart wrenched. I drove away.

My house wasn't far, less than half a mile away, but I'd hardly got started when I was seized by a fresh determination. I suddenly had an idea how I might still persuade Grace Chadwick. It wasn't so important to see her myself, I realized, as it was that she be *seen*. Almost before that thought had fully taken hold, I knew who could help me—Samantha Sanderson. I remembered a half dozen times I'd seen her giving Grace a ride into or back from town, and Glenn Rothenberg as a doctor had Grace's confidence. Both were people she might listen to, and I was quite certain I could persuade them to do their best to present Grace with my arguments on Heather's behalf.

I made a couple of necessary phone calls, to the plumber about a leaky faucet and to the TV repair people to come and adjust my aerial. I arranged with a local gardener to mow my lawn and put my flower beds in shape, and finally I took off for Vineyard Haven to pick up the children from sailing class. Then, as they filled me in on all the latest details of their lesson, I headed for the Clam Shell Theater, which was out beyond Vineyard Haven on a wide reach of land known as West Chop.

I skirted Vineyard Haven itself with its crowded Main Street, comprised mostly of shops and boutiques, by taking a couple of back-street roads and the super shortcut provided by someone's private driveway. Just before reaching the Mink Meadows golf course, I slowed at a familiar blue-and-white sign adorned with symbolic tragicomic masks and turned into the driveway of the theater itself.

Set among a grove of trees, it was a fine old mansarded barn, a big one, which Samantha Sanderson had bought and renovated with mostly volunteer help: local youth aspiring to be actors; charitable ladies; the occasional civic-minded journeyman in the construction business, and others like Essie, who before discovering ballooning had found going to the theater momentary escape from the monotony and hardness of her life.

As I pulled up, I saw Samantha herself in paint-stained shirt, jeans, and sneakers carrying a heavy five-gallon can of paint and headed for some big canvas scenery flats lying on the lawn. They were left over from last summer's production of *The Merchant of Venice*, and some cast members were already hard at work painting them into Victorian London for the next week's opening performance of *Victoria Regina*.

Samantha was perhaps thirty—it's always hard to tell with actresses; they usually look so young yet so worldly at the same time. She'd come to the island first as a summer resident about ten years ago, then as a permanent resident five years later when she had begged, borrowed, and scraped together enough money to buy the barn. She was an attractive and energetic young woman, a natural blonde, physically quite like me at her age, slender and bosomy but shorter, and still showing her early training as a dancer in her vitality and strength. She was capable of tackling almost anything from roofing to plumbing and had always done an enormous amount of work herself around the theater.

Despite physical similarities, she was quite different from the youthful Margaret Barlow. I had always been naïvely outgoing, while Samantha was reserved and often cynical. I never quite knew what she was really thinking. She also had a self-assertiveness about her that I suppose was characteristic of so many in the "me" generation.

She spotted me at once and put down the paint can, wiping her hands on her jeans and smiling. "Hello, Margaret. What brings you?"

I said hello back and after some pleasantries asked if she had a few minutes to spare, which she said she did.

I followed her into the semidark silence of the theater. We went down its middle aisle and up onto the stage, where Nancy and Christopher immediately discovered a rack of Shakespearean costumes.

"Try them on," Samantha said. "Go ahead. Have fun."

The children fell to, and she turned to me and said, "While we talk, do you mind if I go on doing what I'd planned? I was going to experiment a little with my makeup for next week."

We went to her dressing room, behind the stage, a small rather airless little place with a mirror surrounded by bright lights, a dressing table heaped with pots of makeup, a wig stand on which there was a gray-white wig, and a costume rack with Victorian-style dresses. Samantha sat at the dressing table, flicking on the lights. I sank rather gratefully into a comfortable chair—but not before my eyes fell for a second on a messy stack of personal papers at one corner of the dressing table. The topmost sheet was a bank statement, and most of the printed figures were red. I looked away quickly, but not quickly enough. Samantha realized I'd seen it. She forced a smile. "In the red as usual," she said. She put a pot of cold cream on the statement.

"I'm sorry," I muttered, embarrassed. "I didn't mean to look."

"No problem, Margaret." She suddenly looked wan and defeated. Then she pulled herself together with almost theatrical cheer. "So," she said. "What's up? Outside of murder. My God! Isn't it awful? Glenn and I had the police out here for hours asking the most ridiculous questions, just because we help the old lady out occasionally."

She began to apply a base makeup.

I explained why I'd come. It took a while, and when I had finished, she had already experimented with powder and grease-pencil lines. She was remarkably skillful and quick. Right before my eyes she'd aged years. She waited a minute before speaking, studying the effect she'd created in her mirror and obviously thinking at the same time about my request that she speak to Grace about the Mikeles. Finally she said, "Of course, I can always try, Margaret, but do you really think even if Grace should say yes that it will do any good?"

I misunderstood. "It must!" I cried. "They'd have a decent home, not three dreary rooms in the back of a garage."

"Oh, I didn't mean that," Samantha said hurriedly. "I meant, do you really think it will actually take any suspicion away from Algar? Some people might have an idea that Grace was letting the Mikeles move into March House because she was frightened not to."

I hadn't thought of that. But it was a logical thought if someone believed Algar guilty, or at least a primary suspect.

"That presumes Algar's guilt," I said, "and for the sake of argument I'm willing to do that. If he was guilty, wouldn't his presence at March House be the safest thing possible for Grace? He'd hardly need her dead anymore unless he were stark raving mad, which he isn't, or wanted to murder her out of spite, which would be ridiculous. He'd have his home, finally, and only a few years of Grace's presence at worst."

Samantha smiled suddenly and said, "And if he isn't crazy but there's someone around who is, then there'd be a man at the place to protect her? All right, Margaret, you win. And I hope Heather Mikele realizes what a good friend you are."

"You will speak to Grace, then?"

"Of course. Or Glenn will."

Samantha took a gray-white wig from its stand on her dressing table and put it on. It was uncanny how much she suddenly looked like Queen Victoria. She put her hands on her ribs and laughed. "I'm going to need a lot of padding," she said, "and something in my cheeks."

She puffed out her cheeks, pulled her head down into her shoulders somehow, and slouched. The effect was electrifying. She was fat and aging. I told her so.

She took off the wig. "I've barely scratched the surface with this one," she said. "But I did want to get some idea of what I was in for." She dove into a large jar of cold cream and began to wipe off the makeup. "Glenn is planning to drive Grace into town today," she said. "He could bring her by here, perhaps. I'll try to catch him before he goes. The thing to do is to get the old girl in a good mood. And that isn't easy, you know. Why, just last week . . ."

Whatever she was going to say remained unfinished. There was a wail from the stage. We rushed out to find Christopher threatening Nancy with a theatrical sword. Samantha and I rescued her, and five minutes later I was driving home with Samantha's last admonition in my ears. "We'll give it our best shot, Margaret, but don't be too hopeful. She's very peculiar about her house, you know. She seems to feel that just allowing someone in the front door robs her of her own hold on life, and she's not ready to give that up yet."

But it was all to no avail. When we drew up to the

door of my own home in Edgartown, Heather was seated on the front step with the twins, both of them tearful. The roof of their world had fallen in. The police had come to pick up Algar for questioning, and I'd been right: He had no alibi for his whereabouts on the night of the murder. Worse, a brand-new spinner, the flashing metal lure used by surf fishermen, had been found in the bushes on the other side of the fish pond.

The police, however, had gone away empty-handed from the little apartment behind Ed Rupert's garage. Neither Heather nor the girls had seen Algar since early that morning. He had disappeared.

EIGHT

The police were watching the ferries and the airports, and Algar still had to be on the island, unless he'd somehow got hold of a small boat. That in itself might not be so difficult, given the Vineyard's seagoing character, but using one, if he were successful, would be a different matter. The Coast Guard had been alerted and had surely sent out a patrol vessel. The sound between Martha's Vineyard and Cape Cod is less than four miles wide and not an easy body of water to cross, unseen, even at night.

I took Heather and the twins inside and put on a no-nonsense manner I didn't really feel. "After lunch, you'll go to the garage and collect your things. You're staying here with me."

Heather didn't argue. She seemed numb, and grateful to find someone making decisions for her. I set the children to chopping cucumbers, peppers, and mushrooms, and washing lettuce for a salad, an occupation that was a little risky at their age, I admit, but I thought the danger of a sliced finger worth it just to keep them occupied. While they chattered and made an unholy mess of everything in the kitchen, I forced a good stiff drink down Heather, put water on to boil, and got busy making a Bolognese sauce I knew the children liked.

When lunch was over, I bustled the whole crowd over to the garage and a half hour later brought them right back with their suitcases. I put Heather and the twins in the guest room I called the Blue Room. In the old days, it had been the sewing room of Captain Samuel's various wives, and, like my own bedroom, it had a lovely view of the harbor. While they unpacked, Christopher and Nancy "helped" by testing out the beds to see how good they were as trampolines.

When I could get a free moment, I slipped away to the library and called George's former law partner in New York. He promised to line up a first-rate trial lawyer in Boston. I needed to talk to Heather alone, so when she and her girls came down, I sent all four children out with money to buy lobster for dinner—Christopher can always manage to eat two, but where he puts them I can't imagine—at the new fish market near the town dock. "After you've paid," I said, "treat yourself to ice cream and then pick up a copy of the new *Vogue* for me from Peter at the bookstore."

If those errands wouldn't keep them out of my hair for a while, what would? The door slammed behind them. Then their voices faded down the street. I sat Heather in the living room and without further ado asked her point-blank the sixty-four-thousand-dollar question. "You know Algar, Heather. If you don't, who does? You've been sharing body, bed, and board with him for twelve years. Did he or didn't he kill Rose?"

She hesitated. "Margaret, it isn't that easy."

My heart sank. I didn't let her finish. I had to know. I hardened my voice and repeated my question.

Something changed in her eyes. They had been guarded, almost hostile. Now they became hurt, as though

I had suddenly broken through some sort of defense. Her face had turned chalky white, and she looked like a chastised child. "He didn't do it, Margaret. He didn't. He was going to, I think, but he didn't."

"Going to?"

My alarm must have been very obvious. The words finally rushed out of her. "After dinner that night, we had no water. They'd shut it off in the garage so they could get more pressure for car washing. Algar went around and got in an awful row with Ed Rupert and had to back off when some of Rupert's redneck friends threatened him. They'd all been drinking a lot of beer. That made Algar even angrier. When he came back, he said he'd had enough. He was raving. 'I'm going over to our house and knock some sense into that damned old woman.' That's what he said. And said if she didn't say yes at least to our moving into the barn, that he'd brain her. It was almost ten o'clock. I begged him not to go, but he wouldn't listen. I'd never seen him like that. Never." Heather broke off. Tears of fear and abject misery rolled down over the dark fatigue shadows beneath her eyes.

I waited until she'd got control of herself, then asked, "And then what? Did he see Grace?" And, given the time of Grace's death, I tried not to imagine the worst.

If possible, Heather's tortured eyes grew even more pained. Her voice was barely a whisper. "Yes."

"And?"

"Oh, not that way. I mean, he didn't even talk to her." She bit her lip, hesitating.

I said gently, "Take your time, Heather, but trust me. Whatever it is, you know you can't keep it to yourself."

She found a tissue in her dress pocket and blew her nose. "By the time Algar got there, he said he'd cooled off. But he still wanted to try to reason with her. He said he realized she might have gone to bed, and he didn't want to upset her if she had—she'd never listen to him then—so he left the car down the road a ways and went into her place on foot."

"And was she still up?"

Heather nodded. "Algar thought she wasn't at first. The house was all dark. He said he went around back thinking perhaps she was in the kitchen, but it was dark there, too. He was standing in the middle of the lawn trying to think what to do and sort of giving up and deciding to come home when he saw lights. A car came down Tea Lane and pulled into the driveway. When the door opened and the interior light went on for a moment, he saw it was Rose Perkins and then remembered it was her car—that big Cadillac. She got out, came around the house to the back kitchen door, and called out for Grace.

"There was a moon, but Algar was standing in the shadow of those two maple trees in the middle of the lawn, and she didn't see him. When her back was turned, he slipped around to the other side of the fish pond and stood in the bushes. Rose knocked and called out again, and a light finally went on in the back hall by the kitchen. Grace must have asked who was there, because Rose said who she was and then the door opened and Grace came out. She and Rose talked a moment. Then they walked toward the fish pond. Algar said Grace seemed very angry and he thought he heard her say something like, 'Rose Perkins, I won't have it, it's absolutely none of your business.' And Rose said something like, 'You're not being reasonable' and 'It's for your own good.'

"Then, Algar said, he thought Grace suddenly struck Rose—it wasn't all that easy to see with bushes in the way and shadows everywhere, but he thought Grace hit her across the back of her neck, here." Heather put her hand to the base of her neck. "And Rose kind of buckled at the knees and Grace got down and sort of rolled her into the pond."

It took a moment for me to put together what

Heather had said. I just stared at her. "Grace attacked Rose?" I couldn't comprehend it.

Heather nodded.

"What did Algar do?"

"He said he did nothing at first. He just stood there. He was like you are now. He simply couldn't believe it. Then he came to life and pushed forward and saw she was holding Rose underwater. That did it. He shouted and started around the pond. But it took a moment. His jacket got caught on some catbrier. He thinks it was then that he lost the spinner. By the time he got to Rose, Grace had disappeared. He tried to pull Rose out, and that's when something hit him. It must have been Grace—who else? Algar thinks she was probably hiding in the shadows of the two maple trees, the same way he had. He said one moment he had Rose by the hair and the next he was facedown in the grass. She caught him right there. Right where she'd hit Rose." Heather put a hand to the back of her neck again. "He thinks he heard a door slam. Maybe the back door. By the time he got to his knees, it was too late for Rose. She was all tangled up in weeds, and it took time to get her out. He tried mouth-to-mouth for ten minutes, then gave up."

"But, Heather, why didn't he call the police?"

"The police!" Heather echoed bitterly. "Do you think they would have believed him? That frail old Grace Chadwick, aged eighty, had killed Rose Perkins and attacked him, too? All Algar could think of was to get out of there just as fast as he could."

For a moment I was oblivious to Heather. I didn't even see her, and she was sitting right in front of me. I instead saw Algar Mikele standing in the moonlight on the back lawn of March House, the wet inert body that had been Rose Perkins at his feet, the dank darkness of the weed-choked fish pond, the dark outlines of the big old Victorian house, its gabled roof peaks and chimneys silhouetted black and jagged against the night sky. Of course he ran. Who wouldn't have? It would have been Grace Chadwick's word against his—the word of a venerable senior citizen whom nobody would ever believe capable of murder against the word of a sullen, brooding man with every reason in the world for wanting her dead. Indeed, why hadn't Grace herself called the police right then? I couldn't understand that. I said so to Heather.

She said, "I couldn't understand either. And Algar couldn't. Unless, he said, she is counting on his keeping silent because nobody would believe him."

"But why did Algar put Rose back in the pond?" I asked.

"He didn't. Grace must have come out again when he was gone."

"Oh, my God," I said. "How awful."

Heather had begun to cry again, and I pictured Algar's flight then. And in the silence when the distant sound of his car motor had died away, I could almost hear the click of the back door opening and its faint, rusty-hinged protest. I saw the bent form of Grace Chadwick as she came out and fluttered back across the lawn to the pond. I saw her bend and bit by bit roll an inert Rose back into the water.

I shivered involuntarily. If it was true, Grace had to be mad. Stark raving mad and with the strength that only madness can give someone.

As though reading my mind, Heather said, "It's true, Margaret." Her eyes begged. "You must believe me, you must. Algar would never make it up. He wouldn't lie, not to me. I know everyone thinks he's strange, even you, but he loves me and the children. He'd never do this to us. He'd never kill someone."

"Of course he wouldn't," I said. But would he, I thought? I felt numb. One thing was almost certain. If Algar was telling the truth, it was doubtful anyone but his wife would ever believe him.

I silently fixed us some drinks. Questions poured

through my mind. Did frail elderly ladies go mad? None that I had ever heard of. They went senile, perhaps, or suffered from Alzheimer's disease, pathetic lost minds; but criminally insane, their eyes blazing with the need to kill, the sudden violence of youth surging through slack, long-atrophied muscles and brittle bones? It made no sense at all. And, once again, I wondered what Rose was doing there at that hour. Had Grace enticed her somehow? And why? Why kill Rose Perkins, of all people?

"Is that all Algar heard them say to each other? Just what you told me?"

Heather nodded.

"And Algar was sure Grace couldn't possibly have mistaken Rose for someone else?"

She shook her head. "No way. Rose announced herself and called her by name, remember?"

I think it was when Heather said this that I suddenly realized how I might possibly shed light on Rose's strange visit. Seeing Heather sitting there so utterly down and miserable, I thought of Estelle Perkins and her spoiled rich insolence. Had her extraordinary behavior yesterday perhaps been a cover-up for something? She had never been that bad as a child or even as a college girl, in spite of promiscuity and pot. Could she have deliberately been putting on an act to get rid of me?

I glanced at the old Seth Thomas clock on the mantelpiece. George had enthusiastically bought it at an auction the first year of our marriage. It said two-fifteen, and I tried to think of what George would do in the circumstances I now found myself. George was like Essie; he believed in action. To hell with talking; he got up and did things. What would he do now, I asked myself? Wait days, weeks, possibly months, while the police crucified Algar and thus his wife and children? Or would he, with an inside track, try to help them?

Heather was waiting expectantly for me to speak, to do something, anything. I rose abruptly and said,

"Round up the children—they can't be far—and take them down to South Beach. Nancy will show you where all the things are in the hall closet—the mats and the soccer ball, all that. And mind the undertow if they insist on swimming, though why anyone would want to so early in the season escapes me. The water is still freezing cold. I'll be back for the lobster supper if Christopher hasn't eaten it all."

I went to the door, then stopped. An odd thought had struck me.

"Heather, did Algar say anything about Rose's car?"

"Rose's car?"

"It wasn't at Grace's when I got there," I said. I kept the rest of my thoughts to myself. The police might have moved it, but I didn't think so. I'd had the impression they were too occupied with Rose herself to bother with anything else. Who had moved it, then? A possible witness to the murder? Or an accomplice? Someone who might also have seen Algar's car, even Algar himself?

I heard Heather reply, "No, Algar didn't mention it."

"Never mind," I said. I went out and got into my station wagon and headed up-island toward West Tisbury.

On the way, I thought of Essie and her rejection of my theory that there hadn't been a case of mistaken identity, that Rose indeed had been the intended victim. I couldn't wait to see her and enjoy my triumph, although it would have to wait until I had better proof than just Algar's word. Besides, I had something else to do before I saw Essie.

Perhaps—I'm not sure—if I had gone to see Essie at once and told her everything Heather had told me, things would have turned out differently and I wouldn't have foolishly taken my own life in my hands. But I didn't.

NINE

Driving once more up the carefully tended maple-lined driveway to Rose Perkins's Rookery, I thought at first there might be nobody at home. I didn't see any cars parked in front of the house. But when I peered in the garage window, both cars were there: Estelle's small Alfa Romeo convertible, which Rose had given her as a college graduation present, and Rose's Cadillac.

I immediately felt off stride. I hadn't expected to see Rose's car. Perhaps the police had brought it back, after all? But if they hadn't, who had? Estelle? If so, it would mean she knew her mother had gone to Grace's. But when would she have collected the car? The night of the murder? Early the next morning before Rose was discovered?

Nothing made sense. If for some reason Estelle had desperately needed the car on the night of the murder, surely she wouldn't have just taken it and left her mother stranded at March House. She would have looked for Rose to offer to come back for her. And not finding her anywhere there or back home, either, wouldn't Estelle eventually have called the police? Or—and the thought persisted—if she had indeed gone to March House, had she actually discovered her mother's body and chose to say nothing? With Rose dead, Estelle stood to inherit well and be free to lead a life-style uninhibited by conventional restrictions.

My head in a whirl of conjecture—some reasonable, some not—I went to the front door, rang the bell, and waited. I confess now to a sudden attack of nerves. Once more I had a mental picture of violent death; of night shadows on the back lawn of March House, of Rose being struck and falling into the fish pond, of Grace fluttering and scurrying. For the first time since I followed Glenn Rothenberg to Rose Perkins's body, I was frightened. Was it because I now felt Estelle might somehow be involved? Something told me to go home, to forget it all, to let Heather and Algar take care of their own problems. They weren't children, after all, and I wasn't their mother. I had my own children and their children. And I had Essie, the wonderful world of ballooning we'd discovered, and the marvelous and exciting things we'd planned for the future.

I had nearly made up my mind to back off and leave when the door was yanked open and it was too late to escape. Once more I found myself face-to-face with Estelle. She was in a pale yellow sarong that she'd obviously just wrapped around herself, since her hair and shoulders were wet and the sarong dry but her slim body beginning to show through it. I could hear laughter and shouts from the swimming pool across the living room and hall.

She said brightly, "Hi, Ann—"

And then she saw it was I and not her celebrity neighbor. Her expression changed so rapidly it was almost amusing.

"Oh . . ." she said.

Her lower lip pouted unpleasantly, and that did it. My nervous fear evaporated. A kind of instant rage seized me. I dispensed with any formality. "I want to talk to you," I said. I stepped into the doorway.

"I'm afraid I'm busy now." It was snapped out and ugly. And she tried to close the door in my face.

I did something I'd never done in my whole life. I think now I'd probably fantasized about it the day before, when I drove away from the house, but never seriously thought I ever would. I struck her. Hard. And right across the mouth.

I'm not a muscle baby. I don't work out in health clubs the way Estelle clearly did; I'm still basically slender and, remember, not much more than medium height. But I do lead a vigorous life and play a fair game of tennis. It was a backhand slap that stung my knuckles and sent a shock wave right up to my shoulder. It knocked her across the hall into a table, upsetting an expensive vase that crashed to the floor. And it drew blood. Bubbles of it welled at once on her lower lip.

She let out a half shriek and put her hand to her mouth. I didn't give her a chance to do anything else. I knew Rose's house. I grabbed her arm, and when she yanked away with a strength that surprised me, I seized the hair at the back of her neck. "In there, young lady! March."

I propelled her bodily into Rose's study a few feet down the hall, flung her down into a chintz-covered easy chair, and closed the door firmly behind me. It was psychological intimidation; she could have resisted me easily, but she didn't. She lost her sarong in the act and just sat there naked, her eyes wide in astonishment. I picked up the sarong and flung it in her face. She held it protectively against her.

"Don't you ever speak to me in that tone again," I said.

"François!" But the cry was halfhearted.

"Forget it, Estelle, unless you want him up on a drug charge. And yourself with him."

She turned white. "You bitch."

"Me? You think you can flash pot and coke in front of everyone you know now that poor Rose is dead and have them all bullied silent to protect her the way they did when she was still alive?"

"What do you want?"

"Information."

"About what?"

"About how your mother's car found its way back from Grace's place to your garage."

She leaped to her feet, clutching the sarong, and started for the door.

I picked up the telephone on Rose's desk, wondering how Fisher had missed that one, and dialed a number. Hearing me do it, Estelle stopped short.

The phone was answered with, "State police, Trooper O'Connell."

I didn't speak. I held the phone out so she could hear. "Hello? State police?"

She sat down again, all the fight gone out of her. I hung up.

The door rattled. Then François appeared, dripping wet with a towel around his waist. He looked first at me, then at her. *Mais, qu'est-ce qu'il y a?*

Estelle didn't answer. His eyes shifted rapidly again, from one of us to the other, and I stared him down until he retreated, closing the door behind him. I was sure he'd hang around on the other side, listening, but I didn't care.

I said, "Well?"

"It got into the garage because I put it there."

I ignored the almost sneering petulance. "Oh? You went to March House and got it?"

"Hardly. How would I have known it was there? It was in the driveway."

That was something I had not expected, and I was unable to hide my surprise. "In the driveway? Yours?"

"Down by the road. I found it in the morning. I thought it must have run out of gas or something. But it hadn't."

"Did you tell this to Lieutenant Fisher?"

"No."

"But why on earth not?"

"Because he never asked." She was even more petulant now. She had touched her mouth and was examining the blood on her fingers with an expression of disbelief. "Any other questions?"

I handed her a tissue from a box on the desk and decided on a new tack.

"Yes. Why did your mother go to Grace's in the middle of the night?"

"I don't know."

"Yes, you do. Rose never went anyplace without telling you where she'd be and why. It was part of her always treating you as though you were ten years old."

She looked up sharply. For an instant I thought she might start to tell the truth, but a curtain came down again behind her eyes.

She said, "I wasn't with Rose that night." She dabbed at her mouth with the tissue. "François and I went to Menemsha."

"I see. And what time did you get back?"

"I don't know. Ten-thirty. Maybe eleven."

"And Rose wasn't home then?"

I sensed hesitation when she shook her head. "No."

"But didn't you think it strange that she was out and that there was no note to tell you where she'd gone or when she'd be back?"

"Her door was shut. I thought she had come home and was in bed."

"But how could you have thought that when her car wasn't here?"

Her expression became more sullen than ever. "I didn't look in the garage. Why should I have? The door was shut. It usually is when there's a car in it."

She had me there. I knew she was lying, but her lies had successfully shut me out. Some of my initial adrenaline surge slowed, and I began to feel vaguely unsure of myself. I knew I had to come up with something before I appeared foolish, and she sensed it. I had to keep talking, so I tried a wild shot, a complete fabrication.

"Estelle, I think you ought to know something. I think you ought to know you were seen at Grace Chadwick's around midnight. You drove up to March House with François, walked around the back of the house, called for your mother, then came around the front and drove off in her car."

I knew at once, of course, that my shot had missed—and by a wide margin. For the first time some of the sullen fear I'd inspired faded from her eyes. She stared at me and laughed. "I don't know where you got that from. I never went near the place."

I tried not to sound defensive. "There was a witness. A reliable one."

"Well, whoever it is, they're lying. I was here. All night. You can ask anybody. When Rose didn't come home, we all waited for her until nearly two o'clock before we gave up and—"

She broke off, realizing she'd contradicted herself. A minute earlier she said she'd been out, came home, and thought Rose was in bed.

In seconds the tables had turned again, and she was back on the defensive. Her smile was gone. She sat there, miserable, twisting the bloodied tissue in her fingers. Then suddenly she began to cry. I waited until she turned tear-filled eyes toward me. "Margaret, I know you hate me, but you've got to believe me. I didn't go to March House. Honest. I don't care what anyone says. And I *did* find Rose's car at the bottom of the driveway in the morning. I don't know how it got there, but it started right up, so I drove it to the garage. Then I went to look in on Rose, and she wasn't there. The bed hadn't even been slept in. First I was a little worried, but I decided maybe she'd got up early and made the bed and had gone somewhere, maybe down to Ann's. And when Ann said she hadn't seen her, I thought maybe some friend had come and picked her up. They often do."

"By lunchtime you weren't seriously concerned?"

She shrugged. "No, I wasn't. Not really. I mean, what Rose did was her business, no? I'm not supposed to be responsible for my mother, am I?"

I had to admit to myself that she had checked me once more. But I knew she was still holding something back, so I persisted. I ignored her questions and said as aggressively as I could, "Then you didn't go to Menemsha for dinner after all—unless your saying you were here all evening is another lie."

"No."

"Where did you go? Or didn't you?"

She hesitated again before she said, "We went to Ann's. Rose went, too."

It was the first time I felt she was telling the truth.

"So you were with Rose?"

"Yes."

"And she came home with you."

She didn't answer. She stared at her hands.

I lost patience. "Come on, Estelle, either you tell it to me or to Fisher. Make up your mind." I waited.

She finally shook her head and said, "No. She went to March House. Grace called while we were still at Ann's."

This time it was my turn to stare. I could hardly believe what I'd heard. "Grace called Rose? At Ann's?"

"Yes."

"At that hour? But how did Grace know she was there?"

She shrugged helplessly. I tried again.

"What did she call about?"

"I don't know." Her voice rose. "Honest."

"And Rose went? Just like that?"

She was crying again, like a child, and she nodded.

"It was about eleven. We'd already finished dinner. Grace said she had to see Rose right away. The rest of us didn't get home until about one-thirty. I thought Rose would be back and in bed. When she wasn't, I called Grace. Rose once told me she stays up half the night, usually. She said some old people don't need much sleep. But there wasn't any answer, so I guessed Grace couldn't hear the phone or had gone to bed. I figured Rose was on her way back, so I went to bed myself."

It rang true. I could picture it—Estelle, probably befuddled by pot or too much to drink and mostly interested in bed with François and probably with Italian Trunks and the androgynous girl, too, the moment Rose was asleep. I could see her waking early with a hangover, remembering the night's events and then not finding her mother. She would have gone outside and seen Rose's car covered with nighttime dew, and she would have yanked the door open expecting Rose to be asleep in the front seat, perhaps, and found the car empty. I almost felt sorry for her.

"Estelle, do you know why Rose went to Grace's house so late at night and just like that—just because of one phone call? You must."

My persistence finally paid off. She suddenly surrendered. I guess she'd had enough. I certainly had.

"I'm not sure," she said, "but Rose had some sort of business with her. It could have been that."

"What sort of business? And don't tell me you don't know. Rose confided everything in you."

"She wanted to buy out Algar Mikele and give the property back to Grace."

It was a sudden bright shaft of light. I knew I

had finally stumbled on to something very important. I said quickly, "Well, at last. What was the deal?"

"Deal?"

"Nobody spends a lot of money for nothing. What did Rose expect in return?"

Estelle's voice was barely a whisper. "I think she said Grace was to make a new will and leave March House to her."

The shaft of light got much brighter. "Ah!" I said. Then I thought of Grace, old and infirm and with precious time running out. Why would she agree to such a scheme unless she saw an uncomplicated way to have once again some money of her own that was free from Arthur Heston's constant and onerous supervision?

"And how much," I asked, "was your mother planning to pay Grace for this new will?"

Estelle looked surprised. "I . . . I don't think anything. I mean, she never mentioned it."

"Nonsense. Why would Grace do it otherwise? Heston would buy the house back for her if Algar finally caved in. How much was Rose going to give him?"

"I . . . I think a hundred and twenty thousand."

The figure caught me by surprise. For a moment I simply stared. Under her option, Grace only had to pay Algar ninety thousand. Rose almost certainly would have learned that.

"Why so much?" I finally asked.

"I don't know," she said. "I think Rose said she thought Algar wouldn't take less. March House is worth much more, isn't it? And he'd need that much to buy something else at today's prices."

"Had she actually talked to him?"

"I don't know. Honestly, I don't."

She sat miserably shredding the bloodied tissue and I thought, *She's telling the truth, but something is still odd somewhere. Rose has never shown any interest in March House or Grace or in real estate. Why did she suddenly decide to take advantage of Grace's deal with Algar? There is more to surface yet, somewhere.*

As though none of it mattered, Estelle suddenly looked up from her hands, her eyes desperately anxious, and said, "You won't tell the police, Margaret, will you? Please."

I knew then that I'd heard everything she had to say. "If you mean the drugs," I said coldly, "it's your business what sort of mess you make of your life."

I opened the study door. I was right about François's listening. He jumped back, eavesdropping written all over him. I laughed contemptuously and went out the front door, got into my station wagon, and drove slowly down the driveway.

Just before turning onto Middle Road, I stopped and looked back. I could see Rose's house, Estelle's now. Nobody had come out to make certain I had really left. I stayed there a moment, adding up what I had learned. Leaving aside temporarily how Rose got involved in the first place, I'd found out a lot, but I still hadn't discovered why she had gone to March House so urgently and so late at night and I still didn't know who had brought her car back. I decided, however, to take things one at a time, to first concentrate on what I'd learned from Estelle which seemed all important. I summed everything up this way:

Rose wanted to buy out Algar Mikele and give the property back to Grace in return for Grace's leaving it to her. It was a good deal for Grace—she'd have Algar off her neck forever with no more fear of him and once again have money that didn't come from her Heston controlled trusts; it was a good deal for Rose—the property was worth far more than what she'd offered. It was a good deal even for Algar—he wouldn't clean up but he'd have enough to buy something else, far less fancy of course, but suitable, and he'd get himself out of hock at the same time and put an end to his family's misery.

But then, Grace murdered Rose, and that didn't

make any sense. If you don't like someone's business proposition, you don't have to kill them; you just have to say no. Especially if you are a frail old woman.

And that didn't make any sense either—Grace killing even a sparrow, let along another human being. No matter how hard I tried, I simply couldn't picture Grace stunning Rose, rolling her body into a pond and holding her head underwater, and then, according to Algar, attacking him.

The more I thought of it, the more it seemed utter nonsense. Algar had to be lying.

Sadly, I headed down Middle Road for home. But something kept nagging; Heather, her belief in Algar, the way the twins adored him, and, in an odd way, Algar himself. In spite of his morose character, his anxiety for his family didn't strike me as characteristic of a murderer.

With that thought an idea flashed into my mind that was so startling I nearly stopped the car dead in the road. Heather's twins had told Christopher that Grace was a witch. They'd said they had seen her flying across the lawn at night. Of course, that had to mean running, since nobody flies, and witches don't exist. But what old woman who needed help to get across the street by day could run about at night like that? Suddenly Algar's story seemed true again, and I saw a question that begged for an answer. Could Grace somehow be two people, a nighttime Grace and a daytime Grace? A nighttime Mr. Hyde and a daytime Dr. Jekyll? No, that was as impossible as the existence of a witch.

Unless—my thoughts leaped one step further—unless nighttime Grace wasn't Grace at all but an impostor, someone in old-woman's clothes who had enticed Rose over to daytime Grace's house just to murder her! Someone who had driven her car back to The Rookery perhaps to throw suspicion on Estelle and François.

I don't know why I did it, whatever suddenly prompted me to. I don't know what I expected to find, but I turned up Tea Lane and drove its dusty length to March House. Samantha had said Grace Chadwick would be in town with Dr. Glenn Rothenberg; I'd have the place to myself. What stupidity! Clearly, where I was concerned, the awful reality of murder had not yet sunk in all the way.

TEN

It was useless, I decided, to try to hide my station wagon. I drove right up to March House and parked before the steps of the wide, sagging, wooden veranda that spanned the whole front of the building. If caught there, I planned to brazen it out—say I'd found the door open and feared Grace might have been taken ill. Or I'd say whatever else came into my head. I've always been good at making things up on the spot.

There is almost nothing I can think of more silent than an empty house. It's a silence that lies outside as well as within. Standing by the station wagon, I felt it envelop me like a muffling blanket. Darkened windows stared wordlessly at me like secretive eyes. Moss-stained brick was as rigidly mute as the worn, paint-peeling woodwork of the eaves that capped it, and the soundless slate roofing and lifeless chimneys even higher above. I heard an occasional birdcall, the distant whirr of a locust, and the blood beating in my inner ears. Nothing else.

I went up the steps and crossed the veranda to the front door and rang the bell—just in case Grace had decided to stay home. I waited, but no one came. I rang again, hearing the bell sound distantly within. I lifted the handle of the lion's-head brass knocker and, bolstering my courage with aggressiveness, slammed it back down hard three times. The silence persisted.

After a minute or two, I went around back to try there. I don't now recall exactly why or how I thought I'd get in; I think I had some silly notion that I might find a ground-floor French door unlocked, perhaps one in the living room that faced the back lawn. Country householders don't usually take the scrupulous precautions city and suburban people do if they're just going out for the afternoon. Of course, I found everything locked and the living room curtains drawn. But then to my surprise I saw that the kitchen door in the servants' wing beyond was ajar. I went over and cautiously pushed it open all the way. Sunlight fell on the worn linoleum of a narrow hall where a swarm of houseflies rose and fell in a loose spiral.

There has always been something frightening to me about an open door in a supposedly empty house. A door doesn't open itself unless there's an exceptionally strong wind, and if Grace had not left this one open by mistake, did it mean someone else had entered the house and might still be in it?

All my courage evaporated. I found it hard to use my voice. When I called out, "Grace?" it took effort and sounded weak and thin. The reply was continued silence. Beyond the sunlight down the hall, I could see only shadows. I stepped across the threshold.

I called again. "Grace?" Now my legs had begun to feel helpless, too, like legs that won't work in a dream. Then, distantly, I heard a faint sound. I froze, listened, and at first decided it was the rhythmical tick-tock of a grandfather clock. I remembered there was one in the front hall, which was beyond an intervening dining room and a butler's pantry, both of which I now remembered lay at the kitchen hall's end directly in front of me. But then I realized that to hear the clock at this distance, the dining room and pantry doors would have to be open, and I could see that the latter was not. What was the sound, then?

To my left, a narrow winding staircase rose to servants' sleeping quarters, disappearing rapidly into darkness. I fought down an awful feeling that someone might be standing somewhere up there just out of sight. To my right was the open kitchen door. Was someone there who might suddenly come out or just be waiting? I took a deep breath and stepped into the doorway, and I think if there had only been old Grace Chadwick herself hunched innocently over the kitchen table shelling peas, that I would have screamed and run.

There was no one, but at once I realized from where the sound came. The sink, a deep old-fashioned copper-lined one, had a leaky faucet that dripped rhythmically. Force of habit as well as the desire to stop the steady sound made me want to shut it off, but if I were to go in to do so, I would have to come out again without knowing if, while I was in the kitchen, someone had entered the hall either from outside or by coming down the servants' stairs. I didn't want to face that.

I kept moving along the hallway, in shadows now, the sunlight behind me. I went past a cold larder, a small servants' toilet with the seat missing, a door I thought must lead to the cellar, and then I reached the butler's pantry. It had a swing door with a small window in it, which I forced myself to peer through. Anyone could have been there, and I wouldn't have been able to see who it was, the pantry was so dark. I pushed the door open, its spring hinges protesting. But once more there was nobody, nothing, just a small musty room shrouded in gloom. I suppose it hadn't been used for years.

I pushed open a second door and found myself in

the dining room. The table was covered with a sheet and sheets covered a dozen chairs and a sideboard and all the paintings as well. Big double doors gave onto the front hall. They were open, and now I could finally hear the dirge-slow sonorous sound of the grandfather clock.

I went to the hall, which was cool and had a musty odor, and stood looking cautiously around me. In spite of the fear that gripped my chest like a cold hand, I was able to think what a magnificent house it must have been in the old days when it was filled with light and the movements of people—the owners, their friends, servants, children, and their pets. The hall was large and went right up to a domed skylight with a dozen panes of colored glass that admitted an oddly tinted kaleidoscope of light that filtered down onto a magnificent open stairway leading first up to a wide half-landing before it turned to rise to the balconied second floor.

Off the hall, I saw closed doors that guarded the family living room, which I had tried to enter from outside and which I vaguely remembered had two large fireplaces; the dining room I had just left; a book-lined library; a billiard room with its huge green baize-covered mahogany table, overhead fringed lamp, and cue racks; and finally, the room in former days used only on very special occasions, the front parlor, where I had pictured Grace Chadwick talking to me on the telephone.

I started slowly up the stairs, whose dark red tread-wide carpet was nearly threadbare. Halfway, I stopped. Had I again heard something, not in the house this time but outside? I waited, trying to block out the sound of the grandfather clock, and then I was certain I'd heard something. Tires crunched on the gravel driveway. Through an arched Palladian-style window over the front door, I could look down on my station wagon. All of a sudden there appeared the familiar blue-green of one of Bert's half dozen Vineyard Haven taxis. Before I could worry that it might be Grace coming back unexpectedly, a man got out, a fairly tall man dressed in baggy khaki trousers and an old sweater. For a moment I was puzzled. Who on earth was this? Then I recognized the balding gray head, the long neck thrust forward from narrow stooped shoulders, the jowled jaw, and the heavy paunch. It was Arthur Heston, minus his usual pinstriped suit and briefcase.

The taxi pulled away, and Arthur stood a moment, studying my car, then came toward the front door. I was standing on the half landing midway between the hall and the balconied landing of the second floor and was directly under the skylight. Thus I was fully exposed should he look, by chance, through the same Palladian-style window over the door through which I could see him. Without thinking and in what felt like three steps, I fled to the relative safety of the full landing above, completely forgetting my fear that someone could be up there.

The first doorway on the landing directly at the top of the stairs opened on what appeared to be an unoccupied, shuttered-up bedroom. I ducked into it. Standing in half darkness, I could still see Arthur until he came up on the veranda and neared the front door below my line of sight. Had he recognized my car? His footsteps sounded heavily, and then there was the sound of the doorbell. It was located on the second-floor landing quite close by, and its shrill sound shattered the silence and made me jump involuntarily, reminding me that I might not be alone. I shrank deeper into the shadowed room, expecting at any moment to see someone appear from one of the other rooms off the upstairs hall beyond me.

Nobody did. Getting no answer, Heston used the knocker, as I had done. It sounded terribly metallic and loud. I thought he'd go on forever until I heard his footsteps again as he retreated to reappear momentarily again through the Palladian-style window, before he disappeared, to walk—as I guessed correctly—around the house to the back. I remembered thinking that perhaps he hadn't recognized my car because he hadn't called my name. But he had to wonder why nobody answered, when the car indicated quite positively that someone might be in the house.

That, of course, is when I made my great mistake. I should have answered the bell and the knocker. I should have come out of hiding and quite openly descended the stairs to greet him. I could easily have bluffed my way out of an awkward situation. My story of worrying about Grace when I'd found a door open would have worked. Even if he didn't believe me, Heston would not have dared challenge me.

But foolishly I didn't do anything. Caught snooping, my good sense evaporated. Like a child, I lost my head and hid from him.

Somehow certain now that except for Heston I was alone, I came boldly back out on the landing, and in less than a minute I heard his distant shout at the kitchen door. "Grace? Grace! Hello?"

There was silence again but not for long. I heard the dining room door to the butler's pantry swing abruptly open and shut. Almost immediately after there was his heavy tread in the front hall directly below me. I was just able to duck out of sight before he called out again.

"Grace, it's Arthur."

Getting no answer, he started up the stairs. I slipped behind the door of the room just before he reached the landing. Standing only a foot or two from me—I could see him through the open space between the door hinges—he called again and proceeded down the hall.

My eyes had become accustomed to the darkness of the room, and it no longer seemed so menacing. It was just what I had guessed it to be, a small bedroom with ornate Victorian furniture.

I waited, holding my breath. I heard Arthur's returning footsteps. He reappeared to stand once more right outside my door. I could hear him breathing, almost feel the heat of his body. I had ceased being frightened. Instead, I was embarrassed beyond description. I could think only of how ghastly it would be if he should discover me. It was too late to bluff. I would be caught hiding like a common housebreaker. No explanation could have rescued me.

But he didn't discover me, although now I wish he had. He looked down at the hall below, making up his mind what he should do. Then, with a vague sound of frustration, he went back downstairs.

I crossed to one of the bedroom's two windows and looked through the slanted slats of the closed shutters. Presently, I saw Arthur crossing the lawn. He reached the barn, entering by a small access door to one side of the big main doors, which, when open, would admit a hay wagon with a full load.

I waited for what I was certain was at least five minutes, and when he didn't come out, I guessed he must be fiddling with the old Lincoln, as he always did when he visited, getting it ready for its annual trip to Vineyard Haven and Edgartown. I glanced at my watch. It was nearly three-thirty. I couldn't stay there forever; Grace would be coming home soon with Glenn Rothenberg or Samantha.

I went back out onto the landing and, far more confident now, proceeded down the upstairs hall the way Heston had done to the room at the end.

ELEVEN

It was a large corner room. Its open shutters and raised blinds let in plenty of light, which revealed a shabby old chaise longue, a big and ornate walnut wardrobe with a mirrored door, an exquisite old-fashioned dressing table that I guessed to be French, a Victorian marble-topped dresser, a sagging secretaire, and finally a massive four-poster with a canopy and heavy drapes in tattered dark brown velvet. Two of the room's windows were partially raised, and a breath of air stirred their age-yellowed organdy curtains.

I went to the dressing table. Its top was cluttered with a silver-backed hand mirror and matching brush and comb, a "junk" box in which Grace kept a hodgepodge of lipsticks and rouges, so incongruous to her age, and a large jar of cold cream. A wastebasket filled with rouge- and powder-stained tissues testified to the amount of makeup she hid behind during the day and had for so many years now, along with hat, gloves, scarf, and dark glasses.

I went next to examine the secretaire. I don't know

what I expected to find; certainly I had nothing specific in mind, and I soon quailed at the confused mass of old papers, letters, and clippings that jammed every pigeon-hole and cranny. I could hardly open drawers for the accumulation of many years' worth of objects. String, sealing wax, rubber bands, paper clips, old pen nibs, erasers, and baggage tags fell out helter-skelter; all the bits and pieces hoarded by an eccentric old woman.

It was hopeless, I realized, to think I would discover anything there to unravel the mystery of Grace Chadwick, and I put back everything I'd disturbed where I thought it had come from, although I very much doubted Grace would know someone had been there no matter how much rummaging about I did.

I glanced around the room again and then, depending on how you look at it, stupidly or innocently ignored something very important. There was a dusty glass-doored bookcase with three shelves fixed to the wall above the desk; each shelf contained slim leather-bound personal diaries, many yellowed with age and dating back to World War I and 1917. I opened one. I think it was for 1926, and the few pages I turned revealed nothing of any interest, only shopping lists, observations about the local weather, and the occasional remark noting whom she'd dined with or had seen that day. I put the diary back. I had no time to indulge myself in the petty side of Grace Chadwick's life. Thus, what I mistakenly paid no attention to was the absence of any diaries for the five years previous to the present. The last one was for the year prior to her illness. Probably I thought she'd simply become too old to bother anymore. Whatever, I shut the bookcase doors.

My attention was next caught by two silver-framed photos on the dresser. One was of Arthur Heston taken about ten years before, and one was a composite of four photos—two baby pictures, a picture of a little boy about three years old, and one of a boy about six. Clearly, they were all the same child, and the resemblance to Arthur Heston was extraordinary. I didn't know what to make of them. Was Grace that fond of the man that she kept baby photos of him? It seemed very odd.

On the wall near the four-poster, which didn't seem to have been made up for some time, there were two old and badly faded family photos. In one I recognized Grace as a lovely, smiling young woman playing croquet with her mother and father on the back lawn. Judging from their clothes, the year must have been approximately 1920. How different the house and grounds looked then, so open and uncluttered, the trees half their present size and the lawn fringed by well-tended flower beds. In the background, I could see the fatal fish pond, not a murky, sad, weed-choked thing encroached on by the undergrowth of adjacent woods, but a bright little jewel set amid exotic plants and flowers, and the undergrowth still yards away, where it belonged.

In the second photo, Grace, her parents, and friends were grouped around a garden tea table. With a start I recognized the Pecks, Essie's grimly puritanical parents. I'd seen photos of them in Essie's house. The Reverend Peck held a little girl by the hand, a dark-eyed somber child I realized would have to be Essie. Both features and hair, although childish, were quite similar to those belonging to Essie today. I had never seen a picture of her as a child before, and I found it very strange to see her as she was more than half a century ago. How short life is and how quickly it passes.

There was something about both photos that bothered me. I wasn't sure what, but something in them was not right. It was Grace, I finally decided, but it wasn't how different she looked then. There was something else I couldn't understand. It was just a feeling I had.

I turned away finally and opened the wardrobe. At first I saw nothing but old dresses. Then, casually rummaging back to one side, I ran into something that sent chills through me. One dress felt damp around the hem. I pulled it out into the light. It was made of faded dark blue cotton, and at knee height I noticed grass stains—where Grace or someone else had knelt while pushing Rose's body into the fish pond? The thought horrified me. I suddenly felt the murderer had to be standing directly behind me and I had to force myself to turn and look to reassure myself. When I put the dress back, my hands were shaking, and all the fear I'd felt on first entering the house had returned.

Even if I had wanted to stay, I couldn't any longer. I had to get out at once. I started for the door, fighting away panic. Then, glancing back into the room one last time, I saw something that stopped me dead in my tracks. An inexplicable feeling of dread rose through my body to my throat. I could hardly breathe. In the mirror of the wardrobe, I had seen the reflection of another slightly-opened door across the room just as it swung open a little further. I didn't scream. I couldn't. I stood frozen, helpless, waiting until my eyes could tell me the worst—who was there and what would happen to me.

The door silently opened even more, wide enough for someone to come through. Incredibly, nobody did. What appeared instead and close to the floor was a small gray face with prominent black eyes that stared back at me in startled silence. It was a squirrel. For a moment neither of us moved. Then with a startled chatter it dashed for one of the open windows and in a flash had disappeared back outside where he belonged.

My terror ebbed, my heart slowly returned to normal, and with it my curiosity. I had seen the door when I'd first come in and had thought it concealed only a closet—the wardrobe and damp, grass-stained dress had distracted me from investigating it closely. But now, opening it all the way, I saw a darkened room. On the far wall, a mirror faintly reflected the bedroom I was in.

I made up my mind quickly. I looked out into the

DAVID OSBORN

upstairs hall, hearing only the grandfather clock downstairs. I went to one of the windows and peered down at the empty lawn. There was no one there either. Arthur Heston must still be tinkering with the old Lincoln in the barn. I was fairly certain he hadn't come back to the house and that there was no one else there.

I went into the room. Once again, I don't really know what I expected to find, but it certainly wasn't what was there. In the daylight coming through the open door to the bedroom, I saw an old-fashioned nursery complete with crib, teddy bears, a dollhouse, children's books, a hobbyhorse, and an open toy chest filled with every kind of plaything. All of it, although dusted and clean, was obviously very old. There didn't seem to be any window. If there had been one once—and there must have been—it had since been sealed.

I found a table lamp, turned it on, and looked about, nonplussed. Whose nursery was this? When was it used? Was there a connection between the baby photos of Arthur Heston and the fact that Grace never married and lived all her life with her mother and father?

I very nearly missed noticing the two wigs, and I suppose I would have if they'd just been casually lying about. I would have thought they were simply part of a child's dress-up costume and not stopped to consider that dressing up was something older children did, not a child still in a nursery.

But they weren't just lying about. They were on a doll's head, one over the other. And the doll's head had no body. It gave me quite a start when I first saw it. It belonged to a very large doll and was spiked down onto an old-fashioned hat stand sitting atop a small dresser. The head looked very human, and for a split second I thought it was and that there was someone in the nursery with me. If there had been just one wig, I probably would not have thought anything of it either. I would have simply thought I saw a doll's hair. But with one wig slightly askew on top of the other, I looked closer and I saw both were white, the hair fine and wavy.

I hesitated, then put one on and looked in the mirror, a charming little oval-shaped thing with a sculpted frame of porcelain shepherds and shepherdesses. An old woman stared back at me. I snatched the wig off as though I'd been burned. I felt my own hair prickle at the nape of my neck. And then—who knows what prompted me?—I opened one of the dresser drawers.

Lying in it, casually as though just thrown in, was a pair of narrow-cut, paint-spattered jeans and a pair of sneakers. And lying next to them was an open box of .22 cartridges. The box was new and the cartridges were packed tightly together but with a small number already removed. I didn't count how many. Why should I have? I simply stared.

A common enough sight in any country home is a rifle; people own one to shoot rats or stray cats that kill songbirds, or even to give themselves a sense of security. But I hadn't seen a rifle anywhere, nor could I ever remember being aware in the past that Grace had such a weapon. She just didn't strike me as the sort of person who might use one. What could the cartridges be for, then? A pistol? And why were some missing?

I didn't touch anything. I slowly closed the drawer, and whatever further thoughts I might have had at that instant were abruptly interrupted. What sounded like a muffled scream came suddenly from very far off, followed by some sort of a heavy sound, equally distant, a faint thumping that could be felt more than heard. Neither was repeated. I came out of the nursery at once and stood in Grace's room listening, beginning to think my imagination had played tricks on me. I heard nothing except complete silence broken momentarily by the rustle of some sparrows under the eaves.

The silence and the accumulation of fear and tension I felt made terror rise in me once more. I'd had enough of being alone in a big empty house where murder had occurred. All I could think of, suddenly, was escape.

Heedless of whether I might run into someone or make a noise, I dashed out of the room and down the hall and stairs. I didn't stop until I reached the kitchen door. Arthur Heston had shut it. I yanked it open and almost leaped out onto the lawn.

There I spun around to look back at the silent moldering old mansion, convinced that eyes were watching me from every window.

And I was standing there like that, trying to calm myself, when I heard the sound again, human but too awful to describe. It was not a scream this time but more of a bubbling moan, a stifled cry of extreme agony. It came from the barn, and I thought, *Oh, my God, I did hear something upstairs. That's Arthur Heston. He's had an accident—perhaps he fell from the loft.* And it occurred to me that Grace's old limousine might have fallen on him somehow if he'd jacked it up.

Heart in my mouth, I shouted, "Arthur?" There was no answer. I ran across the lawn to the access door of the barn and called again. "Arthur?"

Without thinking, I went in.

If the house was dark and gloomy, the barn was more so. The small round windows high up at each end barely filtered enough daylight through years of dust and cobwebs to pick out the massive traverse beams and uprights of the two huge open haylofts that occupied most of the barn's space right up to the roof.

I made out the old Lincoln, its big shadowy form immediately in front of me, its two old-fashioned headlights like giant eyes. It appeared to be tilted to one side.

Then I saw what looked like a man. Arthur? He was slouched down on the passenger's-side running board as though kneeling, his head inside the car.

All this I saw in a second or two and had hardly registered any of it when I felt rather than heard the faint rushing sound behind me.

There was a violent blow across the back of my neck. Darkness immediately closed in, and I saw nothing more.

TWELVE

My first awareness was of cold on my face and a familiar male voice I could not immediately identify.

The darkness faded, and now I could distinguish some vague shapes. I discovered the cold was a water-soaked cloth, and finally I identified the familiar features of Peter deBord bending over me.

"Take it easy, Mrs. Barlow. You're okay." I struggled and managed to sit up, and he said, "You fell or something."

I began to take in my surroundings: March House, the lawn behind it, and the driveway beyond with my parked station wagon. I was lying on the grass just outside the barn, whose two big doors were now open. But I couldn't fit Peter into the picture. He belonged in Edgartown in the bookstore or out in the harbor windsurfing in a wet suit. Why was he here? Why was I? I felt nauseated, and my head was splitting.

Thoughts were jumbled. I began to remember. I'd come to nose around and I'd been in the house. Peter explained his own presence. "I biked by to deliver books to some people down the road and saw your car and the small barn door open."

And then as I half turned to look back into the barn, he said quickly, "Don't look, Mrs. Barlow."

But it was too late. Even as he spoke, I remembered what I'd seen before—a man crouched on the running board of the big old Lincoln limousine. He was still there, legs buckled beneath him, as though he were kneeling, and his head still inside the car, held that way by the door's thick window, cranked up as tight as his neck would allow. One wheel was off the Lincoln and the car had come down from the jack that held it up, probably because of his struggles. It was Arthur Heston.

"I haven't called the police yet," Peter was saying. "I didn't want to leave you."

He went to wet the cloth again at a water spigot by the small barn door. He came back, held the cloth to my head once more, and, after a minute or two, helped me struggle to my feet. As I stood up, I turned for a second look and now could see Arthur Heston's face through the Lincoln's windshield; it was almost black, his tongue an obscene protruding sausage, and his eyes blood-red and bulging like those of a fish. A hand could barely fit through the space between the window top and the door-frame.

"You'd better sit down again," Peter said. He must have thought I was about to faint, and I guess I nearly did.

"Not the house, Peter. My car." I couldn't yet remember why the mere sight of the house terrified me.

We reached the station wagon, and Peter steered me around to the front passenger's seat. I sank gratefully into it.

"I'll drive you home, Mrs. Barlow. I'll put my bike in the back. But I think we'll have to wait for the police first."

I told him where the phone was, and to be careful. He loaded his bike into the car, then went to call, and I slowly came to my senses. At first I could only remember going into the house. But slowly it all came back; Grace's room, the photos of Arthur Heston, the nursery, the wigs, the paint-stained jeans and the sneakers and the box of cartridges, and the cry like an agonized scream followed by the strange thump, which I now realized was probably the old Lincoln falling off the jack.

I shuddered imagining it; Arthur jacking the car up and working at the wheel, perhaps, and pausing to go to the car's window to talk to whoever killed him. It would surely have been someone he knew and trusted. No stranger could have hidden in the front seat of the car, taking the chance that Arthur would not notice. Perhaps the conversation through the open window had even been pleasant or jocular, although it was hard to imagine Arthur's being jocular with anyone. And while they talked, his murderer would have slid over to the passenger's side, if not already there, gotten hold of the window handle, and struck like lightning. Whoever it was would have had to be very quick to beat Arthur's almost certain instinct to pull his head back as the heavy plate-glass window suddenly cranked upward toward his unprotected throat—and the killer would have had to have been strong, too, to help the window mechanism hold Arthur's head like a vise against his violent death struggles.

I was glad when Peter returned and got in the station wagon with me. For all I knew, the murderer could still be around someplace and, in my imagination, sitting there alone in my station wagon, was about to come after me. Peter reported that the police were on their way, and in what seemed no time at all, there were distant sirens that grew rapidly louder, and suddenly the driveway was filled with police cars and an ambulance. There was complete chaos then, to which I did not contribute until Lieutenant Fisher appeared by the door.

I could see he recognized me at once, but he proceeded as though he had not. He reintroduced himself with a definite emphasis on the "Lieutenant" in order to set himself apart from the rest of the officials, including Otis Cramm, now crowding the barn. I hadn't really paid too much attention to him the first time we met. I'd been too shocked by the sight of Rose's dreadfully mutilated face. Now I took the time to consider him more carefully, and he made me think immediately and rather ridiculously of another Fisher, Beatrix Potter's Jeremy Fisher, the frog who, while angling from a lily pad, was almost devoured by an enormous and predatory trout. The Homicide officer's mouth was wide and slack like a frog's mouth; his skin was sallow; his eyes bulged unattractively, and his thinning hair was inadequate cover for a rather big head, which seemed strangely flat on top and to have no intervening neck between it and his narrow shoulders.

"You the lady who found the body?"

I confessed that I was, and Peter told him how he'd found me lying unconscious on the barn floor.

He dismissed Peter with a curt glance and continued to question me, completely disregarding what I'd just been through and the state I was obviously in.

"Did you see who it was?"

"No. No, I didn't. I heard only a faint sound," I said.

"What were you doing here?"

His accusing manner got my back up. I've never much liked the police to begin with. Few, I agree, are as stupid as Otis Cramm, but, just the same, most can't tell the difference between the worst sort of criminal scum and an educated well-intentioned citizen, and the so-called career of "law enforcement" too often attracts neurotics who need badges, guns, and authority to make them feel as adequate as the rest of us.

I found Lieutenant Fisher to be no exception. Instinct told me to be very careful of him or I'd end up needlessly badgered, perhaps even a suspect. Thus I think I surprised myself by the quick lie I told him.

"I was driving by," I said, "and saw Arthur by the barn. We're old friends. I stopped to say hello."

His expression never altered. "You went in the house first?"

"House? No."

"Didn't make him coffee or tea?"

"Tea? Good heavens, no."

Before I could muster my thoughts to wonder what made him ask me, he told me. "The motor of your car is stone cold, Mrs. Barlow. Would that be because you were unconscious for a long time? There are also two unwashed cups in the kitchen sink, and I believe Miss Chadwick lives alone."

"I don't know how long I was lying in the barn," I said honestly. "And it must have taken you some time to get here."

"Nine and a half minutes," he interjected. "It took us just nine and a half minutes." His expression was unpleasantly victorious. "In this weather, it takes a motor thirty to forty minutes to cool off. At least."

With a slightly sinking heart, I briefly remembered my bumper sticker, which bravely said QUESTION AUTHORITY. I hoped Lieutenant Fisher had not noticed it. Thinking of it myself, however, buoyed my courage and I imagined what Essie might have said in my circumstances. She was hardly one to quail before the law. On the contrary, policemen invariably provided her with scornful amusement, which she made no attempt to hide.

So I looked Fisher right in the eye and smiled with as much apparent merriment as my raging headache would allow. "You win, Officer."

He literally flinched at the sudden demotion from lieutenant.

"I confess to modesty. I did go in the house—to the

bathroom, actually, the one upstairs in Miss Chadwick's bedroom. There's no seat on the one downstairs."

Essie, disguised as me, won the day. Fisher retreated, his frog face more sour than ever. "You didn't touch the body?"

"Oh, my God, no." This time I wasn't making believe.

For young Peter this was the last straw. He leaned across me and said angrily, "Hey, Lieutenant, give it up. Mrs. Barlow ought to be in the hospital, not sitting here answering questions."

My inquisitor reddened. I thought for a moment he would detain Peter. Then, surprisingly, he retreated. He flipped open his notebook and found my name. "Margaret Barlow. South Water Street. Edgartown?" When I nodded, clapped the book shut and said, "If you leave the island, Mrs. Barlow, let us know. We'll want to talk to you later on."

Muttering something about "cops" under his breath, Peter put the car in gear and unceremoniously shot out of the driveway, oblivious to the fact that he left Fisher about to say something else.

"Are you okay, Mrs. Barlow?"

I leaned back and closed my eyes. I wasn't. My head and neck hurt dreadfully. "Thank you, Peter, yes. And you agreed not to call me Mrs. Barlow, so please don't. You make me feel eighty."

He laughed. "And regardless of how you might feel right now, that's still forty-odd too many, no?"

I managed a smile. "You're sweet, but I should be so lucky." Glancing at him, I thought, *I just hope the woman who finally gets this one realizes how lucky she is.*

"Home or doctor?" he asked.

I suppose I should have gone to a doctor, but I couldn't face anything except aspirin and bed. Besides, I figured I didn't have a concussion. I could tell now my neck was what had been hit, not my head. "Home will do," I said.

"Sure?"

"Sure."

Turning onto the main road from Tea Lane, Peter said suddenly, "Why did you tell him what you did?"

"What's that?"

"I mean all that business about the upstairs john."

"You didn't believe it?"

"No."

"Don't you think he believed it?"

"Cops never believe anything."

I thought a minute, then said, "If I told him what I really was doing in the house, I would have been taken in for a week of questioning."

"What were you really doing?"

"Not today, Peter."

"Sorry."

He sounded slightly hurt. I touched his arm. "No offense. I will tell you. Just not right now."

We didn't talk anymore, and before I knew it I was home. Peter put the car in the garage, turned me over to Heather, who had just walked back from the beach with the children, and went off on his bicycle to the bookstore. Heather got me to bed fast, and I managed to persuade her not to bother with a doctor.

"Not even Glenn Rothenberg?"

"Especially not Doctor Rothenberg."

Something in me suddenly shied away from him. He practically lived with Samantha. On the way home with Peter a couple of very nasty images kept forcing themselves into my mind: Samantha in paint-stained jeans and sneakers carrying a heavy five-gallon paint can as though it were an empty sardine tin; Samantha appearing the next week as an eighty-year-old woman in *Victoria Regina*; Samantha's thoroughly red bank statement; Glenn Rothenberg always driving Grace around.

But was it really Grace he was driving?

I hadn't told Lieutenant Fisher about the nursery and what I found there. I was beginning to think I should have, because a whole new thought about nighttime Grace and daytime Grace was beginning to creep into my mind. Was it ludicrous to think that the person posing as Grace Chadwick would dress up like her in her bedroom and even leave in her wardrobe the dress that was worn to commit the murder?

Suppose, I thought, I was wrong and nighttime Grace and daytime Grace were the same Grace after all, but that Grace wasn't Grace? Suppose there was no real Grace at all?

THIRTEEN

The irony of what I'd been through, Essie said, was that all the time help had been right at hand. She had been less than five hundred yards away transplanting herbs from the field she'd sold to the one she'd kept. She had been out of sight, to be sure, and out of hearing, but close by just the same.

"I can't get over it, Margaret, and I know Owen Fuller was home, because I saw him in his barn when I left."

She sat on the edge of my bed sipping the herbal tea Heather had made and that Essie was polite enough to praise and not say was inferior to her own.

It was evening, about seven o'clock. Essie had been in town at the Harbor Bookstore looking for her secateurs she thought had slipped through the hole in her creel. When she heard from Peter what had happened, she'd come right over. Keeping my mind as much as possible off my aching neck and head, I told her almost everything, from the time I'd driven up the lovely avenue of maples to Rose Perkins's Rookery to the moment Peter finally chauffeured me to safety from the obnoxious Lieutenant Fisher.

I say "almost" because I had left out the part about discovering the box of .22 cartridges. I was certain if I mentioned them, Essie would have tied me to the bed. Two people had already been brutally murdered and two attacked—Algar, if he was telling the truth, and me. If my suspicions were correct, the cartridges along with the jeans and sneakers belonged to the murderer and meant someone around was armed and thus doubly dangerous. One could perhaps fight off being drowned or choked, but no one could fight off a well-aimed bullet. I also hadn't yet told her my idea that someone might be impersonating Grace. Faced with Essie's practical-minded presence, I'd decided to see whether, if given the whole picture, she would not come to the same conclusion on her own that I had.

Once Essie had ascertained that I wasn't exactly at death's door, she severely reprimanded me for going to March House on my own, without her. "Nobody would have dared attack both of us," she said, and she was right. But it would have been mostly because of her, I thought. Essie was far more able to cope with violence than I. I didn't say so, however. My pride denied her the compliment. With a twinkle in her eye that took some of the bite out of her annoyance, she added, "Besides, I would have loved to sneak about March House. I've been wanting to for years."

Now, once more going over the details about the secret nursery and the baby photos of Arthur Heston, she was still as astonished as I.

"Can you imagine, Margaret, what trouble the Chadwicks must have had trying to hide Grace's pregnancy?"

"We don't know he was hers," I said. "He could have been a baby brother."

But I hardly believed my own suggestion, because I had formed images of the young and lovely Grace who had played croquet on the back lawn suddenly facing what in her time and especially to her narrow-minded parents was the ultimate disgrace of illegitimate childbirth. And then for years having to hide Arthur Heston for his annual visit certainly seemed, at any rate, to substantiate that he was hers.

"Or," I said, with almost no conviction now, "he was possibly just a lifelong friend and not connected to the nursery at all."

"Possibly," Essie echoed, "but that's not nearly as much fun."

"Shame on you," I said. I could see the islander side of Essie's character creating racy headlines in her mind to help fill long lonely winter nights. I brought the conversation back to what I felt was more important. "The sneakers and jeans," I said, "belong to a woman, I'm certain, someone young and slender." I hesitated, remembering how yesterday, while repairing traps on the *Janet B*, Essie had belittled any suspicion of Estelle Perkins. Then I said warily, "Someone like Samantha Sanderson."

Essie smiled. "Samantha now?"

"The jeans would fit her perfectly."

She shook her head. "I think you're putting too much importance on them," she said. "There must be a reasonable explanation. They could belong to Samantha, of course. Got caught in a storm or something. But they're more likely to belong to someone helping Grace in the house."

"But who?"

Essie shrugged. "A local girl or some college kid employed for the summer, I suppose. Rothenberg should be able to tell us."

"But why change clothes in a nursery," I insisted,

"if it's supposed to be secret? Grace would have kept it locked, surely."

"The clothes didn't have to be changed there to be there," Essie replied. "Grace could have put them there after they were changed someplace else."

"What about the wigs, then?" I demanded. I think I nearly held my breath. Surely she would see now what I was driving at.

I was wrong. Essie looked blank. "Wigs?" she said, and then brightened. "Oh. Why were they in the nursery? Grace's vanity, I suppose. She's always been terribly vain. Look at all that ridiculous makeup. She probably didn't want anyone to see them. Especially not Arthur Heston if he came into her room, which obviously from what you tell me he was quite in the habit of doing."

It caught me by surprise. I'd never considered that the wigs were Grace's. I'd only thought of them as part of a disguise. I tried to keep chagrin out of my voice. I said, "I didn't know Grace wore a wig."

"Oh, yes," Essie declared. "She told me all about it one day, I remember. She lost almost all her hair from chemotherapy before she went into remission, and of course it never grew back."

I swallowed my disappointment. "If you're right," I said, "and the clothes and wigs don't actually mean anything, then perhaps Rose's wanting to buy out Algar becomes the only possible clue we have at the moment— that is, if Estelle wasn't making it up."

Essie looked confused. "Clue? I don't follow. Clue to what?"

"To some sort of motive for Rose's murder."

Her answering tone was one of patient forbearance. "Margaret, I can't see how Rose's wanting to buy out Algar would make someone want to murder Grace. On the contrary."

"Oh, Essie, please!" I exclaimed. "Do stop insisting

Rose's murder was a mistake. Whoever killed Rose meant to kill her, and nobody else."

"You keep supposing that, Margaret."

"I'm not supposing it," I said hotly. Then I remembered I hadn't yet told Essie about Algar's witnessing Rose's murder. "Oh!" I added guiltily, even apprehensively. My omission could be worse an affront than my sneaking around March House without her.

But to my surprise when I'd repeated everything Heather had said, she didn't seem at all annoyed. What she did, though, was put on a certain expression she always used out of courtesy to appear merely skeptical when actually she didn't believe a word I said.

"How interesting, Margaret, dear, but I'm certain you've made allowances for the poor desperate man's having to stretch the truth a little."

"On the contrary," I said firmly. "I'm positive he did not."

"I see." Essie sniffed diffidently, and that suddenly got my back up. She'd proved me pretty much wrong so far, and I expected she'd prove me wrong again—Essie always had a more logical way of looking at things than I—but I was now determined to present my theory about Grace not being Grace, come what may.

"Let's get back to jeans and wigs," I said. "Just suppose you were mistaken there. Suppose the wigs aren't being used because Grace is nearly bald and the jeans and sneakers weren't left there by some local girl or college student. Suppose they belong to the murderer."

I waited. Essie didn't answer for a moment. She stared at me with an expression of incredulity and then finally said, "Correct me if I'm wrong, but what you're now suggesting is that whoever killed Rose and Arthur and attacked you, and presuming it was the same person— I still only say presuming, mind you—that this person has been impersonating Grace?"

"I'm suggesting more than that."

"Oh?"

"I'm suggesting," I said, "that Grace did not miraculously go into remission."

"You're saying she died?" Essie's eyebrows arched pointedly.

"Yes."

"Six years ago?"

"Yes."

"And all this time you think someone's been pretending to be her?"

"Yes," I said.

Essie let out a low whistle. "That's quite a thought," she said.

"I can't believe an old woman as frail and sick as Grace was could enjoy such a remission. And an impersonation would explain everything."

"Well, not quite everything," Essie returned cautiously after a moment. "It wouldn't explain, for example, how someone managed to keep her death a secret all this time."

I started to protest.

Essie held up one garden-worn hand. "And it doesn't explain why anyone would want to impersonate her for so long and then, according to you, use the impersonation to kill Rose Perkins and Arthur Heston. How do you explain that?"

"I don't know," I confessed. And indeed at this point I didn't.

We were silent then, Essie deep in thought. I could see I'd shaken her thinking, but I wasn't sure how much. After a moment she said, "If you seriously think someone is impersonating Grace, do you have any idea who it might be?"

I shook my head. I was suddenly far less certain than I had been earlier. "I don't know that either," I said. "I really don't. I have suspicions, but only suspicions."

"You're saying an impostor would have to fit the

jeans and sneakers. So we're back to Samantha again, aren't we? Or even Estelle?"

"Perhaps," I answered.

"Who else, if you're right? If the murders weren't committed by a lunatic and were premeditated, as the police claim, wouldn't the murderer have to be someone connected with Grace? Or Rose, if you insist."

I didn't answer this time. Essie's practicality was getting through to me. I thought once more about both young women and Rose. If, as Essie had pointed out the day before, it was hard to come up with a motive for Estelle's murdering her mother, it was even harder to ascribe one to Samantha. In spite of my dark thoughts about her slender body easily fitting the jeans, her acting ability, and her red-ink bank account, why on earth would she want Rose Perkins dead? I could see no possible reason.

Essie broke into my thoughts. "Tell me something honestly. If Algar hadn't reported the scene he said he saw, would you have suspected an impersonation?"

I looked up at her hard. It was a question I had hoped to avoid. Under normal circumstances, I think pride would have brought an instant defensive retort from me, one that would be highly protective of Algar. But Essie's tone, like her concerned expression, was different than it had been before. I felt no anti-Heather jealousy there. She was trying to be helpful, not dig at me. My momentary irritation with her faded quickly and I responded in kind and tried to clear my head of any theorizing that might color an honest answer.

The jeans, the wigs, the damp dress—Essie was right, they didn't prove an impersonation. On their own, they just led to speculation. What about the children, then, saying they'd seen Grace Chadwick flying across the lawn at night like a witch? Their story, as I'd once thought, could be childish imagination stimulated by the moon-silhouetted gabled roofs of a dark and menacing house, or they could have simply seen Owen Fuller. What they reported didn't indicate an impostor. And what about Arthur Heston and the blow I'd been struck? Both suggested someone quick and strong, but there, too, I had to admit, like it or not, that everything rested on Algar's telling the truth.

Essie was waiting for me to speak, her expression anxious but trusting me to be truthful to myself as well as her.

"No," I said finally. "If I hadn't heard Algar's story, I don't think I would have."

She must have realized how difficult the answer had been for me to give. She didn't ask me then if I really believed Algar or not. Instead, she suddenly seized one of my hands and said, "Oh, Margaret, dear, forgive me for being such a cynic. I must seem like a dried-up old schoolmarm sniping at everything. But do try to see why. There you lie, clobbered by some awful maniac, with Rose and Arthur already dead. I understand your desire to help poor Heather and her children, I really do, but you have me scared beyond reason. All our wonderful dreams and plans for the future—please, please don't lose sight of them and go on sneaking about playing detective and end up getting yourself killed. And don't say it could never happen when it so easily could. If Algar is truly innocent, Heather has nothing to fear. A good defense lawyer and a jury will find him so."

I wasn't sure about justice and Algar. If Algar wasn't believed, there seemed to be such a very strong case against him. But Essie was right about the danger. What on earth was I doing playing detective? What had happened so far wasn't make-believe. It was all very real. All the time I'd been in March House somebody had silently been around, somebody very dangerous. The terror I'd felt there came back to me in a rush. My hands and skin under the bedclothes were clammy and my mouth dry. I could hardly muster words beyond a whisper and the weak smile of abject surrender. "You win," I said.

Essie didn't try to hide her relief. There were tears in her eyes. "Will you promise me you'll leave any more investigating to that horrid Fisher creature?"

"I promise," I said, and at that moment meant it.

But long after Essie had gone back to Menemsha, and after Heather had fed me hot soup and given me more aspirin and Peter had kindly telephoned to see how I was, and when everyone was asleep and comforting darkness enveloped everything, I knew I had made a dear friend a promise I could not keep. Regardless of the danger to me and the risk to all the dreams Essie and I shared, it was too late to turn back. I had to go on. If Algar wasn't telling the truth, nothing made any sense. I simply couldn't accept that the damp dress, the jeans and wigs in a nursery, children's stories, Heston's violent death, my aching neck, and a box of cartridges meant nothing.

Besides, not giving Algar the benefit of the doubt would have meant destroying Heather's only hope. For surely, if I didn't believe him, nobody else would. Until there was proof to the contrary, I had to.

FOURTEEN

I stayed in bed the next day trying to think clearly, but it wasn't easy. It was difficult not to relive the terror I'd felt at March House from the silence of the place when I'd arrived; the dark butler's pantry and sheet-draped gloom of the dining room; the slowly opening door of the secret nursery; Arthur's death cries; and the shadowed barn with the big round headlights of the old Lincoln limousine fixed on me like malevolent eyes. It was hard not to think of the first rustling sound behind me, which I knew, even before the blow, was something terrible.

But I didn't. I forced my fears to the furthest corner of my mind and concentrated on the possible evidence that could prove Algar's innocence. If someone was indeed impersonating Grace Chadwick, then Grace Chadwick was dead and would have been for years. That someone was entering March House at will and climbing the stairs to Grace's bedroom. There, standing amid long-forgotten toys, the intruder would don one of the white wigs taken from the doll's head in the nursery and select a suitable dress from the wardrobe in Grace's bedroom. Whoever it was would then sit at Grace's dressing table, applying disguising lipstick, rouge, and powder as the dead Grace had always done. Finally, adding a hat and a scarf worn high around the neck and sometimes dark glasses, the new "Grace" would go out to face the world.

How often was this done? Grace went to Florida all winter, so the sham would have to be played out only in the spring, summer, and autumn. Summer was the real test, because the majority of people who knew Grace well were summer visitors. "Grace" would never need to put in an appearance more than once a week, I thought. She'd need to do nothing more than be seen on the edge of the road by the rural mailbox or being driven to town by Glenn Rothenberg. Man or woman, the person doing this was skillful. I remembered only too well my own phone conversation with "Grace," the old quavery voice, and the capriciousness of advanced age.

The impersonation would have started immediately upon Grace Chadwick's death, which had somehow been kept secret. Perhaps she too had been murdered! It would not have been hard to kill her, I guessed. A pillow over her face while she slept in her great four-poster would have finished her quickly without a struggle. Next would come the rapid withdrawal from Vineyard social life, already begun by the real Grace on the grounds of illness and age. Everyone had accepted it. Why not? People didn't pay that much attention to other people. Essie knew Grace well and she'd been fooled. Rose Perkins had been duped, too.

In my mind, I saw the impersonator hurriedly putting on last touches of the disguise when headlights on Tea Lane announced Rose Perkins. I saw "Grace" making the rapid, scurrying descent of the now-dark stairs; I heard Rose call out; I saw the back door open and the meeting on the shadowed lawn; I saw the blow to Rose's neck and the fluttering figure kneeling beside the stagnant, weed-choked fish pond to hold underwater the head of the inert woman rolled in there to be drowned.

But what about the police? Surely Fisher would have interviewed "Grace" extensively. Wouldn't he have seen through the disguise? The answer was, why should he have? With no reason to suspect an impersonation, he would have seen only what the impersonator wanted him to see—an eccentric, semi-senile old woman answering his questions with non sequiturs and hostile demands that they all go away and stop littering her property and blocking her driveway.

In the back of every policeman's mind, there had to be two questions: How accurate was the information he was getting? How would the person interviewed stand up in court as a witness? Where Grace Chadwick was concerned, Fisher could only have concluded she would be useless on both counts and decided his best course would be to relieve himself of one more unnecessary burden by staying as clear of her as possible.

All right, but how about her handwriting? I wondered. What about checks and tax forms, among other things? Simple. If she wasn't a suspect, the police would not have checked her papers in the first place, and even if they had, an old person's handwriting gets shakier by the month, making forgery a cinch.

Only Arthur Heston could have stood in the way. Was I wrong to think the impostor fooled him, too? He knew Grace Chadwick better than anyone. Would he have seen through her disguise? If physical difference didn't make him suspicious, then perhaps he would have noticed a difference in her speech or daily habits, or he could have tripped her up on intimate family knowledge. Well, if Arthur indeed had discovered the impersonation, then he was either a blackmailer or an accomplice, and in either case he became a threat that had to be eliminated.

I could easily imagine them both, Arthur and his

killer, a faceless unidentifiable "someone," in the half light of the barn seated in the front seat of the big dusty old limousine. I remembered the musty smell of unaired leather seats and horsehair stuffing and could picture the killer looking out at Arthur through the tall upright windshield. Perhaps considering what was about to take place, the murderer had gripped the varnished walnut steering wheel that was once so competently maneuvered and cared for by a liveried chauffeur now long dead.

Heston—balding, narrow-shouldered, big, and soft of belly—would be bent over the front wheel he was removing. What would this pair be talking about? I wondered. Blackmail? Heston threatening, expression and voice angry? Or maybe they were conspiring on what to do about the ongoing police investigation.

And all the time the murderer, sliding closer to the window, waited until Heston put his head inside the car—in anger? Out of curiosity? It made no difference. The trap sprang. Like lightning, a steel-strong wrist spun the handle. The heavy glass surged upward and touched Heston's naked throat. He reacted, but he was too late.

How long did it take to die? A minute? Two? All the while his flailing hands desperately tried to force the window back down, a test of dying strength against the leverage of gears and handle that gave equal strength to whoever held it up ever tighter against him.

How long after I'd heard his first scream of terror and dashed down the stairs out of March House before I heard his moan of surrender to death? Had sparrows, frightened by his final throes, fluttered and screamed in the barn's high eaves? Had the killer, holding the handle fast against Arthur's desperate struggles, laughed or spat out words of venom as his vision darkened and the life went out of him?

Out in the Edgartown harbor beyond my windows, a tall-masted ketch came gliding in under power, emitting a faint, muffled rumble of exhaust from its auxiliary motor, its sails half lowered and fluttering in a light wind, the voices of its bronzed shirtless crew calling out as they readied to catch the mooring buoy. Sanity.

The barn slowly left my mind. Why? I asked myself for the hundredth time. Why impersonate Grace? To what end? And then, asking this question just once more, the answer was suddenly so clear and so obvious that I wondered why I hadn't seen it all the time. The impersonator would take Grace's place, go into "remission," and "stay alive" until Algar Mikele became absolutely desperate and virtually bankrupt; then, vetoing Algar's sale to anyone else, buy back March House from him for the lowest sum possible, resell it for a small fortune, and cease the impersonation. People would wonder about Grace Chadwick's sudden disappearance but would never find her.

Everything around me became electric sharp and bright: soft patterns of light across my ceiling, objects in my room, the hulls and masts in the harbor, clear voices out over the water.

The whole scenario was suddenly so simple. Of course, there was always the chance that Algar might not go broke and have to sell, but that was a gamble worth the risk. I remembered my first reaction when Estelle told me Rose wanted to buy him out and I'd wondered, then, how much Rose had planned to pay "Grace" to will her the property. Had Rose indeed died because she'd become a threat to the impostor's whole scheme? It seemed reasonable to think so. And Heston! Why put up with him if blackmail was his game?

In spite of myself, I felt the now-familiar chill of horror creep up my body once more. And once more the darkness of death filled my mind with its images. Grace, the real Grace, old and frail, her body wracked by cancer, lying upstairs in March House on her chaise longue and trustingly accepting into her room someone who would soon murder her. Or sitting old and lonely at her kitchen table just as I thought I might find her, in despair at the relentless pain of cancer and the inescapable approach of death, and welcoming the knock at her door. She would be smiling and welcoming as her murderer sidled behind her and raised a hand, far younger and stronger than hers, to strike life from her.

I felt the back of my neck, still sore from the blow I had suffered, and was overcome by fury. There might have been a fourth person dead if the murderer had struck me harder.

I rose to sit for a long time, looking out my window at the comforting familiarity of the summer harbor; the Edgartown Yacht Club and the Reading Room, another private club, both bulky shingled squares projecting at the end of their weathered piling wharves into the boat basin; the fancy brass-railed yacht-club launch picking up crews from moored yachts; and the myriad small craft ranging from tourists' outboard motor whale boats, hired for the day, to dinghies from private yachts. Essie and I had eliminated Samantha and Estelle for lack of motive. Now, all of a sudden, I had a motive that would fit not just both of them, but anyone who knew about Algar's deal with Grace; anyone desperate enough to see opportunity in age, illness, and reclusiveness, and cold-blooded enough to risk an impersonation, to say nothing of murder.

Suddenly I felt very lonely. And vulnerable. If I should need help, where would I turn? I felt confused, too, my mind a storm of conflicting ideas, impressions, and suspicions. If I needed to talk things out, to whom could I talk? It couldn't be Essie because I was going to break a promise to her; it couldn't be Heather because it was conceivable she might be lying to me.

And then I thought of young Peter deBord. No, I told myself at once, that was impossible also. I hardly knew him. I put him out of my thoughts, but he kept coming back. But why not? I thought quickly. He'd had something of a baptism that very day, to say the least, and the most he could tell me was that I was crazy and to stick to my grandchildren and knitting.

I didn't think that Peter would say that, however. I had the impression he didn't regard me as an over-the-hill widow. In fact, quite the contrary. My impression was that he found me quite attractive. For a few moments I allowed myself the feminine luxury of remembering two occasions when I'd caught him glancing at my legs, and on another furtively sizing up my figure. I began to feel a trifle foolish, and I think, sitting there, I actually blushed.

Oh, for God's sake, Margaret, cried my common sense. *You're twice his age. Control your fantasies. What is his mind like?*

His mind was fine, the more sensible side of Margaret Barlow decided; and on that I finally went back to bed and drifted off into late-afternoon sleep with a last comforting thought. If that disgusting Fisher creature were to find my fingerprints all over Grace's bedroom, I'd already provided myself with an excuse, whether he cared to believe it or not, for my presence there.

FIFTEEN

"**B**ut Margaret, don't you think you should tell all this to old Frog Face?"

Peter and I were sitting on a sea- and time-worn overturned skiff that smelled wonderfully of caulking, old paint, seaweed, and fish. An elderly lobsterman we both knew had drawn it up above the high-tide mark on a bit of pebbly Chappaquiddick beach just by the cross-harbor ferry dock. The little Edgartown–Chappaquiddick ferry would rest not a moment longer than needed to discharge its open-deck cargo of three cars and reload before its five-minute return journey to Edgartown, where it would repeat the day-long process.

The sun was warm and bright, the harbor surface that glassy calm that often occurs when the wind drops between early morning and early afternoon. Scores of yachts big and small lay motionless at their moorings, and beyond them the docks and wharves of Edgartown were just beginning to bustle with the daytime activity of summer visitors.

Peter had been windsurfing, catching whatever wind he could out on the sound, and was wearing a sleeveless, short-legged wet suit zipped open to his waist. His skin was bronzed, his hair dark and salt-flecked, and his eyes very blue. I, feeling a little like a college girl on a clandestine date, was at my preppy best in white Bermuda shorts, a lavender-colored linen shirt with a matching cardigan over my shoulders, and lavender espadrilles and wondering what on earth had got into me to try to look twenty years younger than I was.

We'd been on the beach for half an hour, and I'd told Peter everything. He'd listened silently without comment, occasionally nodding or shaking his head, all the while toying with a handful of tiny shells he'd scooped up from between his bare feet, or carefully picking out small flat stones and skipping them out across the now-glassy water. He seemed to find neither murder nor my involvement with it particularly surprising.

I thought of Fisher. "I don't think he'd believe a word I said, Peter," I remarked. "And by telling him the truth now, I'd have to admit I lied before—'suppressed vital evidence,' he'd probably say—and that could really get me in a lot of trouble. I'm certain I'm not high on his list of favorite people."

"Maybe you're right," Peter acknowledged. "But what's the alternative? You won't let me do the obvious."

"I most certainly won't," I said firmly.

Peter had suggested following "Grace" on one of her trips to town and, at an opportune moment, yanking the wig from her head. I had immediately reminded him of the box of .22 cartridges in the drawer of the nursery. "But you don't know she has a revolver," he protested.

"And you're not going to be the one to get her to show you if she does or doesn't," I countered, "or get yourself locked up for assault by old Frog Face if for some crazy reason I've made a mistake and she really is Grace. I'm not going to try it either, so forget it."

Peter made vague noises of protest about being able to run faster than any old woman could scream and then said, "Okay, you're the boss. So getting back to what you and Essie talked about—jeans and sneakers and wigs and Samantha and Estelle Perkins. Now that you've figured out a possible motive, what about them? Back to square one, no? And if Samantha's a possibility again, what about Rothenberg? Do you think that would make him suspect, too?"

"Would he be in it with her? I don't know."

"They've been shacked up for a couple of years now," Peter observed. "How could she possibly fool him? He'd have to see through any disguise, wouldn't he?"

He was right, I thought. Samantha and Glenn Rothenberg were obviously lovers and had to know each other very well, physically at least: too well surely for him not to be able to see through any type of physical disguise. And even on the very remote chance Samantha could have fooled him with a disguise, how long could she possibly have got away with the endless lies and fabrications she would have had to come up with to cover her complete disappearance as Samantha whenever she was with him as "Grace"?

"You're right," I said. "Logically, if she's the impersonator, he would have to be in it with her."

I had voiced an opinion, but something in me balked just the same. I could see Samantha killing someone but couldn't accept Glenn's possible involvement in such a crime, even if he was just a silent partner. Was it because he was a doctor and I was raised to think doctors, like judges, are beyond reproach? Or was it because of his personal charm? I couldn't decide. My brain said one thing, my instincts another.

Peter skipped a stone that nearly landed on the board of a passing surfer friend who was paddling his way through the calm water. They exchanged a few friendly insults, and then Peter turned back to me.

"Somehow I can't see Estelle Perkins doing it. She's wide open now to be suspected, I agree. But actually drowning someone or cranking a window up on Heston's neck?" He shook his head. "I'm not sure."

"Do you know her?"

He shrugged. "I've seen her around."

I felt an odd twinge. Jealousy? I told myself not to be idiotic. "And?"

He grinned. "Estelle needs to be run. If she doesn't shape up, she gets knocked on her ass."

"I agree," I said. I was beginning to feel bitchy. "How about him?"

"The Frenchie? No way. Not actually doing it, anyway."

He was right. I could see François plotting, never doing the dirty work himself since he was too much of a coward. But urging someone else to do it? Oh, yes! As I remembered Estelle, however, huddled wet and naked and little-girl sullen in the chair in Rose's study, I found myself agreeing with Peter's assessment and not sure at all about her guilt or innocence either. Then who else? My mind was searching everywhere for a murderer candidate when Peter suddenly asked me something that at that moment seemed quite unrelated. He said, "What was it you think you saw and found strange in the photographs?"

"The ones of Grace when she was young?"

"Right. You said they were on the wall by the bed."

"I don't know," I said. I tried to remember the photos: Grace, her parents, the croquet equipment, the tea table, and the fish pond. It was something about Grace herself; that was as far as I could get. "Do you think it's important?" I asked.

Peter shrugged. "Maybe not. But there are too many dead ends." He was thoughtful. Then he said, "You know, whoever we're looking for has really screwed up, at least where buying and selling March House is concerned."

"How so?" I asked. "If and when Algar shows up, he's going to need money more than ever."

"And keep his mouth shut about Grace killing Rose just to get it? Maybe you're right. But I bet whoever we're looking for won't chance that now. Would you?"

Would I? I stared at the little car ferry tirelessly churning its way toward the Chappaquiddick dock, but I didn't really see it. Instead I saw myself as the impostor, for years untroubled but now suddenly thrust into the limelight involuntarily. I saw myself buying March House from Algar and then, even if I got away with it, calling more attention to myself by selling it again for a price that would surely make Fisher wonder. I saw myself as someone who had suddenly lost control of a situation just because I had lost control of myself. The very purpose of the murders I'd committed had now become self-defeating, and I tried to imagine myself continuing the impersonation of Grace Chadwick and couldn't. Now, I thought, I would have to spend all my energies covering whatever tracks I might have left.

I said to Peter, "It makes things even worse for Algar if our murderer decides enough is enough. There won't be any new mistakes to take suspicion away from him."

He stared silently at a lovely yawl drifting slowly through the harbor entrance, its sails slack, its crew casual as they moved easily around the deck. "Alice," he said suddenly.

"Alice?"

"I think you have to find out about Alice."

The name and his remark were both totally out of context. I asked him, "Who on earth is Alice?"

"Alice Webb," Peter said. "The maid."

"What maid?"

"At March House." His tone had that touch of

forced patience a boy would use when he realized a girl was pretty but not terribly bright. "There was a maid there when I was still in school and used to deliver the *Gazette*."

I shook my head. "I don't remember any maid."

"Sure you do. She was a dreadful old hag, and I'm positive her last name was Webb. She was the sister of that Chilmark grocery-store lady, Dorothy. Remember her?"

I did and laughed. "Old Gums."

"Right. Her teeth always slipped out when she started shouting at kids she caught poking around in the candy bin."

Suddenly I did remember Alice, a lean, mean little creature scurrying around Grace's house, with wispy gray hair and a black, scraggly woman's mustache, and long hairs, too, on her chin. I told Peter I remembered her. "What do you mean I need to find out about her?" I asked.

"I mean, where is she now?" He put his handful of shells down next to me on the overturned skiff and began sorting them out, chucking those he didn't want over his shoulder into the water.

"Well," I answered, "I should think she's either sitting behind a stove someplace or in a home. Or dead. She wasn't exactly a debutante, was she?"

"If she were alive, she'd be the one to tell you whether Grace was really Grace or not, no?"

I mentally kicked msyelf for being so slow.

"You're probably right," I confessed. "But suppose she can't be found?"

Peter shrugged. "If she isn't alive, she may have said something once about the nursery or Arthur Heston to someone in her family that could be helpful—and unless asked point-blank, they'll never step forward with it, especially not to the police. You know how these country people are."

"But they might open up to me?"

"Maybe. Worth a try, no? You could start with Dorothy if she's still around."

"Peter, you're a genius!"

He grinned and straightened up from the shells. A gull was flying by low over the water. He skipped a stone at it, which, on the second skip, nearly scored a hit. The gull flapped away screaming, and I thought him an incorrigible small boy.

"Do you want me to come with you?" he asked. "It would have to be later in the week. I can't get off today or tomorrow." He glanced at his underwater wristwatch.

I checked the time, too, and saw it was nearly eleven-thirty; I knew this week he had to be at work at noon. "I'm going right now," I said. "I can't see how asking a few questions about Alice could get me in any trouble."

"As long as you don't get some crazy idea into your head about going back to March House."

I shuddered. "No way," I said.

The breeze had finally come up a little, and the harbor surface had begun to be disturbed with dark ruffling "cats' paws." Peter pointed at the skiff. "Those are for you."

I looked down at the three shells he'd picked out and left there, lovely sun-bleached little things with soft pink interiors. Peter had dragged his board into the water. He turned to face me again, framed against the morning summer sky and the water and with me thinking he really was too beautiful for words and telling myself simultaneously to behave. He said abruptly, "Margaret, why do you have such an age complex?"

I was speechless. Almost. "Me?"

He smiled. "You. It's ridiculous. You're in your fifties, I'd guess—although you certainly don't look it—so why not just accept it? That's not old."

And then, before I could find some sort of answer, he was in the water and righting his board, the rising breeze immediately catching its sail. "I'll race you back!" he shouted.

The ferry was just pulling in. I rose from the old skiff clutching the seashells tightly and ran up from the beach to catch a ride. The last I saw of Peter as I crossed back over the narrow harbor neck to Edgartown, he was already halfway up the main harbor to the yacht club, a lean black-clad figure angled straight back just above the wind-ruffled water, the white-and-red sail of his windsurfer a bright splash of color in the sunlight.

And it was just at that moment and just because I was watching Peter and remembering him restlessly skipping stones as we talked that I suddenly knew what—in part, at least—was in the photos of Grace Chadwick that I'd found strange.

I recalled watching Peter, scooping up stones, launching one after the other out over the water; I recalled the photos of Grace sipping tea, the cup poised delicately in one hand, and lining up her croquet mallet on a ball to send it through a wicket.

Grace, like Peter, was left-handed.

I thought of a third person, slim and young in her paint-stained jeans and sneakers as she lit a cigarette while we sat and talked in the dressing room of her theater.

Samantha Sanderson was left-handed, too.

I wondered if Fisher possibly had any forensic evidence that might indicate which hand the murderer favored. If so, I knew he would hardly tell me. I was going to have to continue wondering.

SIXTEEN

An hour later, after Heather took the four children down to South Beach with a picnic meal and a new softball Christopher insisted I buy because he said the old one was "unwrapping," I once more headed up-island. I passed the central commercial airport and drove along South Road, the main east–west highway on the island's Atlantic side, and when I reached Beetlebung Corners and the village of Chilmark, I pulled up at the grocery store.

It was unpainted with a surrounding covered porch and looked like a slightly disreputable roadhouse, hardly in keeping with the "quaint" colonial appearance of so many New England shops brightened up for tourists and natives alike. Inside, it was no orderly suburban supermarket either. Modern freezers jammed with six-packs of beer, soft drinks, and cheap wine vied for wall space with sagging old shelving crammed with dusty tin cans, packaged goods, and stacked boxes of vegetables all barely visible under a minimum of fly-specked fluorescent lights. In an odd way, however, the shabbiness and disorganization seemed far more in keeping with the relaxed summer-in-the-country atmosphere of Menemsha and the western half of the Vineyard than with bright and bustling Edgartown and Vineyard Haven with their socially chic atmosphere.

There weren't too many shoppers, only a few summer visitors looking for the freshest possible early sweet corn, and here and there a local islander, distinguishable at once by dress as well as by accent—and more often than not by excess weight, a common problem among country folk in these days of soda, junk food, and six-packs.

The proprietor was at the cash register ringing up a sale; he was a sallow fellow in his fifties, with a thin chest, a large stomach, and wearing, quite inappropriately considering the weather, a gray cardigan over a shirt too dirty to be outside a laundry basket and unbuttoned too far down his large torso for decency.

I waited until he'd rung up a sale, then asked if Dorothy Webb still worked there.

He regarded me with watery and vaguely hostile eyes, and even by taciturn country standards he took a long moment before answering.

"Dorothy? Can't say she does."

"Could you tell me where I might find her?"

"Chilmark cemetery, I reckon."

"Oh? I'm sorry to hear that." In spite of the bad news, I felt foolish the way well-mannered people do when good breeding is disdainfully taken for snobbery. "Actually," I said, "I was looking for her sister, Alice. I'd hoped Dorothy could help me locate her."

I waited. From experience I knew it would take a moment or two for another answer. And I was right. He rang up several items for another customer before he spoke.

"Alice?"

"Yes."

"She's up to the cemetery, too." He smiled as though the news should have been welcomed.

It wasn't. My heart sank. Even though Peter and I had agreed that Alice or Dorothy might be dead, for some reason—over-optimism I suppose—I hadn't really expected them both to be. I'd thought one at least would still be around. Senile, perhaps, hard to get through to, but not the shut door that death meant.

I asked him how long Alice had been gone.

He rang up another sale and suddenly became quite garrulous. "Been gone a couple of years now. Her niece Suzy lives up at Lobsterville." His island accent was thick. "Married to Henry Simmons. Got a plumbing business in Vineyard Haven. If you want to know more, ask her. She'll tell you, I reckon."

"Thank you." I fled without looking back. I didn't want to see him staring after me, which I knew he was bound to be doing.

Outside, I allowed myself a moment of dejection, but then the usual optimistic Margaret took over again. Dorothy alive, I thought, would have been too easy, so I'd at least give the niece a try!

I drove off to Lobsterville. It's on the north shore and west of Menemsha, from which it is separated by Menemsha Bight, the narrow jettied entrance to Menemsha's harbor and pond. Many years ago Lobsterville had been a prosperous fishing establishment, but was now nothing more than a mile-long row of near-shanty houses built on the dunes beyond a pebbly beach and separated from each other by beachweed, brush, and brambles, a haven for the island's large skunk population.

A narrow dirt road provided access into the area. On the most beautiful of islands, Lobsterville is an ugly place and, in my view, a blighted retreat for a number of unfortunate souls who cannot afford better and are forced to live with the kind of neighbors who would turn any place into a slum, regardless of its location.

After I had passed a dozen houses or more, I saw a rusty mailbox that read H. SIMMONS. It was at the road's edge where a sandy driveway led between a number of automobile carcasses to a small bungalow incongruously painted bright canary yellow, a choice made worse by bright red shutters. A laundry line fluttered with a full complement of men's and women's underwear, none of it from famous designers, to be sure, but indicating that the owners at least believed in washing. I drove up and saw that the windows and the door were open. I found a small notepad with a pencil I always keep in the station wagon's glove compartment, got out, ducked the laundry, and went to the door and knocked.

A woman's voice cried out from somewhere within, carrying over the blare of a television set. "Who's that?"

When I didn't answer, she appeared in the doorway, and I got a surprise. I don't know what sort of person I expected to see—probably someone who fit the junkyard surroundings, someone about forty and overweight with coarse features and the graying lank hair of one who has given up any hope of maintaining her femininity.

The woman who appeared and said "Yes?" and made no attempt to open the screen door that stood between us was young, perhaps in her early thirties, and looked like someone out of *Bonnie and Clyde*. She was slender and flat-bosomed, and her hair, the color of bright new brass, was tightly permed around her head. Her face just missed being pretty because of a narrow nose between close-set eyes as cold as those of any ferret and by a rodentlike mouth barely disguised by too much lipstick. She was wearing a shirt over a bathing suit, and garish platform sandals.

I found my voice. "I'm trying to locate Suzy Simmons."

"You've found her."

I introduced myself and told her I was looking for information about her aunt.

"Alice? What did you want her for?"

Her tone was hostile, and I suddenly decided not to tell the truth. "Massachusetts Bureau of Statistics," I said glibly. "I'm checking figures on highway fatalities." I put on a sympathetic look and glanced at my notebook. "We had your aunt down as one, let's see, two years ago now, is that correct?"

I held my breath and waited for an answer. I was pretty certain, of course, that Alice of all people had not died in a car crash. I'd only said what I did because I thought it would elicit more of an immediate answer. People love to prove officials wrong. I wasn't disappointed, but I was looked over carefully before she replied.

"You people from the state sure get your nose into everyone's business, don't you?" she said.

"The information is confidential," I answered quickly. "You're not obliged to answer." I put on the expression of an overburdened petty official. "But it sure would make my day easier, Mrs. Simmons. I've been traipsing around forever on this one."

She studied me again. "It wasn't an accident," she said suddenly. "No car to it."

I managed to look surprised and make some sort of a questioning noise. I think I just said, "Oh?"

"Where did they get that? It was her heart. And it wasn't no two years ago, neither. It was five years. She was up in Boston with Miss Chadwick. You can ask her. That's the old woman she worked for. Still around. Lives on Tea Lane. Big house. Everyone these parts knows it. Kind of a crazy old lady. Alice went up the odd day to help out."

"You said Boston?" For appearance's sake, I made a note.

She nodded. "Miss Chadwick brought her back. Far

as I know she paid for the funeral, too. I don't think anyone in the family went, except my other aunt, Dorothy. She could tell you all about it, but she's dead, too. Alice wasn't real popular."

I wasn't surprised by this sudden candid revelation. Certain country people are often like that. Once they feel safe to confide, they tend to open up completely. I made another note or two and gave her my best apologetic smile. "Heart, not automobile; and five years, not two. I'll correct our records. I guess we were wrong once again. Somebody in the office must have got her mixed up with another Alice Webb. That, or a computer went berserk. They usually do. I'm sorry to have taken up your time."

My admission of bureaucratic fallibility turned the trick. I was rewarded with more confidences.

"Oh, that's all right. October, I think it was—I mean, when she died. They took the ferry and then the train from Falmouth. I remember Alice once saying Miss Chadwick wouldn't fly."

"What was the trip for?"

"Had to see the murdered guy, I think, the one in all the papers."

"Heston?"

"That's him. Came down every summer, they said. Her banker or something. Can you imagine? Getting it the way he did?"

"I read about it this morning," I said. "It sounded just horrible."

"Have to be someone strong as anything to choke the life out of a man like that with just a car window."

I got her back to Alice. "Presumably your aunt died in a Boston hospital, then?"

"Alice? No. Died in a hotel, I think Dorothy said. Went out just like that, if I remember right." She snapped her fingers. "Same place Miss Chadwick always stayed in once a year."

"You don't remember the name?" For appearance's sake I made another note and poised my pencil.

She shook her head. "The hotel? Oh, not anymore. I did, I think. Someplace fancy, I remember."

"The Copley Plaza? The Ritz? The Atheneum?"

"That's it!" she exclaimed. "Atheneum. Something like that."

She waited for me to ask another question. I couldn't think of one, and so far I'd got nowhere. Alice Webb died five years ago in Boston, where she'd gone with Grace Chadwick, who brought her body home. So what? I suddenly felt a little desperate. There was nothing further I could "officially" ask Suzy.

"The old lady sounds like quite a character," I ventured casually and tried to look as though I was really checking over my notes. "Your aunt probably had enough stories about her to write a book."

"Well, not really," Suzy said. "Alice wasn't one to talk much anyway." She laughed. "Just complain."

I made one last stab. "Your aunt didn't ever mention a nursery, did she?"

"Nursery?" A confused look came into Suzy's eyes and I sensed immediately I had made a mistake. A nursery had nothing to do with checking up on Alice Webb's cause of death.

I said quickly, "Somebody in the office the other day was talking about some old lady who they said kept a secret nursery for years. But it probably wasn't the same person." Then I pretended to remember something. "Oh! Your aunt's age. I don't have it here."

"I couldn't be sure. Around seventy, I guess." To my relief Suzy's smile came back. "Listen, maybe it was the same person. Alice never mentioned a nursery, but Dorothy said she used to complain about a room Miss Chadwick always kept locked, and once a key was missing, I think, and she accused Alice of stealing it so she could nose about. Alice wouldn't go up there for a month.

I bet that's what it was, a nursery. That's crazy." Suzy's close-set eyes flashed. She was completely hooked. "Say, why don't you come in and I'll put some coffee on while we figure it out. Henry will be back soon, but he won't bother us."

She swung open the screen door, and I felt a stab of panic. Her appetite for gossip had turned things around. I saw myself getting in over my head with endless new fabrications to hide my real identity—and all without learning anything new.

I said, "That's really nice of you, Mrs. Simmons. I'd love to, but I can't. I've got four other calls to make before I'm finished. Maybe the next time I come this way."

She looked disappointed. "Okay." Then she looked anxious. "We're not going to get sent a bunch of forms to fill out now, are we?"

"Heavens, no. That's the end of it. And I'm much obliged."

She told me I was welcome, and her tone was still friendly. "Don't get to see people out here very much."

I headed back to my car. Halfway there, I had to step aside to allow Henry Simmons to pull into the yard in a battered pickup. He was a dark surly-looking brute, and I recognized him at once. He was one of the men who were always hanging about Ed Rupert's garage drinking beer.

He got out of the truck, gave me a glance, and without a word headed for the bungalow. His wife opened the door as he reached it. I was back in my station wagon by that time and couldn't hear what they said. It wasn't much, though. Without looking back, he jerked his thumb in my direction, obviously asking her who I was. She was still replying when he pushed past her and went inside. I began to feel sorry for her, married to him, but then I thought she could probably hold her own. I wondered how long it would be before he remembered my car and told her I didn't work for the state.

I drove away trying to assess what I had picked up. A persistent inner voice told me that I was missing something, but the more I tried to see what it was, the more hopeless it seemed. My ideas became completely muddled and based on pure speculation and not solid evidence.

Then something quite ordinary happened to make me put murder and everything else concerning March House to one side for the moment. I was back on the highway—I'd taken South Road—and as I crested the hill approaching West Tisbury, I had a wonderfully clear view of the sky before I dipped down again into woods and pastures. There were only a few clouds, and the sun was high and warm. I suddenly yearned to be up there in the blissful cool silence with Essie, the world far below an unreal toyland place one could escape from, look down on, and laugh about.

The thought brought home to me with a crash all my very real money worries. I desperately needed cash, even the small amount Doris Ketteridge usually paid me. On top of Essie and ballooning, I now had Heather and the twins on my hands, and I was behind on mortgage payments on my house. Meanwhile, I had been on the island almost a week and hadn't yet gone in to see Doris. She would have to have heard I'd arrived with the children—news travels fast on the Vineyard—and she had to be anxious about my absence. Or, if she was annoyed, she might even have already arranged for someone to take my place. Little could she know how very necessary my half day of work with her actually was.

I resolved that at least for the next few days I would concentrate on putting my own house in order. Although ever mindful of Otis Cramm and his odious radar, I pressed down on my accelerator and made as good time as the road would allow. My first stop was going to be the Edgartown Craft Shop.

SEVENTEEN

Summer suddenly advanced rapidly, and with that advance came the swelling human tide of seasonal residents. Tourists would soon spread across the Vineyard into shops, streets, supermarkets, and other public facilities. Already most of the beaches except for the Chappaquiddick eastern shore were becoming crowded. Gays by the hundreds had gathered, appropriately I suppose, to cruise about, most of them stark naked, at the foot of the exotically colored cliffs of Gay Head. Socialites and the superrich were filling the deck chairs and chaise longues of the exclusive Chappaquiddick Beach Club, exchanging the latest winter spa gossip and "preppie" news while they looked out from their safe-from-the-public sanctuary at the sailing races going on around the various buoys of Nantucket Sound.

I had been welcomed warmly by Doris Ketteridge when I finally stopped in to see her. I had been helping her in the Craft Shop on weekdays from noon until closing time at seven. In the morning, I'd take my grandchildren off Heather's hands and drive them to sailing school or to South Beach or to play tennis if it was not a sailing day. In the evening, after dinner, we all played games— Clue, Monopoly, Hearts—or had puzzle races. Then I always read to all four children before they went to bed.

Twice I went up to Menemsha after they were tucked in to join Essie in work on our balloon equipment, getting it ready for France. Balloons don't take care of themselves; the huge air bag had to be ventilated and freed of any possible insects or rodents that might have taken refuge in a hidden fold, and the bag's many seams had to be carefully scrutinized for any sign of dangerous renting; propane bottles had to be checked for pressure and leakage, the burners lit to make certain they burned evenly and correctly; the ridiculously small tungsten steel pins attaching the gondola to the steel-bag frame had to be inspected for any sign of metal fatigue. Essie and I took good care of the equipment in which we had invested so heavily.

Algar Mikele was still missing, and the police continued to search for him everywhere. But I think if it had not been for Heather's presence in my own home—and the haunted dark-circled look to her eyes and the absent way she picked at her food and seemed to lose track of what anyone was saying—I might have decided to abandon my futile role of amateur sleuth. But Heather, along with her children, was a constant reminder of the serious problems they faced.

On Saturday, we had a pleasant surprise. I went to Essie's for dinner with, mind you, all four children and Heather. Essie insisted that I take them along and was wonderfully kind to Heather, never once mentioning Algar's disappearance or anything to do with the murders. After dinner we all sat out on the beach toasting marshmallows in a campfire Essie made of driftwood. With the darkened Menemsha pond and the far-off lights of Menemsha village and its fishing fleet as a backdrop, Essie perched on an old stump like a little brown gnome and regaled the children with marvelous adventure tales of old Vineyard whaling ships and their captains. I was terribly grateful to her for shrugging off her jealousy of Heather, and I think Heather, even if just for a few hours, nearly forgot her troubles.

It was Fisher who finally brought our contentment to an end. The police lieutenant showed up suddenly on Sunday night just as we were sitting down to eat. He insisted on interrogating Heather for half an hour, bothering her with a score of questions about Algar that had already been asked several times before. Had she communicated with her husband? Received any letters or phone calls from him? Where did she think he was? Who were the friends he might contact? Et cetera, et cetera. Of course, he upset her to no end, and the children twice as much. But he didn't seem to care at all.

This did more than just upset me. I was infuriated. I took a page from Essie's book and told him right to his face that unless he had a warrant and unless I was advised otherwise by my lawyer, he could not come into my house again. He made no reply. He simply smirked with all the condescension of a person taking advantage of the full authority granted to him. When he was gone I kicked myself for not having used the occasion to try and discover, without alienating him, how far he was getting in his investigations.

The damage was done. I was back in it, and from the moment he left I could think of nothing else. Monday morning I awoke very early, long before the rest of the household. Standing in my kitchen waiting for the coffee machine to complete its task, I thought back to when I had left Suzy Simmons and to my feeling that I had somehow missed something that lay half hidden in the simple information I had gained about her aunt's and Grace Chadwick's trip to Boston and Alice's subsequent death there.

Giving events time to settle in my mind enabled me now to see things more clearly. I realized the missing "something" about Alice Webb's death was that it had occurred almost at the same time Grace Chadwick went into her miraculous remission. Alice knew Grace well; she saw her several times a week at different times of day and in all sorts of moods. An impersonation would be impossible with Alice around. She would have seen through the disguise at once. In talking to both Peter and Suzy Simmons, I had developed a picture of Alice, a sour, badly educated backcountry islander who was hardly the type to be a blackmailer. But could an impostor take a chance on that? The more I thought about it, the more Alice's demise in Boston began to look all too fortuitous. Did she truly die of a heart attack?

I felt a now familiar chill of fear run through me. Another murder, something to make a death look like a heart attack? Or was I seeing things that simply were not there?

The coffee maker gurgled and hissed to a stop. I poured a cup and asked myself more questions. If there was indeed more to the story, did the trip to Boston figure into a premeditated plan, or was Alice's demise there just convenient happenstance? And if there *was* premeditation, and if Alice Webb was enticed to Boston to be got rid of, didn't that mean the murderer would have had to get rid of Grace at the same time? Or was the real Grace simply a useful pawn to be disposed of after she fulfilled the function of shipping Alice back home?

Several cups of coffee later, my household awakened, and I met Heather as I went back upstairs.

"I've something I must do this morning," I told her. "Could you take the children to their sailing lesson?"

She assured me she could, and I showered and dressed and left the house just as she was serving breakfast. It was a cloudy morning with a fresh southeasterly breeze. The misty air smelled of the sea, and trees swayed.

I drove to Vineyard Haven and the Bache-Turner Funeral Home. Bache had died years ago, but Len Turner still ran the place. I was lucky—it was only a quarter to nine, but they were already open. A black Cadillac hearse and a flower car were out front ready for the day. I found the sight of them depressing.

An overly brisk young man in a dark polyester suit greeted me at the door, one of those too clean-cut all-American types. I tried not to visualize him in a smock or white doctor's coat or whatever those people wear to perform the nonpublic side of their jobs in their establishment's back rooms. When I said I'd come to see Mr. Turner, he showed me along a deep-carpeted, air-conditioned corridor where piped-in "beautiful" music was already filtering out from hidden stereo speakers. A polished oak-paneled door, replete with a brass knocker, opened into Turner's office, an immaculately dusted place with an uncluttered executive desk adorned with framed photos of bright teen-aged grandchildren, just the right number of healthy houseplants, and a deep, shiny, green-leather couch and matching chairs for grieving clients.

Turner appeared almost at once—big, fleshy, and florid. He, too, wore a somber suit and tie, although in contrast he also wore a large gold watch and several exotic gold rings that seemed to have half sunken into fleshy fingers. He greeted me with all the professional good cheer he'd brought to bear on a community that had rewarded him with presidencies of several important civic organizations.

"Go right ahead and tell me what I can help you with, Mrs. Barlow. I'm a little short of time since we have a service in half an hour. Poor dear old Mrs. Trent. We'll all miss her, won't we?"

I made no comment on Mrs. Trent, whom I didn't know. I favored Turner with a polite smile and came straight to the point. I told him I needed some information, but I didn't tell him why. I planned to wait until he asked me and then give him a story about writing a book on local color and native families who'd been on the island for a number of generations. He looked a little disappointed. Clearly he'd thought I was there to arrange a funeral, but to his credit, he recovered at once and gave me his full attention.

"I'm interested in Alice Webb," I said. "She died about five years ago in Boston, I believe."

His puffy eyes narrowed. "Webb, Webb. Alice Webb." Then he favored me with a knowing and slightly conspiratorial smile. "Ah, yes, one of those Webbs from down in Chilmark. There was a sister, Dorothy, I believe. Yes. Both buried there, if I remember correctly. What was it you wanted to know?"

"I wanted to verify the cause of her death," I said. "I understand it was a heart attack."

To my relief, he didn't ask me what my business was. Instead, he studied me intently a moment, then said, "Our records are confidential, Mrs. Barlow, as you must know, but since what you are looking for is pretty much public knowledge, I don't mind confirming it for you. Let's see if I still have her file."

He rose to pull out one of three drawers in a steel file case and extract a folder, which he spread on his desk. "Alice Webb, yes. Died the eighteenth of October, 1980. She was sent down from Boston by Hartman and Hartman. Good people. Very reliable. They took care of everything up there, preservation of the remains, all that. We had nothing to do here except arrange for the burial. The casket was sealed."

"Sealed?"

"Bolted or screwed shut. They often are these days, especially when they come from out of state. If nobody in the family specifically asks to see the deceased, we don't bother to open the casket." He scanned what upside down appeared to me to be a letter. "In this case, apparently," he said, "the sealed-coffin request was a last wish of the deceased herself." He smiled. "It says here she didn't want anyone to see her dead."

"I see." I had just barely managed to keep my excitement out of my voice. In my mind, a sealed coffin could mean only two things. Either the body inside was not in a condition to be looked at by anyone except hardened undertakers, or somebody didn't want the body to be seen and had ordered the casket sealed. I didn't believe for a moment that Alice Webb had issued any such instructions as her last wish. People who die suddenly of a heart attack usually are in too much pain to think of such a thing; murder victims usually don't know what hit them.

I moved on. I didn't want Turner to think I was interested. I said, "I believe Grace Chadwick paid the bill." When he looked up in surprise, I added hastily, "Her niece told me that. Suzy Simmons, the plumber's wife."

"Ah, Simmons, yes. Yes, Miss Chadwick paid all expenses here as well as in Boston."

"Would the death certificate have been registered here or there?"

"Oh, there," Turner answered, "at the Boston medical examiner's office. But I have a copy, if you'd care to see it."

His telephone rang, and as he swung in his chair to answer it, his fingers plucked one of several photocopied pages from the file and flicked it casually in my direction.

So much for confidential records, I thought. This was indeed Alice Webb's death certificate, a printed form bearing the great seal of the Commonwealth of Massachussetts. I concentrated hard and read fast, as though the paper could be plucked back just as readily as it had been offered. Age: sixty-seven. Cause of death: cardiac arrest. Time of death: two A.M. Then I read the name of the medical examiner along with his signature: *Glenn Rothenberg.*

My heart almost stopped and I hardly heard Turner say, "Glenn Rothenberg signed it. Young pathologist. You might know him. Spends summers here. Back then he worked for the Boston medical examiner." He had finished his phone call.

I returned the certificate. "You didn't by any chance receive correspondence from Miss Chadwick on the matter?"

"Oh, no. We just sent her a bill, she sent us a check, and that was that." Turner now seemed anxious for me to leave. "Is there anything else, Mrs. Barlow?" He closed the file.

I said no. I had learned more than I'd ever dreamed I would. I had verification that Alice Webb had indeed died in Boston, where she'd gone with Grace Chadwick; I had proof of a sealed coffin; I had Glenn Rothenberg's signature on the death certificate.

Turner had risen and was glancing at his gold watch. "It wasn't much of a funeral," he said. "Her sister, Dorothy, rode down to Chilmark in the hearse, if I remember, and Miss Chadwick followed along in that big car of hers. Heston always used to take it out when he was here. Got someone to drive it for her. Otis Cramm, I think. Nobody else came."

Two hours later, after telephoning Doris to tell her I couldn't come in and rushing to put on unaccustomed makeup, panty hose, a city dress, heels, and jewelry, I was on a commuter plane to Boston. I left a note for Heather telling her that I'd gone to see a lawyer on her behalf and asking her to look after the children and not to tell anyone except Essie. I didn't quite know what I was after. I only knew that every time I asked questions, some sort of completely unexpected information turned up.

During the flight I tried not to speculate too wildly, but it was difficult not to. Glenn Rothenberg's signature could mean he was an accomplice in the impersonation scheme, which assuredly would point a finger at Samantha as the most likely suspect for the police to interrogate. It could also mean nothing more than an extraordinary coincidence. If he had met Grace when signing the death certificate, he would not necessarily have recognized a change in her two years later when he came to Martha's Vineyard for his first summer, other than that she appeared healthier.

The Atheneum is a grand old neo-Edwardian hotel with high, frescoed ceilings, marble columns, potted palms, and big brass ashtrays. A rather too-smart-and-too-pretty-for-her-own-good receptionist sent my name into the manager, who, it turned out, was not there. I was seen instead by the assistant manager, a pale seedy young man I would have thought more suitably placed at the Bache-Turner Funeral Home. My courage grew the moment I laid eyes on him, for I sized him up at once as someone who could either be sexually bullied or awed without too much difficulty.

I went to work on him with everything I had, making him feel he had a chance to be the most important man in my life, and at the same time treating him like a naughty little boy. It was a technique I called my swinging door, and it worked then, as it had often worked for me before. I gave him my correct name but told him I was a writer who had been commissioned by the "wealthy" Webb family to do a lengthy family history for publication. I explained that Alice Webb, a spinster, had apparently died at the Atheneum five years ago and that I needed the precise date she had been registered at the hotel, either by herself or by a friend with whom she was traveling, a Miss Grace Chadwick.

To my relief, he seemed only too anxious to be of service. "We're computerized now," he told me proudly, and led me into a small records room that seemed entirely devoted to every conceivable electronic office device.

He switched on a computer terminal and began punching keys. Green lines flowed across the screen, and within seconds I was looking at an entry.

Chadwick, Grace, Rm 1247. 10–17–80. Sngl. Departed 10–19–80. Verify File 2124—5B. Webb, Alice, Rm 1248. 10–17–80. Sngl. Decd 10–18–80. Verify File 2124—5B.

"Both rooms seem to have been registered by one person and on one card. Do you want to see it?"

"Oh, yes, please," I said. "Authenticity makes for such good atmosphere in any book."

I could scarcely believe my luck. A registration card had to be signed, and the signature would have to be the real Grace's. At a later date I might be able to find a sample of the impostor's handwriting, preferably another signature, which could be professionally compared.

He moved to another terminal and began punching in more information. "This one is programmed for graphics," he explained. "We've had it only a few months. We can put one million registration cards on just one floppy disc. Makes storage a cinch."

Once more, green lines flowed. And all of a sudden, like magic, the facsimile of a hotel registration card complete with Grace Chadwick's signature appeared.

"Now watch this," my young man said. He pressed a key and a third machine in the room hummed to life; in moments it had printed out the registration facsimile on a standard-size piece of paper. He handed it to me with a triumphant smile. I gave him the best thank-you I'm certain he ever received and tucked it quickly into my handbag.

Extricating myself from his eager invitation to give me a guided tour of other interesting modernizations in the hotel wasn't quite as easy, but I eventually managed to do so and got him to show me personally into a taxi. I had only one more stop to make, and it was an important one. I gave the driver the address of the Hartman and Hartman Funeral Parlor in South Boston.

Half an hour later, and after paying an exorbitant taxi fare run up in impossibly heavy traffic, I found myself standing on the sidewalk in a bleak working-class Irish neighborhood outside a shabby two-story brownstone proclaiming itself "Hartman and Hartman—Where the Heart Reigns." Some people simply can't leave bad enough alone, and to add insult to injury there was a modern plastic wall clock with no hands set in a window against a background of purple drapes beneath which were the printed words: DEATH IS TIMELESS.

In spite of Mr. Turner's unblinking assurance that Hartman and Hartman were "good people" and "very reliable," all I wanted to do was turn and run. It was already afternoon; I didn't see how I could ever get back home in time for dinner. But it was silly to have come so far and not see this through. I raised one reluctant finger and pushed hard on the round porcelain doorbell.

EIGHTEEN

I was as surprised by the person who answered the door as I had been by Suzy Simmons. I expected a middle-aged South Boston Irish version of the Chilmark grocery-store proprietor and someone bearing the usual inscrutable expression morticians all seem to wear.

What I saw instead was a young woman whom I thought would have been better cast as a hostess in a disco. She had layered dark brunette hair and wore sexy tight-fitting black jeans, black boots, and a shiny white satin blouse with spangles around a very low-scooped neckline. Her figure would have been the envy of most movie stars, and in spite of enough lipstick and eye makeup for a nightclub stripper as well as a serious overdose of exotic perfume, she was very pretty.

"Yes? Can I help you?"

No funereal tone there. Even a bright smile. While she waited for my reply, she shifted a wad of bubble gum from one cheek to the other. I might have been coming there to inquire about buying a used car or renting a room.

"Yes, I hope so," I countered, remembering my real mission. "I've got problems."

Unlike her professsional colleague, Len Turner, she looked immediately and genuinely sympathetic. "Yeah? Gee, I'm sorry. Who is it? A relative?"

"Oh, it isn't that," I replied hurriedly. "I mean, it's not about a funeral."

She looked a little surprised and made a rapid appraisal of my clothes and jewelry. Then she laughed. "No, I guess not," she said. "Like, if it was, you wouldn't call on us at any rate. Well, come on in anyway and let's hear all about it."

I followed her inside to find myself in a large, low-ceilinged, and carpeted room with curtained walls and four rows of steel folding chairs that faced a sort of raised dais. There, to my consternation, I saw on a wheeled catafalque an open bronze coffin. In it rested the ashen-gray remains of an elderly man, unnaturally red about the cheeks and lips where someone had been overly enthusiastic with lipstick and rouge in an attempt to make him appear lifelike.

"This way," said my guide. "We'll be more comfortable in the office. We've got a wake on this afternoon. Another few minutes and you wouldn't have been able to get through the door for the Irish. That's Paddy O'Shaughnessy, but I guess you never knew him."

"No," I said. "I never had the pleasure."

"Huge family. Sixteen kids, forty grandchildren. That's what I heard, anyway. Wow! Can you imagine? Like, he must have kept his poor wife busy—what do you think? I guess she'll be coming to celebrate getting a rest."

I somehow summoned up a laugh and, averting my eyes from the waxen remains of the once Irish satyr, followed her through parted curtains into a small office so cluttered as to bear little resemblance to the room I'd just left and none at all to Len Turner's office. Under rather glaring fluorescent lights, I saw two beat-up old wooden desks stacked with papers and folders, a sagging wooden file case, and a Smith Corona that must have almost predated me. Least appropriate of all to a funeral home was something that dominated the room—a very large Pirelli bathing-suit calendar where the pool-wet thigh-length T-shirt on the stunning sexy June model left absolutely nothing from her knees to her neck to one's imagination.

The young woman grinned when she saw me look at the calendar. "She's something else, huh? If I want to turn Chuck on in a hurry, I drag him in here."

It was insane, but for the first time that day I began to feel normal. I liked this girl. We came from different worlds, spoke different languages, and had absolutely nothing in common, but I felt an immediate rapport with her. She was absolutely straight.

"Sit down, sit down," I was ordered. An old half-stuffed office chair was summarily pushed in my direction. "I'm Angela. Angela Wykretowicz—don't try to spell it—not Hartman. My husband, Chuck, and me, we bought out old Casey Hartman a couple of months ago. We keep the name because everyone in South Boston knows it. All we did was add the clock in the window. Cute touch, huh?"

I quickly agreed.

"Want some Coke?" She winked. "I meant the drinking kind? We only use the real thing when we go on vacation."

I accepted. She went to a machine in a corner, blew a large bubble-gum bubble, hit the machine hard a couple of times, and pressed the selection lever. Two cans of Coke rolled down the chute with a clatter. She brought them back to the desk, sat down on a rickety swivel chair, and propped her delightfully slender legs up on a pile of papers next to a photograph of herself and a big dark-haired guy who looked like a wrestler and whom I took to be Chuck.

She opened both cans and pushed one toward me. "You want more, there's plenty. I live on the stuff. Especially when it's hot, like now. Okay, tell me."

I introduced myself. Then, God only knows what got into me—the girl should have been a shrink; she had that rare knack for making a person feel completely safe to talk—I told her everything. All of it, nonstop for about fifteen minutes. She listened wide-eyed, occasionally interrupting to say, "Wow!," "You're kidding," "Hey, crazy!," or "Like, can you believe it?"

When I finished, she rose, got us two more Cokes, blew another bubble thoughtfully, then said, "You know what, Margaret? Wanna bet something? There was a switch."

"Switch?"

"Sure. Grace what's-her-name dies, see? And someone tells the doctor and old Casey Hartman it was Alice Webb. So Grace goes back in the coffin instead of Alice. That's why it was sealed. Good-bye, Gracie. Forever. Who would ever find her in Alice's grave?"

The simplicity of her statement stunned me. I'd thought of everything but that.

"That's quite an idea," I said, and remembered Essie had said virtually the same thing to me when I told her I thought someone was impersonating a long-dead Grace Chadwick.

She shrugged. "Listen, I'm no genius, but it happens." She blew another bubble. "We used to work in Jersey—Fort Lee—me and Chuck, mini-Mafiaville, know what I mean? We'd get guys in there and sometimes gals we knew weren't who they said. That's the way some of the mob used to disappear when things got too hot for them, you read me? Pick some poor slob up off the street they figure nobody would miss, plug 'em, give 'em their

name, put on dark glasses, and go to their own funeral."
She laughed. "We never asked. You're gonna step up to
some godfather type and say, 'Hey, chief, that's not
brother Squalini in the box, it's just some smelly old
wino'? Forget it. Like, you'd end up in the box instead."

"But what about Alice?" I asked.

She laughed. "Hey, like I said, one gets put away,
one disappears, right? In her case, permanently. In the
bay, most likely. They find them every other day floating
around. Oughta rename it Stiffville Creek. Really. Last
week, they even pulled one out of the Thames River. One
of the Harvard kids was rowing and hooked it with an
oar, can you beat it? So who's going to be looking for her,
anyway? They got their Alice back, right? They *think*.
So a few days later the city morgue gets her, if the fish
haven't first. They keep her the legal six months, un-
claimed, and then dump her on the medical students, and
that's that."

I'm afraid I was so nonplussed I simply stared.

"You don't believe me?" Angela asked.

"Yes, of course I do."

She ignored my protest and got up suddenly.
"Wanna see if I'm right? Come on. But listen, like, let's
get level. You trusted me when you told me all this, so I
trust you. It doesn't go out of here, okay? You come back,
like, with the cops or somebody and expect me to play
fair, I'll say I never saw you in my life. Chuck and me
don't want no trouble."

I didn't know what she had in mind to show me,
but I agreed and followed her out of the office through
another door and into another room I'd just as soon forget.

It was cold and stark and looked like a morgue—
which it was. It was all bare tile walls and floor with
glaring overhead lights, and smelled of death and form-
aldehyde. There were two metal-topped worktables with
floor drains under them. A sheet was spread par-

tially over one table, not even half concealing the body of a young woman whose face had been slashed to ribbons.

Angela gave it a casual wave. "Look at that," she said breezily. "I've got to make her look like Miss America by tomorrow. Wow! And I've got two more in the fridge, and Chuck's in Maine on business—he said. My guess is he's fishing. Whatever, and it better not be some broad, and me stuck with all the work. He comes home, I'll kill him."

We skirted the corpse and arrived at an old wooden file cabinet on which were piled bottles of embalming fluid, various unattractive-looking tubes and surgical instruments, and some large packages of cotton.

Angela yanked open a drawer. "Let's see. Webb, right? Alice Webb."

The drawer was crammed solid with old dusty files that looked as though they hadn't been touched for years. "These are all Hartman's," she explained. "Chuck was gonna throw them out, but I said we should wait for the statute of limitations to run out, you can never tell. Like, in case there's ever a dispute. You know, someone accuses you of burying the wrong person." She laughed. "Like someone in the Webb family, for example." She pulled a thin file. "Webb . . . here we are."

She casually laid it open on the unoccupied worktable. There were photos. "This her?"

I forced myself to look, and I don't suppose I'll ever forget what I saw. Stretched out naked on the same table was the wasted body of an elderly woman, the wrinkled, collapsed flesh gray-white with death, the open eyes staring vacantly, the yawning toothless mouth an obscenity.

There was no question of who it was. Even the starkness of death could not hide the woman's identity. It wasn't Alice Webb. It was Grace Chadwick.

"Grace? Right?"

I nodded.

"See? I told you. A switch."

Angela put the photo back and leafed through some loose papers.

"Yeah. Here you are. Sealed coffin. Requested by the deceased." She grinned sarcastically. "You'd better believe it, huh? Your phony Grace probably told Hartman and the family the deceased didn't want anyone to see her dead. Like they should remember her alive. That's what the ones we did in Jersey usually said. Nobody ever argued. Last wishes." She closed the file and said, "Listen, did you maybe check the hotel guest register for the day she died?"

I mentally kicked myself and told her I hadn't.

"Maybe you'd see some name you knew on it," she said. "I mean, all this would have to have been done by someone she knew, right? And maybe whoever it was came from the Vineyard and stayed at the Atheneum, too."

She put the file away and then the doorbell rang.

"Oh, Jesus, Mother Mary, and all the saints!" she cried with an imitation brogue. "Here they come. The family and friends and all. And stinking of drink, the lot of them, I can promise you. Never touch the stuff myself, Chuck neither. Can't stand the smell. Could you believe it? Like, we get clients in here and I have to put on a mask, they stink so of booze when you open them up."

I left her greeting members of the funeral party: stiff-necked, red-faced workingmen, awkward in suits they wore perhaps three times before they went to the grave themselves; and frail old ladies dressed in black with handkerchiefs held to their mouths against the presence of death. They poured through the front door in a solid Irish phalanx to fill up the chairs lined before the corpse of the former Irish satyr, Paddy O'Shaughnessy.

I had the good luck to catch a taxi back to the Atheneum quickly. I didn't want to see the assistant manager again and I almost had to force myself to ask for him. I was told he had gone off duty and was just starting his vacation. His replacement, ever so much more prissy than he, refused to let me see the guest list for the duration of Grace's stay in 1980. "This list is completely confidential, madam." He wasn't at all susceptible to my swinging-door technique.

I decided, since I couldn't get a seat on a plane until the next morning, to try to talk then to the manager himself. Meanwhile, I took a room for the night at the Ritz-Carlton. I couldn't stand the thought of getting, through some awful twist of fate, the same room at the Atheneum that Grace had taken. Or Alice Webb. I telephoned Heather to tell her I was stranded.

"Oh, Margaret," she said, "I'm so glad you called." She sounded close to tears.

"What's happened, Heather?"

There was no answer.

"Heather?"

"Margaret." Her voice was choked. "There's been another murder."

My heart tightened. I couldn't believe it.

"Heather, no!"

"It was Owen Fuller. And I heard it was just ghastly. I can't tell you right now what they're saying. I don't want the children to hear. Essie found him at lunch-time when she went to get eggs. Glenn Rothenberg told me she was pretty badly shaken. She was with the police all afternoon and she called here twice for you. She sounded terrible."

I calmed her down the best I could and told her I'd be back in the morning. I tried to reach Essie, but there was no answer. I went to the bar, had three stiff drinks, fended off a couple of lonely men, bought a toothbrush in the hotel pharmacy, and went back to my room. I thought of calling Peter but decided I couldn't face talking about murder to anyone else that evening except for perhaps Essie, but she still didn't answer her phone. I gave up, took a hot bath, and thanked my lucky stars when I found a half-empty bottle of Valium at the bottom of my handbag. Half an hour after I retired to my room, I was mercifully asleep.

NINETEEN

I flew back in the morning without time to see the manager about the guest register and feeling terribly frustrated because of it. When the plane landed on the Vineyard, I went straight down to Menemsha to see Essie. The weather had cleared, it was sunny and hot, and she was once again up on the foredeck of the *Janet B* repairing some lobster traps. She looked drawn and tired. Before I could ask her how she was, she summoned a smile and wanted to know how Boston had gone, and I said it was still there and the lawyer I'd seen was a good one. I hated lying to her, but I could see nothing but trouble coming between us if I told the truth. Now in some ways I wish I hadn't, although I doubt things would have turned out any differently.

Then she told me about the murder.

She said the police thought Owen Fuller died at about six in the morning. And she described the horror of discovering his body. "I went over about one-thirty," she said, "the way I usually do on Mondays, to get some eggs. He also had a set of new oars he wanted to sell me quite cheaply for my *Pot-Pourri*." She waved at the little one-stroke motor launch tethered to the stern of the *Janet B*. "The ones I have now ought to last a while yet, but it's always good to have an extra pair around. And he told me he had a good creel to sell cheap to replace my old one. Anyway, I knocked on his front door, and there wasn't any answer. His pickup was there, so I decided he couldn't be far, probably out back in the barn or the chicken coops or at the pigpens.

"But he wasn't in any of those places. I waited around a few minutes, and then it occurred to me since his cows weren't to be seen that he might have taken them across Grace's lawn to his far pasture. I remembered his telling me, oh, a week ago, that he was putting in a culvert to drain his own back road there, and it wasn't a fit path for cows to walk on while he was doing it. One of them was bound to get in trouble. He was going to take them across his 'right-of-way,' he said, whether Grace Chadwick liked it or not."

Essie paused a moment, staring blankly at the trap she was working on. The tide had begun to come in and the *Pot-Pourri*, swinging in toward the pebbly beach below us, had started to rub gently against the hull of the derelict trawler.

"So," she went on, "I headed down the little path through the woods to Grace's. The cows had been along it, all right. I could see that immediately, and when I got to the gate in the stone wall, it was open and there they were, all seven of them, grazing away on Grace's lawn and one drinking at the fish pond. I knew right away something was wrong. Call it premonition if you wish.

"I was right. I went through the gate, and there was Owen himself, right on the edge of the lawn, half propped up against a tree. I called out. He didn't answer. I thought maybe he'd had a heart attack and I went to him. Then I saw the pitchfork handle. It . . . it was sticking out of his stomach. I thought at first he was just holding it, that there was just a handle he'd been using to drive the cows—until I saw the prongs coming out of his back just below his shoulders. And his eyes were open. He wasn't seeing anything, but they were open, and there was a fly walking across one eye!"

Her breath caught. "It was awful, Margaret. I'll never forget it." She shuddered and was silent a moment before she shook off the memory and continued.

"My first thought, of course," she said, "was that he'd crossed the wall at that old stile by the gate as the cows were passing through and had fallen. There were some loose stones on the ground from the wall. I thought a stone had given way and the fork had accidentally gone through him and he'd staggered to the tree and died there. I ran straight back to his house and called the police. The phone is downstairs in his kitchen. While I was talking, I heard some kind of a bang from upstairs. I don't know what I thought the noise was at the time, maybe just a shutter slamming in the wind or something one of his cats had knocked over. I wasn't frightened. It never crossed my mind that it might have been the murderer because it hadn't occurred to me yet that Owen had been murdered. I know that sounds crazy after the way Rose and Arthur died, but it just didn't. It was only later when the police decided Owen couldn't have died by accident that I realized his killer must have been right there in the house with me. I didn't sleep half the night after that. When the police finally finished with their ten thousand questions, I just got in my pickup and drove and drove and drove."

"I tried to call you," I said.

She gave me a weak smile. "I was probably down by South Beach or up by Vineyard Haven. I had to get away!"

"But what made the police decide it was murder?"

"Oh, such a little thing," Essie replied. "Isn't that

always the way? Apparently Owen must have been standing up against the tree when the fork was pushed through him, because the tip of one prong broke off embedded in the tree itself, about an inch in. The police found it. Whoever killed him must have driven the fork through him very hard, and I guess he hung there standing up until he died and his weight broke the prong off."

She stopped for a moment again and then said, "I never fully realized what you went through, Margaret, until it happened to me. I keep feeling the killer was nearby at the very moment I realized what he'd done, and I keep feeling now that he's still around someplace—don't you?—watching everything you do. I feel so terribly exposed."

I knew what she meant, all right. I asked her about Fisher. What had he said? What kind of questions had he asked?

Essie brightened at that and even began to smile. "Fool of a man," she said in a voice that was more like the old Essie. "By the time I got through with him, I don't think he wanted to see me again for some time. He made me retrace all my steps from the moment I drove into Owen's yard. He insisted. 'Everything,' he said. Real bullying.

"So, I thought, all right, if that's what he wants, he'll get it. I took him through every single step I'd made from the house to the barn to the coops to the pigs. I stretched out ten minutes of my looking for Owen into two hours until I thought he'd go crazy with impatience and frustration. Then I kept pretending I'd skipped things. 'Oh, Lieutenant, I forgot,' I'd say. 'I went twice into the chicken coop.' And I'd insist on acting out in the most minute detail how I had retraced each step already described. I mimed lifting the coop door latch, opening the door—everything."

I had a feeling Essie would go on forever with me in the same way she had with Fisher, so I interrupted with a question. "Do the police have any idea why Owen was killed?"

"None," she replied. "Except the obvious and the easiest—that Owen must have found out who the murderer was, caught him skulking about. Or had known for some time."

"And was blackmailing him? That would make both him and Heston blackmailers."

She shrugged. "Not necessarily blackmailers. Owen was a very peculiar man. He might have just enjoyed knowing something and goading about it when he had the chance."

I thought of Owen. She could be right. He was indeed the type to hold a Damoclean sword over someone's head, not for gain but simply for the fun of tormenting. I dreaded to raise the additional question that weighed most on my mind. But I did. "I suppose Fisher still thinks Algar is the one he wants?"

Essie at once looked acutely uncomfortable. "Yes," she said, "I'm afraid he does, although I don't know whether Estelle and François and Samantha all had alibis for that time of day—ones that would bear any weight, anyway. Fisher was hardly going to tell me."

"Did you suggest to him that someone might be impersonating Grace?"

"Your pet theory?" Essie smiled. "As a matter of fact, I did."

"And what did he say?"

She hesitated. "Margaret, what's to be gained . . ."

I didn't let her finish. Not being able to tell her I had seen a photo of Grace dead, and thus knew there had to be an impersonation, completely frustrated me. I almost shouted. "Essie, what did he say?"

Startled, she gave up. "He didn't say anything, I'm afraid. He just laughed."

I felt numb then, and I guess it was right at that point that I realized I had to go to Fisher and make a clean breast of things, regardless of how I felt about him or how much trouble I might get into for having withheld information. I had to because I could only see more and more prejudice building up against Algar, which would thus make it more and more difficult to prove him innocent. All the efforts of the police would go into justifying that prejudice instead of looking for the real killer.

But another more important reason to open up to Fisher was Essie. She had warned me of the danger I could be in if the murderer knew I was snooping. But what about her? Wasn't she in the same danger now? Perhaps the murderer thought she knew something that she might even be completely unaware of, and her need to go to her fields behind Grace's place made her vulnerable.

I had a ghastly image of Essie lying dead amid herbs and wildflowers, killed God only knew how. Someone who could drown a woman and garrote one man and run another through with a pitchfork was capable of the worst. If anything should happen to Essie because I hadn't set the police straight, I knew I would never be able to live with myself.

We had lunch, I feeling desperately guilty because I'd broken my promise to her and lied about going to Boston and hoping my guilt didn't show. Then I went back to Edgartown and stopped by the bookstore. Peter got free for a few minutes and came and sat in my car in the shade of one of the huge elms that lined the quiet narrow side street of old colonial houses around the corner. I told him what had happened and what I planned to do.

He said he thought I was right and grinned. "Why don't you let me carry the ball for you?"

"What do you mean?"

"I mean, let me go to Fisher and tell all."

"You didn't go to Boston, Peter."

"How is he to know? And anyway, I wouldn't have

to tell him where I got my information. I'd just have to put ideas in his head."

"And end up completely victimized, if not locked up."

Peter laughed. "I don't think he'd lock me up. He'd take his spite out on me somehow, but not that, and so what?"

"And you would do all this?"

"Sure. No problem."

"Peter, you're sweet. Don't ruin it by being a total idiot. Now go back to work."

He obeyed and, looking slightly crestfallen, got out of the car. Before I could pull away, he came around to my side and leaned down by my window and said, "You're sure you don't want me at least to go with you for moral support?"

"You're working, remember? I can manage."

He surrendered reluctantly. "Okay. You're the boss. But don't let him bully you. You haven't done anything wrong."

"No," I said. "I just withheld evidence vital to a murder investigation, lied to the police, and disobeyed orders not to leave the island without letting them know." I laughed. "Good-bye, Peter. Thank you."

Then, to my own astonishment—and certainly his— I impulsively leaned toward him and gave him a quick kiss on the cheek before I drove away. When I had gone a hundred yards down the street, I looked in my rearview mirror. He was still standing there where I'd left him, watching my retreating station wagon.

Heather had taken the children off to Chappaquid-dick, so I called the Craft Shop and optimistically told poor Doris I'd be in after lunch. Then I steeled my nerves and called Fisher at the state police station. He was in. I identified myself and told him I wanted to see him as soon as possible.

"Ah, Mrs. Barlow, yes. I think it would be best if you did come in. You're free to bring a lawyer if you want."

"I hardly think I need one," I said. When I put the receiver down, I was shaking. His tone had been as menacing as his words. I knew I was in for a bad time.

TWENTY

I drove to the state police station, which was situated in a large, handsome, late-Victorian house known locally as Sutton Place. Painted a cheerful, slightly deeper-than-robin's-egg blue with white trim, it sat on high ground in the Eastville section of Oak Bluffs with a superb view of Vineyard Haven harbor. A large sign on the well-manicured front lawn said: MASSACHUSETTS STATE POLICE.

I drove up thinking this setup was all a little pretentious and parked between a police cruiser and a motorcycle. Once inside I was greeted by an overly intimidating trooper who wanted to know my name, address, occupation, my reason for being there, and practically everything else about me. Finally he showed me into the rather underfurnished ground-floor room that was Fisher's temporary office. In keeping with that introduction, the next thirty minutes was worse than any anxiety had led me to expect. Far worse.

"You went to Boston, Mrs. Barlow. I believe you

were cautioned not to leave Martha's Vineyard under any circumstances without notifying the police."

That was Fisher's opening shot. I wasn't really prepared for it. Who had told him I'd gone to Boston? I wasn't going to demean myself by asking, and decided now was not the time to wonder. "That may be," I replied, "but I question your authority to place me under such a restriction without some sort of a warrant. I haven't left the country, after all. I haven't even left Massachusetts."

His response was to blink like a frog—expressionless—then to open a file he had on his desk and stare down at it. "What did you want to see me about, Mrs. Barlow?" he asked.

Thinking I had won a round, I launched into my story; I told him everything that had taken place since I first went to The Rookery to bring Estelle Perkins flowers, but I didn't squeal on her for possessing drugs. I thought whatever she reaped from them along with François was her business, and anyway, I am not an informer.

While Fisher sat in cold silence, I went from Estelle to guns and wigs and sneakers and jeans and an old dress that was damp and grass-stained at the knees. "When using Miss Chadwick's facilities upstairs, Lieutenant, I confess to succumbing to my curiosity. I looked around."

Then I told him what Algar had witnessed and about how the twins had seen old Grace flying across her lawn at night like a witch. And I told him I was certain "Grace" was an impostor.

I said, "Surely it would be easy for you to expose this person."

"Ah? And where would the real Grace be, then?"

I took a deep breath. "In the old cemetery at Chilmark. The Webb plot," I said.

"Really? Dead, you say?" There was almost open amusement in his voice.

I forced myself to ignore his tone and explained about seeing Suzy Simmons and going to Boston to see when Grace had been there with Alice and discovering when and how Alice had died. "It would have been the perfect time for a switch," I said glibly. "The Mafia does it quite often, I've heard, down in New Jersey and New York. I think if you open Alice Webb's grave, you'll find I am right."

"I see. And what's your theory, Mrs. Barlow, about Alice Webb herself? In your scheme of things, what happened to her?"

I suddenly had a dismal feeling Fisher was laughing at me. And, worse, I felt he was in complete control of the interview and knew far more than he was allowing. But I answered anyway. "I'd just as soon not imagine, Lieutenant."

"In Boston Bay, perhaps?"

"Perhaps. I don't know."

"I see. Do you perhaps know, then, who signed Miss Webb's death certificate?"

There was no point in lying. Intuition told me he knew. And knew I knew. I took a deep breath. "A Doctor Rothenberg," I said.

"A Doctor Rothenberg. Glenn Rothenberg?"

"I believe so. Yes."

"The doctor we have here?"

"I don't know. It's the same name."

"And do you, Mrs. Barlow, draw any particular conclusions from that? Granted it is the same man?" His tone was openly sarcastic now.

"I'd rather leave all conclusions to you, Lieutenant Fisher—from now on."

"Would you?"

"Yes."

His watery eyes went from mine to which they had been briefly raised back down to the file in front of him. From that point on it seemed all downhill to me. He sat silently another moment, then without a word produced a photograph from among the papers in the file. He handed it to me to look at.

I did and felt sick. It was the ghastly glossy black-and-white picture of Grace Chadwick stretched naked on the morgue table at Hartman and Hartman, the very same one Angela had shown me. I looked at the staring dead eyes, the dark hole of the open toothless mouth, and the flaccid gray-white flesh of the torso and legs. I barely heard Fisher say, "I believe you know who that is, am I correct?"

"Yes," I said. "I think it's Grace Chadwick."

"You've seen this photo before, am I correct?"

"No," I said.

"No," he repeated. Again the sarcasm—enough in the two letters to belittle me even further.

I waited.

He said, "Would you care to tell me where you saw this before?"

"I didn't. I just told you that."

I knew he knew it was a lie. I think at that point I expected to be thrown into a dark room with bright lights shining in my eyes while the question was repeated endlessly until I cracked.

Instead, he retrieved the photo, held it up, and said, "Courtesy of Hartman and Hartman Funeral Parlor; Charles and Angela Wykretowicz, proprietors. Care to tell me about your visit there?"

I looked at him and thought of Angela. I thought about her hard. I thought about her brassiness and cheap sexiness and her callousness toward death; I recalled the grieving Irish tumbling through the front door for the wake, smelling dreadfully of whiskey, and of Paddy O'Shaughnessy's waxen coffined remains in the dreary chair-filled viewing room of the South Boston mortuary, ex-proprietor, Casey Hartman.

There is honor among those harassed by the police.

I'd given Angela my word I wouldn't sell her out, and I wasn't about to do so now. I looked old Frog Face right in the eyes and said, very blankly, "Hartman and Hartman?" Then I let recognition seep into my expression. "Oh, yes. Weren't they the Boston morticians who sent Alice or Grace down here?"

Fisher ignored my question, answering it with one of his own. "You never met Angela Wykretowicz?"

"Angela *who*?" I forced the blank look back into my eyes.

This time Fisher didn't speak for a moment. He closed the file on the photo and looked out the window before he said, "Now, that surprises me, Mrs. Barlow." He emphasized my name in a way that was distinctly menacing. "The detectives who followed you to Boston and never let you out of their sight—except when you closed and locked your hotel door at the Ritz for the night—told me you spent at least thirty minutes with Mrs. Wykretowicz, and when they joined mourners flocking in to pay their respects to one deceased Mr. O'Shaughnessy in the front room, you seemed on the very best of terms with her."

What could I say? Correct. Nothing. I simply gaped and, I am certain, blushed and hated myself for not realizing he would have me followed. I thought, *If he knows Grace is dead, he also knows the "Grace" running around is an impostor. No wonder he sounded amused when I explained why I thought so.*

Fisher now smiled for the first time—with his mouth only, I might add. And even then it was the thinnest smile imaginable, the sort of smile a more natural and acceptable frog might have enjoyed after snapping up a passing butterfly. I put on as brave a front as possible and hoped to God Angela had denied everything, as she had assured me she would. "All right, Lieutenant," I said, "you win, but I've never seen that photo. Mrs. what's-her-name . . ."

"Wykretowicz," he filled in smugly. "That is not what she said, Mrs. Barlow. She said she showed it to you."

I could tell from his expression, or perhaps the lack of one, that Angela had been true to her word. He was trying an age-old police interrogation technique, and it wasn't going to work if I had anything to say about it.

"Oh, do stop it, Lieutenant Fisher, please. We're both too intelligent for that old game. Even if she had shown me the picture, she would have denied it. It would be a toss-up—her word against mine. By law all her records, including her predecessor's, are confidential. She hardly seemed the type to me to confess to revealing them and lining herself up for a felony charge."

It worked. Fisher studied me intently and clearly decided the line he'd taken was pointless. Hurrah for me! Hurrah for Angela! Neither of us had surrendered to bullying authority or bureaucratic regulation. I promised myself to drop her a note of thanks as soon as possible.

My sudden euphoria was dampened almost at once, however, and I heard Fisher's next words with a sort of anticipatory dread. "I have a court order," he said, "to exhume the remains of the person buried in Chilmark under the name of Alice Webb. I will be there in the morning at seven-thirty with Len Turner. I believe he knew both Miss Chadwick and Miss Webb. I'll also have someone from Miss Webb's family along, as well as Doctor Rothenberg, if he is indeed the signatory to the death certificate. And you, Mrs. Barlow. Yes, indeed! You! If you should have some difficulty in accepting my invitation, for whatever reason, Officer Cramm will be at your disposal to help you get to Chilmark in time."

He rose. I was dismissed with Otis as a final slap in the face. I tried a last shot. I had to know. "What about the impostor, Lieutenant? What are you going to do?"

I had hardly got the words out of my mouth when he let me have it. His whole attitude changed. Instantly.

The frog turned into something far more dangerous and far nastier than I could have imagined possible. Nasty, cold, totally authoritative and bullying. The law. And he didn't speak, he snarled.

"Mrs. Barlow! After you leave this room, you will also leave investigating Miss Grace Chadwick and everything else in this case to the Commonwealth of Massachusetts and its appointed professional authorities, and that includes asking hotel managers to show you guest lists. I hope I make myself very clear."

It wasn't until I was outside and had stopped shaking somewhat that I also stopped feeling defensive and became angry instead. The horrible little man. I think I actually said something far less ladylike. I think I called him a first-class son of a bitch, and right out loud, too. He was as far along as he was in his investigation because of me. I was quite certain that if I had not gone to Boston, he'd never have guessed that Grace might possibly be an impostor or that Glenn Rothenberg could perhaps be involved somehow.

Walking to my station wagon, I began to wonder what else he might have discovered in Boston, something I might have missed. My guess was it wasn't the name of somebody Grace knew or the guest list. He would not have been badgering me if he had. He would have had a bona fide murder suspect to bully. I had hardly considered this when a familiar car pulled up. It was Glenn Rothenberg's convertible. Samantha was driving, with Glenn beside her. They exchanged a word or two. Then he got out, looking thoroughly grim. As he headed for the substation and saw me, he managed to greet me affably enough, however, and it didn't seem to me with any semblance of wariness. "Hello, there, Margaret. You, too?"

He said it jokingly, as though he were actually there in his capacity as medical examiner. Of course, he had no way of knowing I'd have a good idea of another reason for his coming. I was even surprised he hadn't been picked up by a police car. Fisher's asking me who had signed Alice Webb's death certificate told me he smelled a connection somewhere between Rothenberg and the murders, especially since a body switch now seemed almost certain.

I managed a pleasantry in return. I think I said, "He'll have the whole island in here before he's through."

Rothenberg laughed and we both went on, he to Fisher's office, I to my car. My path took me past Samantha, who looked unnaturally tense. My finding a motive for Rose's murder had reinflamed my former suspicion of her. I didn't want to speak to her, but there was no way I could avoid it.

"Hello, Samantha." My voice sounded to me like somebody else's, and I found it almost impossible for me even to look at her. I was suddenly frightened as well. Very frightened. I had just remembered the missing pistol.

"We weren't able to talk to Grace yet," she said at once. She sounded defensive and her smile was forced, to say the least.

"So much has happened," I said. "Poor Arthur. And now Owen."

"Yes." She didn't seem to want to say more and fumbled nervously in her handbag.

My inflamed imagination went wild. I was convinced she was going after the pistol. But she pulled out only cigarettes. She lit one, avoiding my eyes.

I said, "Perhaps we can get together again later if you have time."

"Oh, sure. If they find her, of course I'll be glad to."

"Find her? What's happened?"

She finally looked at me. "You don't know? Glenn and I haven't seen her since I last talked to you, and the police have been looking for her everywhere."

"No. I didn't know that," I said lamely. I felt like an idiot, and completely deflated. Of course the impostor would have "gone missing." Only a fool would have continued the charade after Owen Fuller's death. The police must have been all over the place. I made an excuse about rushing to pick up the children and left her, my head in a whirl, and drove away without looking back. I couldn't. Even though the car's interior was summer-hot, I shivered, imagining Samantha as Grace in a wig, hat, scarf, and old dress. It didn't do any good to tell myself I had no real evidence of any kind to justify pointing a finger at her and Glenn Rothenberg. My suspicion was enough.

I tried not to think of Fisher smugly listening to my theory of an impersonation. He had certainly kept the impostor's disappearance secret enough. Nobody seemed to know. Not Peter, not Heather, not even Essie, who had spent a couple of hours with him. Nobody except Samantha and Glenn Rothenberg, and for whatever their reasons, either Fisher's orders or their own caution, they clearly weren't talking.

For an instant it crossed my mind that Fisher might consider me a suspect where Rose and Arthur were concerned, although I was in Boston when Owen Fuller was killed. I thought Fisher might have decided I was somehow in cahoots with someone else, part of a conspiracy. He might think I'd gone to Boston not to get information but to attempt to cover up something. I felt sudden panic but then quickly got hold of myself. The old Fisher I'd labeled stupid might have thought so, but not the Fisher I'd seen today. The Fisher I'd seen today wouldn't think I was brave enough or clever enough, if guilty, to have deliberately come to him with information, hoping to mislead him. And he would have been right. The real Fisher had revealed himself, no matter how much I disliked him, to be far too intelligent to be misled so easily. He also showed me a side of his character that had to be invaluable to any police officer. He had a streak of coldly relentless obstinacy. He was the sort of man who never gave up, and I knew it was only a question of time before he revealed who'd been posing as Grace.

Somehow that revelation, I knew, would prove even more frightening than any other development thus far. Reality always is harder to accept than fantasy, no matter how much one prepares oneself for it.

TWENTY-ONE

The old Chilmark cemetery is on high ground with a view south over the Atlantic. There are ancient graves as well as newer ones, the tombstones so worn that one can no longer read the name of whoever lies beneath them. The grass doesn't get cut as often as it should, and there's a sense of melancholy about the place.

For all that, or perhaps even because of it, the cemetery is a reminder of the many people who live on the island year round, and whose daily lives go right on after the last beach umbrella has been folded late in September and after summer homes by the hundreds are shuttered up. When the main streets of town and village again become the domain of these "regulars," when the crowded harbors are nearly empty, when shipways are packed with canvas-shrouded hulls waiting for another summer's playtime to come around once more after winter's snows and storms are gone, life continues; life and death both.

I had called Essie and told her there was going to be a disinterment, and where. She sounded nonplussed.

"But what on earth for?"

I hesitated. I knew there'd be an explosion of scorn that I wasn't in the mood for, but if she didn't hear it from me, she soon would from someone else. "Fisher thinks maybe it's not Alice who's buried there," I said.

"Not Alice? Who else could it be?"

"Grace."

There was a moment's silence as she took this in, and then she positively sputtered. "Grace Chadwick? Dead and buried in Alice Webb's grave? How absolutely extraordinary! Why on earth would he think such a damned fool thing as that unless he is stark raving mad, which is quite possible, of course."

I so badly wanted to tell her why, but couldn't. So as tactfully as I could, since Essie so hated to be wrong, I said, "He seems to agree with the idea that Grace is dead and someone has been impersonating her."

There was a moment's silence at the other end of the line. I could almost hear Essie swallowing her chagrin because the authorities agreed with me. Then she obviously came to terms with it and said quite reasonably, "An impersonation, maybe. Perhaps you have been right, after all, Margaret, dear. But, just the same, Len Turner doesn't make mistakes like that. He doesn't go around burying the wrong person. And anyway, even if he did, what would that have to do with an impersonation? And where is Alice, then? The man's talking complete nonsense. What on earth is he up to?"

"I don't know," I lied. "But I have to be there."

"You? Why?" Essie sounded astonished and indignant at the same time.

I summoned up a laugh I didn't feel and said half jokingly, "Perhaps our Fisher thinks I'm involved somehow and wants to watch my reaction."

"Oh, don't talk rubbish," Essie snapped. "What time is this idiocy going to take place?"

I tried to put her off coming to lend me moral support, but she came anyway. We stood together, our feet wet from the early-morning dew that still lay heavy on the longish cemetery grass, watching the backhoe strip away sod for a body's length from the plain slate headstone that said simply: *Alice Webb. 1913–1980.*

But let me backtrack a moment. I had arrived early, before Essie, and even before the police and workmen, but I still wasn't the first. Suzy Simmons and her husband were there, standing by the as-yet untouched grave and wearing their best clothes, as though going to a funeral. They looked awkward and out of place. I expected unpleasantness from them and I wasn't disappointed. She was the more aggressive. She immediately recognized me and, without answering my "good morning," almost spat out an angry demand to know what was going on. When I said I gathered the police thought there'd been a case of mistaken identity, Henry Simmons, who up to then had virtually kept his back turned, spun around and lumbered menacingly toward me.

"I know who you are, you damned summertime busybody. You're friends with that hippie artist and his uppity wife back of Rupert's. None of your business how Alice died, I say." He jerked his thumb at Suzy as though she were a dog. "I told her straight off."

"I didn't order this disinterment," I said. "The state police did."

"You stick your big-city nose in our family business again, there'll be trouble, understand?"

Suzy chimed in. "You've got some nerve!" she shouted. "The state office at town hall said they never even heard of you."

I was rescued by the arrival of Glenn Rothenberg and Samantha. No matter what they would have to say, it would be better than listening to a tirade from Henry

Simmons and wife. It was obvious that they had not expected to see me. Fisher, I guessed, had said nothing about my role in the affair.

"Margaret, what are you doing here?"

I could hardly tell Glenn the reason. "I'm not really sure myself," I said. "The lieutenant mentioned something about identification."

Samantha hung on to his arm. "He said the same to us. Maybe he thinks the more the merrier, if that's not too inappropriate an expression for this sort of occasion."

Perhaps because there were other people, I found myself less frightened of her than I had been before and managed to return her tired smile.

Some local people always hate the source that provides them with a living. With the arrival of others they clearly considered intruders on the island, the Simmonses had retreated. They now stood off beyond the grave avoiding Rothenberg, Samantha, and me as we made the sort of forced small talk reserved for the most unpleasant occasions, and in this case trying to find something to say that would avoid the stark reality at hand. Only cemetery workers, undertakers, and hardened police officers can usually manage to put some of their emotions aside to face death and the business of unearthing the remains of a long-dead body.

Then, to my relief, there was the familiar throttled diesel roar of heavy machinery, and a backhoe appeared through the stone-pillared cemetery entrance. Behind it were a state police car with Lieutenant Fisher driven by a trooper, Otis Cramm's radar-ladened cruiser, and the Bache-Turner hearse with Len Turner and two of his morticians in workman's overalls packed into the front seat.

Fisher had no comment to make to anyone when his car pulled up a few yards from the grave site and he got out. Cramm looked his usual awkward self and limited his greetings to the Simmonses—surely the only people he would have felt comfortable with—to a brief nod. For the rest of us he assumed an air of uncomfortable officiousness.

The backhoe was positioned for work, and I was wondering what had happened to Essie when her pickup finally appeared. She was dressed in her old brown dress and rough country oxfords and, as usual, with something, I think her wallet, falling through the hole in her old fishing creel. She'd put on a straw bonnet for the occasion. "Sunday-meeting best" was always her description for the way she was dressed. I was so glad to see her.

She joined me with a low-voiced explanation that the "damned thing wouldn't start, of all mornings." Then Fisher came around from the far side of the grave site, where he had been talking to Len Turner.

"I can't remember that your presence was requested, Miss Peck."

Essie's eyes flashed. "It's a public cemetery, Lieutenant. I was unaware it was off bounds, especially to those with family resting here."

I remembered that Essie's parents were buried at the far end. Fisher stared at her a moment with his watery eyes. Then, without a word, he turned on his heel and walked back to Len Turner.

The undertaker, now recognizing me across the deepening hole and mounting pile of damp earth being excavated by the backhoe, gave me a curt nod. I'm sure that, along with the Simmonses, he held me responsible for his being there, which, of course, I probably was. I shuddered with the ghastly thought that if anything should happen to terminate my existence on Martha's Vineyard, my naked body would probably end up in Turner's fat hands, with their ornate gold rings sunk into the flesh of their fingers, to be drained, viscerated, packed with cotton waste, and God knows what else; I made a mental note to write out a "to be opened on my death" note as fast as possible in which I would instruct Heather and Essie not to let Turner within yards of me.

Essie nudged me, her eyes quietly questioning the presence of the Lobsterville couple. I muttered, "In case the body is Alice's, they can probably identify her," and she nodded. She didn't ask about Dr. Rothenberg, and I surmised she figured he was there because the medical examiner had to be present or represented. But she said something about Samantha under her breath that I didn't quite catch because of the noise the backhoe was making. It sounded disapprovingly spinsterish, though, something like "one of the privileges of being a doctor's house-mate." She obviously didn't regard either one with the same suspicion I did. But then, of course, she didn't know about Rothenberg's signature on Alice's death certificate.

After that, we didn't speak anymore. Like everyone else's, our thoughts and eyes were riveted on the ever-deepening grave and the expectation of what it would soon yield.

The backhoe operator had dug down about four feet now and he stopped work a moment to leave his machine and speak to Turner and Fisher. Turner gave an order to one of his workmen, who went to the hearse and came back with a coil of heavy rope. They'd decided to bring the coffin up rather than try to open it in the grave itself.

The operator spoke a moment longer to Fisher, then started up his backhoe again.

The atmosphere around the grave became even more tense. There was a new expression in everyone's eyes, a kind of revulsion. Up to now, I think all our minds had refused to accept what was about to happen. But now the inevitable was before our eyes, the full morbid horror of decayed death, obviously worse to look at than the dead body before burial. Ordinary death through illness or an accident—even murder—is something that happens to someone else, not oneself. But the cold pitch-dark eternity of a grave and the coffin with its consignment of rotting flesh and exposed skeletal remains is the future of everyone who chooses not to be cremated.

Henry Simmons spoke to his wife in low tones from the side of his mouth. She was biting the nails of her left hand, and her close-set eyes never left the grave. The police had stepped forward, and Fisher had idly picked up a clod of earth and was crumbling it between his fingers, letting it fall powdery back to the ground.

Then the hoe stopped again. Len Turner's workmen approached the grave, and the operator carefully eased the hoe back into the hole and gently raised it, bringing up one end of a half-rotted wooden coffin. My heart began to pound, and I felt Essie hold tightly to my arm. One of the workmen got down into the grave and knotted a sling. It took a few minutes, and by the time he was finished he was sweating heavily. The air had turned sultry and it was already hot out. Then, showering dirt, the coffin was eased out onto the ground. The backhoe operator shut off his motor. There was silence.

Len Turner squatted beside the coffin. In one place it was split open slightly, with dirt jammed in the crack. He gestured to his workmen, and they began to unscrew the lid. I was watching them, fascinated the way one is by something horrible, when I felt Essie pull my arm and heard her say, "I think you're wanted."

I looked up. Fisher was beckoning to me and pointing to a spot beside the coffin. I saw that Suzy Simmons was already there, her narrow face more of a wedge than ever. Biting her fingernails, she'd smudged her lipstick, and it gave a twisted appearance to her hard little mouth.

Essie, defying Fisher, came with me. He didn't try to stop her. When we got there, two of four heavy screws that held the lid shut were already out. The removal of the remaining two seemed to take an eternity. I didn't look at anybody or anything, just at the coffin lid. The turning screws made a horrid complaining noise, a high scream that sounded almost human. Len Turner had bent to lift the lid open. In seconds I would see—what? The decaying remains of the Grace I had seen in the photos? A mummified head with deep eye sockets, the skin stretched parchment-thin over protruding cheekbones, hair wispy, lips eroded back from teeth overprominent in a grotesque death grimace. Would I be able to recognize her?

Turner got a hand on the coffin lid and pulled. It didn't give easily. One of the workmen jammed the flat edge of a wrecking bar into the slight crack he'd opened. There was a splintering noise, and the lid flew back.

I think the first sound I heard after that came from Suzy Simmons—a high nervous laugh that bordered on hysteria. Next I heard Essie say softly, "Oh, for God's sake."

Grace wasn't in the coffin. Nor was Alice. But there was something there. Something lying on the stained cheap nylon. It looked like a naked body, and I knew at once what it had to be. It was the body of the doll on whose bodiless head I had found the two wigs in the nursery at March House.

TWENTY-TWO

There was silence so heavy it was like death itself. Everyone stood motionless and staring, each isolated from the others by their own surprise, until suddenly there was a sound—a low moan. Then Glenn Rothenberg and the state trooper rushed to Samantha, who had fainted and slumped to her knees at the very edge of the grave and was just pitching forward into it head first. Rothenberg grabbed her inert body a split second before it was too late, and her weight would have pulled him in as well if the trooper hadn't got a grip on both of them. They stretched Samantha out on the ground, and Glenn put his jacket under her head and she started to come out of it.

I saw Fisher take that scene in. Then, as he turned to talk to Len Turner, he made notes on a clipboard, and I went over to him. I said, "Do I have your permission to leave, Lieutenant?"

Without looking up, he nodded. Essie and I walked back to my station wagon. We didn't talk until we got there, and she said, "Now, just what do you make of that?" She laughed nervously, as shaken as I was.

"It's more what Fisher is going to make of it," I replied. "Someone didn't want anybody to see the body, obviously."

"Obviously," Essie echoed. "So that 'somebody' dug it up before Fisher could."

I remember I was about to open the car door and I stopped short. "Did what?" The thought had never occurred to me. The first thing that had come to my mind on seeing the open coffin was that someone, for reasons beyond me, had removed the body at one of the funeral parlors. Why a headless doll had been put in its place was something else. I was completely baffled by that.

"Of course," Essie said. She wore that faintly superior look country dwellers sometimes put on when dealing with the ignorance of city friends. "That's why they pulled the coffin out of the grave to open it. The earth had been loosened—not too long ago, either—perhaps last autumn. Couldn't you see? They were afraid of the grave sides caving in."

I remember Fisher talking with the operator and picking up a clod and crumbling it.

"I guess," Essie went on, "the logical answer to 'why' is: no body, no proof of a switch." She added quickly, "Oh, I'm not agreeing with you and Fisher that there *was* a switch, mind you. I'm just speaking hypothesis. But obviously somebody either didn't want anyone ever to know who was buried, or he or she was trying to hide foul play."

I couldn't tell Essie that Grace had died of a heart attack, so foul play didn't make sense. I muttered something about the doll.

"Somebody's way of laughing at the police, I should think," Essie said. She laughed herself. "If you can imagine what Fisher must have thought when he saw it, it *is* rather funny."

I remembered the doll's head in the nursery and shivered. Even thinking of Fisher's surprised discomfiture, I didn't share Essie's amusement. To me, unless the doll's body was some kind of a deliberate attempt to confuse, there was something terrifyingly insane taking place. I couldn't make up my mind what it might be. It could even be a clever act by a totally mad mind.

We couldn't talk further. Essie had to leave. Bad weather had been announced for the next few days, and she had a score of lobster traps to bring in. "And then this afternoon," she said, "I have to go to my fields. I have plants that must come off the land I sold before they flower."

With a promise to get together that evening if we had time, we went in our respective vehicles in opposite directions where the bumpy gravel cemetery drive reached South Road. Perhaps it was just as well. I think we were both still too shocked by the disinterment to make much sense, and I really wanted to be alone to try to make sense of a new thought taking hold of me. I had dismissed out of hand Essie's idea that the missing body had been the victim of foul play, automatically assuming, as I had perhaps misled Angela into thinking, that Grace had died of a heart attack. Measuring Alice's wiry energy, which made one forget her age, against Grace's infirmity and terribly wasted condition, it was a logical error, I suppose, to assume Grace would have heart problems and Alice wouldn't.

Now I suddenly saw things differently. Fisher, I realized, must indeed have been looking for murder evidence since he was hardly the type to waste time on disinterment to verify the presence of a body that, from Len Turner's and Casey Hartman's records, he had to be almost certain was there.

By the time I reached home to give Heather a well-earned morning's rest, had done some of the children's laundry, and had gone to Vineyard Haven's Lagoon Pond to watch them in their first sailing race, I had developed a whole new perception of events in Boston the night Alice Webb died. I perceived Alice, not Grace, as dying of a heart attack and then Grace's being the murder victim, as I had always suspected she might have been. The killer probably saw in Alice's unexpected demise the sudden chance to become Grace Chadwick and eventually drive Algar Mikele into selling March House.

Angela had said there could have been some time between Glenn Rothenberg's signing a death certificate and Casey Hartman's arriving to collect the corpse, time enough, I was sure, to murder Grace and put her in Alice's place. For what better place than the closed coffin supposedly containing the body of a person certified dead from a heart attack to hide someone else whose fatal injuries might have aroused official curiosity should the corpse ever be discovered and routinely autopsied?

Still feeling sore around the base of my neck, I could easily imagine what those injuries might have been. Would Casey Hartman have noticed the shattered vertebrae of an old woman's neck? Probably not. Undertakers don't perform autopsies. But even if he had noticed something extraordinary, there was the signed death certificate. Who was Hartman, called out from lowly South Boston to the prestigious Atheneum, to challenge the official statement or the doctor who had recommended him, for who knew who got paid off and for what these days—and by whom? I could hear Angela saying, "Like, you can get in big trouble rocking boats, right?" In South Boston you learned early not to ask too many questions.

Standing on Lagoon Pond's shore and watching Nancy and Christopher jibe their little Sunfish around a buoy, I tried to imagine how it had all happened. The Atheneum's rooms, like its lobby and most of its loyal older clientele, still reflect a statelier period. In my mind I could visualize the old brass bedsteads, the commodes and wardrobes almost Victorian in their flavor. I could see once-opulent carpets turned slightly threadbare where decades of guests had scuffed their feet. There were lamps whose frayed silken shades made soft light; there were heavy velvet curtains, worn at the hems; there were window frames and bathroom pipes painted far too often, and bathroom tiles, once shiny white, that had turned a dingy cream color in keeping with now archaic plumbing.

I saw Alice in one of those rooms, stricken, lying on a bed and struggling to breathe, her eyes dull with the onslaught of terrible cardiac pain and the shock of fear. Grace and a faceless someone with her who would be her murderer—it had to be someone Grace knew—frantically calling for help. I saw Glenn Rothenberg arrive and remove a stethoscope from his doctor's bag, then close the staring eyes that now saw nothing. He filled out the death certificate, left a copy, heeded a request to recommend the least-expensive mortician possible, and departed, a busy young man with many more pressing things to do than wait for the body's removal.

Alice Webb lay alone and dead then, and far from her island home, her bony work-worn hands folded in final rest across her withered old chest. Grace had retreated back to her own adjoining room, frightened and exhausted, to be calmed by her murderer, whose twisted mind had only just grasped the opportunity that lay there. The ever-watchful Alice was gone. Kill Grace and become Grace.

There are ways to kill without leaving incriminating evidence. Some cancers have complications requiring digitalis or insulin, for example, of which even a massive lethal overdose would not show up in an autopsy. But Grace's cancer had no such complications. There are other traceless drugs and poisons, but nothing was at hand and time was short. The undertaker would soon be there, and a still-warm body might make him suspicious.

Grace Chadwick must have died minutes after the

decision was made. She died and was probably put in Alice's bed, and Alice was hidden.

Forty minutes later, Casey Hartman arrives, breath dense with whiskey fumes. "This is the deceased, I take it. Alice Webb, you say? And the death certificate? Ah, yes, cardiac arrest, I see. Going to Martha's Vineyard? All right. Yes, yes, Bache-Turner. I'll get the address. Just a plain wooden coffin, no extra expense, screw it shut, is that it? Deceased one's last wishes? We'll pass that on to Martha's Vineyard."

Grace on a stretcher, wheeled quickly and discreetly down the hotel corridor to the service elevator and gone forever, via Hartman and Hartman in South Boston, where death is timeless, to a lonely Chilmark grave. There are Indians buried nearby and long-drowned sailors. And the rolling thunder of the Atlantic dies in a whisper over crumbling tombstones and long-forgotten weedy burial plots.

Alice's turn now. Alice in Grace's hat and scarf and wig and clothes. Alice in Grace's wheelchair, in the elevator and through the lobby. The hour was not so late as to seem odd, an old woman going out in her chair for a last airing that day.

Down a quiet street, load Alice into a car, drive to a lonely wharf somewhere in Boston's endless waterfront, remove the dress, the makeup, the wig, and roll the naked corpse into the dark oily waters. One more poor anonymous bag woman dead of unsuspicious heart failure and gone to the ultimate cold.

Back at the hotel, the impersonation begins. Leave the wheelchair in the car, slip back upstairs. There are phone calls to make. As Grace. To Alice's family, to Bache-Turner. But not to Arthur Heston. Arthur Heston can wait. Arthur Heston visited Grace on Martha's Vineyard only two months previous. He'd found her ravaged by cancer, wasted, frail. Time is needed to make a remission believable, a long winter and spring and early summer of letters slowly hinting at it, the rejoicing in rejuvenation until a far more vigorous Grace can, the following summer, be believed.

In the morning, Grace's clothes are donned, the wig and hat and scarf. A face is obscenely coated with Grace's rouge and powder and lipstick. Grace Chadwick returns to March House, wants to see no one, chases people away. But lets word slowly get around. Grace Chadwick isn't going to die. Not just yet . . .

Watching the children work their way windward to another buoy, sails bright splashes of color against the silvery slate-blue of the water and the green of the shore beyond, I tried also to imagine the eventual meeting with Arthur Heston the following summer. I saw the lawyer, balding, narrow-shouldered, jowly, his face betraying his condescension, coming to March House in one of Bert's taxis, paying the driver, walking around to the back door.

I heard his footsteps in the kitchen corridor and through the shrouded dining room into the main hall. I heard him go up the sweeping stairs.

"Grace? It's Arthur."

A quavering answer. And the meeting in her corner bedroom, the shutters half closed, and Grace, in the shadowy gloom, propped up on the pillows of her big four-poster bed. What had gone through the murderer's mind as the curtain went up on the ultimate test?

"There you are, Arthur. Come in, come in. Don't just stand there like a ninny. Sit down. Come to take the car out, have you? Can't imagine you've come just to see me. But find me better, do you? Well, miracles will never cease; I am. I don't intend to die yet, Arthur. Not yet."

And the right touches to make it convincing. Some of Grace's gestures, noticed from long familiarity, perhaps. Grace's left-handedness if the murderer was not. Grace's eccentric imperiousness. Grace's paranoia about Owen Fuller and anyone else who might recently have disturbed her.

Had the deception worked? Had Arthur Heston fallen for it? Believed it because there would have been, in fact, no earthly reason not to; and then retired to the barn to look after his beloved old Lincoln limousine, to remove its dust sheet and prepare to drive it off on its yearly run to Edgartown and Vineyard Haven.

Or had he seen through the disguise and taken the first step toward blackmail that was to turn the Lincoln into a guillotine that would someday choke the life from his body?

I got no further in my dark thoughts. Nature suddenly intervened. A squall line was bearing down on Lagoon Pond, threatening to capsize the six little racing Sunfish. The sailing instructor was among them in a flash with her fast power launch. Orders were shouted, sails were dropped by well-trained kids, and when the drenching rain and wind hit a few minutes later, the whole fleet was in safe tow like so many little wingless beetles, their crews laughing and shrieking under the cold pelting rain as they made the safety of shoal water and a leeward beach.

A half hour later the storm ended and the sky cleared. I got my two children home, happy but furious at the same time because they had been winning. I felt exhausted by my own imagination and was ill-prepared for what happened next. I had hardly walked through my front door and sent the children upstairs to get out of their wet clothes and into a hot bath when the telephone rang.

"Hello?"

The voice that addressed me belonged to the last person from whom I ever expected to hear.

TWENTY-THREE

"It's Estelle, Mrs. Barlow. Estelle Perkins."

I found my voice and replied.

Then she said, "I know this sounds crazy, but I've got to see you."

I heard tears in her voice, but I must confess I neither felt nor expressed much sympathy for whatever might be their cause. "What about?" I asked.

"I can't tell you on the phone, Mrs. Barlow. It . . . it's too complicated. Could I come to see you? Please? I know you don't like me, but I have to talk to someone, and you're the only person I can trust."

I grudgingly began to reconsider. I knew she must have swallowed a lot of pride before calling me. Either that or she was an even more dreadful little bitch than I imagined, and a far better actress. I settled for my first judgment. The fear in her voice seemed absolutely real to me. Besides, I have to admit I was curious.

"Can you give me some idea of what this is all about?"

She hesitated, then said, "It's about a letter Grace Chadwick wrote my mother. I found it yesterday when I was going through her things."

"Oh?" I tried to keep instant curiosity out of my voice. If she was telling the truth and there was a letter, the fact that she'd called me, of all people, could mean it was important. "When was it written?" I asked.

"Five years ago. It was from the real Grace."

That caught me by surprise, also, and I was cautious. "What do you mean, the *real* Grace?"

"You must know," she said. "I heard about the police digging up Alice Webb's grave this morning because they thought Grace was buried there, and the person we've all thought was Grace is somebody else and maybe the murderer."

How on earth did she know all that? Before I could ask, she said, "Suzy Simmons told me. I saw her in the grocery store this morning. She said Len Turner told her."

Given the nature of small-town gossip, that made sense. But I wondered briefly, before I decided to take Estelle at her word, what Fisher would have to say to Turner for such loose talk.

"Perhaps I could drive out," I said. I didn't really fancy her coming into my house because she might have François in tow. Or even awful Italian Trunks and his androgynous girlfriend.

I heard Estelle protest. "Oh, Mrs. Barlow, I don't want to inconvenience you."

I remained firm. "I'll come down after lunch."

I hung up only half hearing her "thank you" and stood staring at my telephone. What on earth now? Before I told Heather I was going up to Chilmark, I must have run through nearly half a dozen explanations; Estelle knew something about her mother's murder she didn't want to tell to the police; she knew the impostor's real identity; she herself was implicated in some sort of plot. I even made François the murderer with Estelle not knowing how to handle that fact. My head was in a whirl.

"Don't go," Heather said when I told her. She looked worried.

"She sounded genuine for once," I said.

"I don't care, Margaret. From everything you've told me she's trouble, and seeing her can only be bad for you."

I gave Heather a hug and a kiss. "Bless you, dear, but whatever it's about I think I can handle it."

"I can come with you," she insisted.

I hesitated. Heather's well-intentioned anxiety had succeeded in kindling a certain hesitation of my own. Suppose she was right and I was wrong? Suppose Estelle was indeed up to no good? The old saw about a leopard not changing his spots ran through my head, but then I reminded myself that old saws don't always cut true, that Estelle wasn't a leopard, just a spoiled degenerate brat barely past her teens. Besides, there were children to consider. If Heather accompanied me, we would have to bring them along, and if there was any unpleasantness, I wouldn't want them around.

I turned down Heather's offer, and an hour later I was on my way, thinking that two trips to Chilmark in one day were quite enough for my liking, but a visit with Estelle could not be as bad as Lieutenant Fisher's little cemetery party at an hour when most respectable people were sitting down to breakfast.

As it turned out, I was wrong. I should have listened to Heather, but hindsight is useless, and what happened had to happen eventually, so perhaps it was just as well I went when I did.

The twenty-minute drive flew by. Once again I found myself at Beetlebung Corners, where the two main roads from Vineyard Haven and Edgartown meet. I took Middle Road just beyond the junction and shortly after turned into the long maple-lined driveway leading to the low gray-shingled silhouette of The Rookery.

Estelle's little Alfa Romeo convertible was parked before the front door, and, getting out of my station wagon, I saw Rose's Cadillac in the garage. Just the same, there was an odd feeling of abandonment about the place, as though everyone had suddenly just upped and walked away.

There wasn't a sound except for the occasional whistle of a bobwhite in a field across a stone wall, and from very far away the haunting cry of a mourning dove. The thunderstorms and squall lines of the morning had fled, but the radio was announcing more and the air was heavy and hot again. I apprehensively went to the front door, my footsteps on the gravel making what sounded to me like an incredible volume of noise to warn whoever awaited me of my approach. I rang the bell and waited.

Estelle didn't take long to answer. The door flew open almost immediately, and there she was. She'd put on a dress and was wearing far less makeup than usual—perhaps to win me over—but what I noticed more at the time were her eyes. They were puffy and red with dark circles under them. She'd clearly been crying a lot and sleeping little.

The smile she gave me was like a child's. "Oh, Mrs. Barlow, thank you so much for coming."

I stepped into the house. She closed the door quickly, almost furtively, I thought, as though she were frightened that someone might rush in with me or be watching from behind a tree or a stone wall.

"Let's go out to the pool," she said, and once again I followed her there.

The house was as silent as outside. We crossed the living room and went through the French doors to the back terrace and took chairs by the glass-topped iron table next to the pool.

"Can I get you something to drink, tea or a Coke or something?"

I declined, wary of her sudden good manners, and at the same time noting the absence of any sign that the pool had been used that day.

Estelle saw me looking about and said, "There's nobody here. Just you and me." When I said nothing, she added, "François left a couple of days ago. And everyone else."

"Oh?"

"It seems there wasn't as much money in Rose's estate as everyone thought. She'd run through most of her capital and she was planning to take a heavy mortgage on this place to buy out Algar. So François suddenly found Ann Alfreda more interesting."

Her tone, to my surprise, was more scornful than bitter, almost amused. Just the same, I couldn't refrain from being bitchy.

"She turned in her two beautiful stallions for François?"

Estelle replied with a tired smile. "I guess. When last seen, they were with Mary-Lou."

I refrained from asking about Italian Trunks. Unquestionably he had to be down below at Ann Alfreda's, too, and inwardly I marveled how such an androgynous wretch as Mary-Lou could attract any man, let alone seduce two and possibly three into sharing her, unless all three were bisexual. The bed scene at Ann Alfreda's ugly house had to be strange beyond belief. What could be left to amuse such people?

I said to Estelle, "None of that bothers you?"

She answered with a strange sadness in her voice. "It did yesterday. It doesn't today." She bent her head suddenly, twisting her fingers in her lap. "You must think I'm a dead loss, and I guess I have been. I don't know how I got involved with those people. I just did."

In spite of her apparent contrition, I balked at being sympathetic, although, to be honest, I felt she wasn't asking for sympathy, and in spite of myself I rather respected her for it. I said a little less coldly, "I'm sure you have had personal problems, Estelle, but François is not the reason you called me."

She seemed to pull herself together. "I'm sorry," she said. "Here." She picked up from the table an old faded envelope I hadn't noticed before. "I found it at the back of one of my mother's desk drawers. I don't know how the police missed it, but they did. It will explain a lot, although in giving it to you to read I have to betray a trust it asks not be betrayed."

"Why are you, then?" I asked.

She was silent a moment, looking acutely uncomfortable. Then she blurted out emotionally, "Mrs. Barlow, I badly need help and advice. I know this is hard for you to believe—probably impossible, the way I behaved to you—but you're the only person I know whom I can trust and whose judgment I respect. Please help me. Please."

I looked at the envelope she held out. Whatever its contents, I couldn't see how they could involve me in anything I didn't want to be involved in. As for betraying a trust, that burden was on Estelle's shoulders, not mine. Nobody had asked me to keep secrets, not even she. I could decide later if I should remain silent.

I glanced from the envelope to Estelle. Her expression as she waited for me to decide was desperately anxious. I took the envelope. Written on it in a woman's clear old-fashioned hand was:

To be opened on the event of my death.

Estelle looked at me and then added quietly, "It seems Grace Chadwick was my grandmother."

For a moment, I was nonplussed, and then seconds later filled with that sort of amazed revelation we all experience from time to time that leads us to say to ourselves, "But of course." For I suddenly realized what it was I'd seen in the old photos of Grace Chadwick and her family hanging by the big canopied four-poster in Grace's corner bedroom; what it was besides noting that Grace Chadwick was left-handed that had struck me as odd and that I couldn't place.

In the photos I had seen a lovely young woman whose face I now realized had seemed strangely familiar. I was looking at virtually that same face now.

I smiled at Estelle Perkins and said as casually as I could, "Yes, I can see that she was." Then I took from within the envelope two folded sheets of notepaper covered with the same handwriting as was on the envelope itself. I looked at Estelle. She was staring off across the pool, her hands still in her lap. There were tears in her eyes.

I read the letter, dated over five years previous:

My dear Rose,

I have something to tell you in confidence, and I dearly hope you will respect this, my last wish, and never divulge the contents of this letter to anyone in the world no matter for what reason. You once said your parents had revealed to you that you were adopted but that they didn't know themselves who your real mother and father were, as it was against the rules of the adoption agency to disclose their identities. In telling you this untruth, they were respecting a solemn pact made between my parents and them to quiet forever the terrible shame I brought on myself and my family even before I attained my majority.

I bore a child out of wedlock. I will take the name of her father, whom I loved with my whole being, to my grave with me. The child, of course, was you.

It is perhaps too late to ask for forgiveness for having deliberately distanced myself from you all these years. As I rapidly approach my death from this dread cancer, I regret it. But I had not the courage to face more than the most casual contact with you. To do so was to remind myself of the agony I suffered the year of your birth, the brutal separation from him I loved by my father and his, the heartbreak of giving away the living reminder of the one and only love of my life.

I have sold March House to pay my bills, for I have no money of my own, only what comes to me from a trust established by my father and which on my death goes for the most part to a charity. But everything in the house when I die is yours to sell if you wish, except for the contents of my safe. Since you have money, I wish you to give what is there to my granddaughter, Estelle. You will find my jewelry, not worth much except in sentiment, and some bonds an uncle gave me that I believe today are still worth a little.

When my parents died and I occupied their corner bedroom, I turned an adjacent dressing room into the nursery you should have had in the hopes that making believe I had been able to keep you would ease some of the pain. Lift the rug under the toy chest. It covers the safe, whose combination is written on a piece of paper tucked inside the head of the brown teddy bear that sits in the crib.

Don't tell Arthur Heston about this. As the trustee foisted on me by Father's will, he has been a necessary evil in my life, pushing himself on me at every chance, first in hopes of getting at least March House when I die, and now with some idea of at least having my old car, my furniture, and what is in the safe. Please burn the baby photos of him. I suspect somehow he guessed of my disgrace when he one day discovered the nursery and hoped to use my loss as a means of ingratiating himself. As if photos of a horrid little boy could substitute for the little girl I loved so much and was forced to abandon.

My dear Rose, I ask your forgiveness and that you accept my eternal love.

Your mother,
Grace Chadwick

I silently returned the letter to Estelle. "I have no need to repeat any of this," I said. "Ever. In fact, I'd much prefer not to."

"Thank you," she said. "That does help. A great deal."

I thought of Rose trying to buy back March House and get Grace to will it to her. Her motive seemed pretty clear now. I asked, "Did Rose never hint at this?"

She reflected a moment, then said, "Not directly, but looking back I see a lot of things. I mean, besides her trying to get March House for herself, of course. Comments she made about what an old fool Grace was to sell March House to Algar Mikele when before she'd hardly ever mentioned Grace's name. Then, the way she became furious when she began trying to see Grace, and Grace refused to see her. I didn't understand it then; I thought it a little odd, but I understand now."

"I suppose," I said, "she must have been very hurt that Grace never told her in person."

"Hurt? No, I don't think so," Estelle replied thoughtfully. "I don't think Rose was ever hurt by anything or anybody. Do you? Honestly?"

I thought of Rose, her shallowness, her determination to be a social lioness. I didn't answer, but I knew Estelle was right.

As though reading my mind, she said, "Grace being Rose's unwed mother didn't exactly fit in with Rose's image of herself holding forth at garden parties and being the big society deal on the island. Perhaps long, long ago before Grace became an eccentric recluse, but not in the last few years." She smiled. "I think I actually understand what Grace went through far better than Rose—giving Rose away and then all those miserable years afterward living with the constant reminder that nursery must have been. Can you imagine doing such a thing? She must have been half mad, but I feel desperately sorry for her just the same, maybe because I'm the same age as she was when it all happened."

Or perhaps almost the same young woman in character, I thought, and if anyone was hurt it was she, and by Rose. I studied her. There was a kind of calm about Estelle I wasn't used to. Had the cataclysm I once thought necessary to straighten her out finally happened? I felt a sudden forgiveness toward the outrageously insulting brat I'd been forced to bully into cooperation a week ago. If any sign of that child still existed, I couldn't see it. Who had I been to judge someone so severely? I thought. I doubted I'd been the easiest girl to have around at the same age. And if I objected to her sexual standards, I thought, well, what had my own mother, unquestionably chaste until my father possessed her on their wedding night, thought about my losing my virginity at seventeen? That had happened on an unchaperoned skiing weekend and I'd followed it up with a not-so-secret ten-day trip to Paris only six months later with a married guy old enough to be my father. Estelle was as much a product of the public environment she grew up in—schools, movies, magazines, and television—as I was at her age by the different forces surrounding me.

"How do you want me to help you?" I asked.

"I wondered what you thought about respecting somebody's last wishes—how important it is, especially if it's difficult to do. Grandmother wanted me to have her jewelry, which she says isn't worth much, and the bonds, which I suspect are worth much more. But it doesn't make any difference what they are worth. I don't care about that. It's that she wanted me to have them. But if I go to the police or make a claim through a lawyer, I'd have to show this letter and reveal her secret. And if I don't and I'm caught sneaking about March House, who knows what could happen. I'd be labeled a thief and maybe even considered a murder suspect. Is her last wish worth the risk?"

I thought of March House and whatever danger might still lurk there. Estelle hadn't mentioned the murderer, but I couldn't think of much else. Somehow "Grace's" disappearance made the whole situation even more frightening. "Grace's" presence there, whether or not she was an impostor, had at least been a *known*. But where was she now? And who was she really? Getting caught by Fisher and the police might be the lesser danger at March House.

All the old demons came back, every fear and terror I'd experienced and had nightmares about. I pushed them back and forced myself to think only of last wishes from beyond the grave. Why did people feel they had to respect them? Any more than they respected the dead person's wishes during their lifetimes, if those wishes were inconvenient. Perhaps, I thought, it was because a life completed was owed some reward after all, some appreciation without judgment even if only from someone who had no part of it. A dying person ought to know things will turn out the way he or she wants them to, and for once have the blessing and peace of feeling their trust in others will not be betrayed. I thought of wishes and I thought of Grace Chadwick, a poor tormented woman imprisoned for life in a narrow world that no longer existed—a life that for her had been mostly unrewarded misery.

I said to Estelle, "Yes, whatever she wanted is worth the risk. You have to honor her wishes."

A look of extraordinary relief came over her, and tears came to her eyes again. "Oh, thank you, Mrs. Barlow." She laid a hand on mine. "It means so much to me to hear you say that. I needed to have someone tell me I wasn't wrong."

"I don't know how you're going to manage it, though," I said. "Surely Fisher must have March House locked and guarded."

Estelle laughed. "Every door and window, apparently, and with red warnings posted on the front door and front gates, and Otis Cramm sitting in his cruiser in the driveway. But I'll figure out something." Then she became serious again. "Just the same, I'm frightened. Oh, it's not what you think. I'm not worried about anyone still lurking around. I'm frightened of opening my grandmother's safe and taking whatever is there. It makes her death seem so final, and death scares me."

"It scares everyone," I said. I made up my mind and stood up. "Well?"

"You're not coming with me?" Her eyes widened. "Don't you want me to?"

"Oh, yes, Mrs. Barlow, but I didn't dare ask."

"I think you'll need someone," I stated firmly, "and I'd like to make up for the other day."

"Oh, Mrs. Barlow, thank you for that."

The look of gratitude on Estelle's face chased away

any lurking March House demons. For the moment, anyway. And the hug and kiss she gave me somehow overcame my bad conscience at bullying her.

Five minutes later, we were in her Alfa Romeo rolling down the front driveway toward Middle Road and the rapidly approaching end of my story.

TWENTY-FOUR

On the way to March House, we tried to think of what to do about Otis Cramm. Even without his presence, the front of the house was visible from the road, so we'd have to try to get in from the back, as I had done. With Otis there, how would we make our approach without his seeing us? If we couldn't use Owen Fuller's drive next door, which was in plain sight of March House, we'd have to push our way through a quarter of a mile of thick damp woods choked with underbrush and catbrier. Somehow Otis had to be distracted.

I was at a loss, but as we approached Tea Lane, Estelle brightened. "Got it!" she said.

"What?" I asked.

"You watch," she said mysteriously. She gave me a quick smile, spun her wheel, and shot down from the asphalt surface of Middle Road into Tea Lane's bumpy dirt and gravel.

We rocked and bounced for a minute. Dust rose behind us in a long coil that drifted away into the thick green bordering woods. We picked up speed and then, as we topped a low rise, March House's rusty old iron front gates came into view, and just beyond them, in the weedy overgrown driveway, the familiar outline of Otis Cramm's cruiser, Otis himself leaning against it reading one of his ever-present hunting magazines.

"There he is!" exclaimed Estelle. She leaned on the Alfa's shrill Italian horn, which I am sure could be heard a mile away. Cramm looked up sharply, and as we went by, Estelle slowed, put out her hand, and made an un-mistakable obscene gesture. "That's to wake him up," she said.

She accelerated again. We passed Owen Fuller's driveway still in Cramm's sight, then, another quarter of a mile down Tea Lane, made a U-turn and stopped.

Estelle looked over at me and said, "Okay? All set?" I had barely nodded, not quite knowing what she had in mind, when she went on. "This time he's on your side," she said. "You're the one who has to be rude."

Before I could reply, she put the Alfa in gear and floored it. We leaped forward and in seconds, with Estelle running the Alfa's gears smoothly through their gates, we were going at breathtaking speed, rocking and bucking and swerving as she dodged holes and ruts with the ac-complished skill of a race-car driver. The noise of stones and gravel thrown up against the Alfa's underside was deafening.

"Get ready!" Estelle shouted.

I saw the March House gates looming again—this time very fast. Cramm looked alert now as Estelle once more leaned on the little convertible's ear-splitting horn.

I was too frightened to say anything. We must have been doing close to seventy-five miles an hour. On the narrow dirt lane it seemed much faster, the trees flashing past as a green blur. I barely had time to turn my head and the gates were right there, Otis on his toes, leaning forward in openmouthed astonishment.

DAVID OSBORN

"Now! Now!" Estelle shouted.

Almost without thinking I obeyed and made the awful gesture and, feeling some strange and wild surge of triumph, added a milder one of my own. I stuck out my tongue.

It was too much for Otis. Looking back, I had a flash vision of the king of radar scrambling into his cruiser; and then again before I could think, we were slowing onto Middle Road. We screeched over the tar surface in another U-turn that almost wiped us out against a passing car and skidded to a halt back on the dirt just at the head of the lane again.

Estelle pointed. "There. See?"

Over the top of the relatively distant rise separating us from March House, I could see the top of Otis Cramm's cruiser, just the blue and white flashing lights, as he pulled out of the driveway and gave pursuit.

"Hurrah!" Estelle cried. "Got him."

The Alfa leaped forward once more. "This time we'll play chicken," she said, "and guess who will win?"

What happened next is still locked in my memory—a scene I'd as soon forget but can't. I wake up some nights thinking of it and break into cold perspiration.

Foot to the floor, Estelle swung the Alfa into the middle of the narrow lane and stayed there. Cramm's cruiser, also in the middle of the road, bore down on us at breakneck speed. In seconds it was right there in front of us. I could see Otis only yards away—his wide staring eyes, his police hat set above his protruding ears, and his stupid little mustache.

Then he abruptly disappeared. Simultaneously there was a sharp bang. We jerked and skidded. Estelle wrestled her wheel back and forth as we slewed sideways down the road. "Damn," she said. "He clipped me."

She got control of the car, slowed, and looked back. As I, too, glanced over my shoulder, I saw Otis's cruiser, only its roof lights now visible above the hump in the road on the other side of March House and half obscured by whirling dust.

I hadn't the chance to see more. We swung sharply into Owen Fuller's narrow concealing driveway.

"It's a hundred to one he didn't see us," Estelle said calmly.

Owen Fuller's house heaved into view, and with it a familiar pickup truck. Essie's old Chevy was parked by the chicken coops.

"Uh-oh. Who's that?" Estelle asked.

"Essie Peck," I said. "She parks here all the time. She has one of those fields back of Grace." I felt for just a moment a great sense of relief. With Essie at hand, we had nothing to be afraid of. In fact, she'd be absolutely delighted to come with us. It would perhaps be a last chance for her to sneak around March House, something she'd missed out on the first time I'd gone there. But in almost the same instant, I remembered the confidence I shared with Estelle. Instead of calling on Essie, we were going to have to avoid her. "I'm sure she won't bother us," I said. "If we go behind the barn, she won't even know we're here."

Estelle hesitated, warily skirting the pickup, then drove around the coops on the wagon track that led behind the barn.

She shut off the motor, and we got out. Her left rear fender was gone. "Everything has its price," she said as we went into the barn itself, where we could look out at Owen's house and driveway. And there we waited.

We decided to give Otis Cramm twenty minutes. He appeared in less than ten, drove slowly around Owen Fuller's house, then back out to Tea Lane. The left front fender and headlight of the cruiser were an irreparable mess, and his left door was banged in. We gave him five more minutes to make certain he wasn't coming back before we left our hiding place.

Once more I felt surrounded by a horrible kind of

stillness, that heavy silence that often comes before a storm when even the birds are quiet. All the memories of my first visit to March House came rushing back. What I felt must have shown in my face, because Estelle took my arm as we went cautiously back around Owen Fuller's chicken coop and said, "Would you rather not, Margaret? I can do it alone."

I forced a smile. "Don't be silly," I said. I've come this far, I thought, I'll see it through. Besides, I didn't relish the idea of waiting all alone at Owen's barn for her return. I'd had quite enough of barns.

Estelle led the way along the little path in the woods to the stone wall stile and gate beyond, where Owen had met his end. I was beginning to wonder how she knew the way so well when she said over her shoulder, "I was here with my mother one day last summer when she tried to pay a call on Grace. We came in from the other end of Tea Lane, and there was a tree across it. We couldn't get past Owen's driveway."

We went over the stile with its fallen stones just as Essie had described, and there, suddenly, was the overgrown back lawn and the scum-covered fish pond where Rose had met her end and the tree where Owen had met his.

Somebody, the police, I suppose, had closed all the shutters—downstairs as well as upstairs—and the kitchen door was shut. There was no sign of anybody. "I bet Cramm's back in the driveway," Estelle said in a low voice.

We tried the kitchen door. It was locked. Estelle pointed to one side. A pane of glass was broken in one of the windows nearby. We went to it, and she put her hand inside, unlocked the window, silently raised it, and without making any noise went over the sill. The window was fairly close to the ground, and I followed easily enough. We found ourselves in a small cold larder whose open door gave onto a short passage leading in turn to the back kitchen hall.

I won't dwell on yet another unsettling walk down that hallway, where narrow back stairs twisted up into darkness; how we went past the kitchen with all my nightmare fears of unexpectedly finding someone seated at the table; or describe the darkened butler's pantry and gloom-shrouded dining room and my dreamlike sense of déjà vu as we crossed the now-silent hall, the grandfather clock finally stilled, the strange light filtering down from the colored-glass cupola. I felt my whole life somehow entangled in March House.

I led Estelle up the sweeping staircase to the half landing from where I had first seen Arthur Heston and now, looking down through the Palladian-style windows over the front door, saw Otis Cramm. His cruiser was back, just as Estelle had suggested, and Otis was standing by it again, watching the road. I found myself thinking of Essie, who usually drove far too fast, and hoping she wouldn't come racing out of Owen Fuller's driveway if she left before us and get a ticket. The speed limit on Tea Lane was twenty-five miles per hour, and Otis was in a mood, I was certain, to ticket anyone his radar zapped at twenty-six.

As far as that went, I dreaded to think what charges he'd have in store for Estelle. Speeding and reckless driving, most certainly. He knew her car. And then what? Assaulting an officer of the law, resisting arrest, for a start. An inflamed Otis would be capable of anything, especially if he'd had a drink or two before filing his official report.

Estelle, however, seemed oblivious to Cramm. She made sounds of delighted victory and seemed prepared to watch Otis forever. I had to remind her why we were there and urge her on to Grace's bedroom. "Cramm is one thing," I whispered, "but if Fisher shows up, we're in real trouble."

The shutters in Grace's room had been closed and the curtains drawn. The room was hot and nearly dark. Almost immediately I fell over a chair and thought the whole world could hear the noise. I tried the lights. None worked. The police had shut off the electricity. Estelle, however, quickly came up with a candle in a brass holder, complete with matchbox. "It was on her bedside table," she said.

How on earth had she seen it? A match flared, the candlewick flickered, flame took hold, and long shadows fell across the room.

"Where's the nursery? There?"

She pointed to its door. I said yes and followed her to it. It was locked, but the key was in the keyhole. Estelle turned it, and we went into the stiflingly hot and airless nursery, the candle flame turning dolls and teddy bears and the hobbyhorse into shadow demons, dragons, and gargoyles on walls and ceiling.

"She said the toy chest," Estelle murmured. "There it is." She put the candle down on it and turned to the little crib. "And here's the bear. Off with your head, Ted." She picked up the worn old teddy bear that sat in the crib, held its body fast, and twisted its head. It came off easily. Her fingers searched inside and with a low exclamation she pulled out a small folded sheet of paper. "Look, Margaret."

She brought it over to the candle, unfolded it, and together we read some numbers that were obviously for a combination lock.

"This is it, we've got it," Estelle said.

I held up the candle while she pulled the toy chest away from the wall and rolled the rug back from where it had been standing.

"And there's the safe," she whispered.

I held the candle down low. At our feet was what appeared to be a small trapdoor with a recessed handle in the floor planking. It came up easily when Estelle tugged, revealing the dusty metallic surface of a safe with its combination dial a small rosette in its middle.

Estelle knelt immediately and asked me to read the numbers. I did. There were three sets, which usually meant three times left for the first, twice right for the second, and once left for the third. She spun the dial left, right, then left again. The tumblers clicked. The safe opened. "Could you bring the light closer, Margaret?"

I obeyed.

Estelle reached into the interior and brought out an envelope. "The bonds, I bet," she said.

She was right. There were four of them, and at first glance in the dim flickering light they seemed to be for some railroad in the West. "We'll look at them later," Estelle said.

I took them, and she reached again into the safe. This time she came up with a tattered old leather jewelry case about the size of a small Whitman's sampler. The clasp was broken and the lid held tight by string. She slipped the string off and opened it. The candlelight shone on an assortment of jewelry. I saw silver bracelets and a small antique engagement ring—"Probably her mother's," Estelle murmured. Her finger poked about, uncovering a cameo brooch, a threaded-gold necklace, and a double string of pearls. And then a small lady's wristwatch with a black strap, a gold watch with a pretty gold-and-diamond fob, and various other items of less importance. "She was right," Estelle breathed. "Not worth much, but oh so pretty, and I'm so very glad to have them." She tied the string round the box again.

"Is there anything else?" I asked. "We shouldn't stay here too long."

Estelle bent low and plunged her hand back down in the safe, feeling. "Wait," she said. "Yes, there is."

She straightened and pulled out what she'd found, holding it up to the candlelight. It was a small yellowed

leather-bound book, and I recognized what it was immediately.

"That could be very important," I said.

"What is it?"

"Grace's diary. And probably the one for the year
she died."

"Why is that important?"

"Because," I said, "she died in Boston, and the diary might say if she planned to meet someone there, perhaps someone she knew well from here."

"And that might be whoever has been posing as
her?"

"I don't know," I said, "but there has to be some
reason for its being hidden here in the safe. All her other
diaries for years back are in a bookcase out there."

"Then let's get it to a decent light and have a look,"
Estelle said.

She gathered up the jewelry box and envelope with
the bonds and started for the door.

"Wait," I said. "We ought to close this up again."

She was almost at the door. "You're right," she
said. She turned to come back and stopped suddenly, listening, then put her finger to her lips warning me to keep
quiet. She listened again, then quickly blew out the candle.

"What's the matter?" I whispered.

"I don't know. I thought I heard someone."

I didn't answer. I couldn't. I was seized at once by
an almost indescribable terror. I remember straightening
from where I had knelt next to the safe in order to close
it. In the darkness I could feel my heart thudding against
my ribs like blows of an angry fist. I strained to hear, but
there was no sound.

Then I felt rather than saw Estelle move away from
me, and she became faintly outlined at the doorway by
the relatively lighter bedroom beyond.

She stood there a moment before stepping silently over the threshold.

And then quite abruptly with an almost violent movement, she turned to face me. The door slammed shut. There was the sound of the key turning in its old lock and I was alone.

I groped through the pitch-darkness to the door and tried to open it, to no avail. It was securely locked.

"Estelle?"

There was no answer.

TWENTY-FIVE

There is almost no way to describe my thoughts. But I think what dominated them all was the bitter chagrin of having let myself be taken in. I was certain I'd been conned right from the very beginning.

It seemed centuries ago that I'd taken Estelle's call and with Heather's anxious warning in my ears had driven to The Rookery to be greeted at the door by a "reformed" Estelle. From then on I had ignored every clue, and each one now seemed all too obvious: her knowledge that only Otis Cramm was on guard; her familiarity with Owen Fuller's property and the path through the woods to March House; her apparent knowledge that the back window with its conveniently broken pane was a way into the house; the candle so quickly found in the dark gloom of Grace's bedroom; the ease with which she'd gone right to the toy chest in the nursery, ignoring everything else there.

How had I ever let Estelle allay my suspicion of her when she so perfectly fitted the role of murderess?

Here was someone strong and athletic who could fit into paint-stained jeans and sneakers; someone who benefited substantially by Rose's death—The Rookery was worth a lot but March House far more if with Rose out of the way she could have bought it back from Algar; someone whose drug-induced morality and associations with immoral degenerates could have made her callous enough to murder even her own mother and make it look like the work of an innocent man. I saw the fine hand of François, perhaps even Ann Alfreda, whose fading career couldn't keep up with the money demands of her jaded life-style. Had Rose somehow originally been party to the impersonation or even the impostor herself until her own daughter betrayed her? Possibly. Rose had the sort of cold grasping character that could turn to murder. Rose, too, could have been the faceless person who'd seen opportunity in Alice Webb's unexpected death. But no one would ever know now. Rose was dead, along with Grace, Alice Webb, Arthur Heston, and Owen Fuller. Who was next?

The terror I'd felt before Estelle locked me in rose in my throat, and perspiration began to trickle down my face and body. Margaret Barlow. Me. *I* had to be next! The damning diary—and it had to be damning; otherwise, why would Estelle have rushed away with it?—was gone. There were no clues to any of the murders, no witnesses, not even Otis Cramm, if she could leave without his seeing her. There was no one except me.

And suddenly I knew how she could make certain of my permanent silence. She had only to set fire to the house. The Chilmark volunteers were good, but no fire department arriving ten minutes after Otis would discover the blaze could hope to put out the fiery inferno that would be March House. It's tinderbox-dry wooden interior would go up in seconds, and I with it.

Panic seized me. I beat helplessly on the door. How long had I been locked in? A minute? Two? How long before I would smell smoke? I screamed for help. For Otis Cramm. For anyone. For Estelle, begging her to let me out. And for Essie, who was so close in one way and so far in another. Could she possibly hear me out back in her field?

Silence was my answer. Silence, then a faint sharp sound. A car backfire, I thought. Estelle's Alfa hurtling away. Then silence again. A silence so silent as to be deafening.

In a frenzy, I pounded on the door and screamed for help again and then finally got a grip on myself.

No door was impenetrable. I would get this one open somehow. I felt its surface. It was made the way doors used to be made—solid. My fingers located the lock. How could I open it? I remembered in a movie someone's pushing a key out, then with a coat hanger or piece of wire pulling the key back under the door—if the falling key didn't bounce too far out of reach. I knelt to feel the threshold, to see if there was enough space under the door for the key to slip through. There wasn't. There wasn't even enough room under the door for a thin sheet of paper.

I began to feel panic again. I explored the door's edges. Could I pry it open? It fit so tightly I almost couldn't find the crack between it and the surrounding jamb. I could think of nothing in the nursery sharp enough to slip into such a crack and strong enough to lever with.

My panic rose. Could I smash the door down or burst open the solid lock? And with what? Something very heavy. *And move quickly, Margaret; time is running out!* A bureau drawer? Not heavy enough. The side of the crib? How could I get the crib apart in the dark? I groped toward it and then thought of the safe. Was it too heavy for me to lift? I found the trapdoor still open. I knelt again, feeling about in the pitch-black darkness, and tried to budge the safe, but to no avail. The safe was firmly wedged between two beams and probably bolted to them.

I desperately stood again. And realized I had not yet smelled smoke. How long had I been here? Five minutes? I breathed deeply. Was the door so tight no smoke could get through it? I listened intently and heard no telltale crackle of flames. Perhaps Estelle hadn't set fire to the house after all. It was worth a lot of money to her. Maybe I was in quite a different sort of danger. What if nobody should think to look for me here? In the summer heat without water, how long would I last? And what about air? How long before I used up every breath of it in that small stiflingly hot room?

The sharp panic I'd been feeling became a dull ache. And then I remembered that when I had first found the nursery, I had sensed a faint draft someplace and had briefly wondered if it was what had attracted the exploring squirrel, who'd so frightened me, into entering the room. I stood very still in the silence and tried to feel it again. And finally did. Was it my imagination? No, air was coming from someplace, ever so lightly to be sure, but there was that same faint draft just the same.

Where was it from? A window badly bricked up? The floor? And I suddenly remembered something else I had noticed when I'd been there before and had forgotten because at the time it seemed to have no importance. Over toward the dresser where I had found the jeans, sneakers and wigs, there was a crack in the ceiling plaster where there had once been a leak from the roof.

I fumbled about, found a chair, took it close to the dresser, and stood on it. I put my hand to the ceiling and quickly found the crack. A slight coolness sifted down from it.

I don't know much about how houses are built, just what I've seen here and there. I did know that plaster in old houses was smoothed over narrow wooden lathing, which in turn was nailed to beams or studding. And I knew that floor planks nailed to the top side of beams—if there were any, and unless there was something terribly heavy on top of them—could be lifted loose by banging them from underneath.

I mentally pictured the outside of March House. At one end, there was a floor above the one I was on, probably servants' quarters reached by the back stairs that started down in the narrow kitchen hall. But above Grace's corner room, I remembered there was nothing but a slanting roof with a couple of dormer windows, which would indicate an attic.

For the first time I felt hope. I needed a tool of some kind. But what? I suddenly remembered something that lay almost at my feet—the old wooden hobbyhorse. It wasn't strong enough to do much damage to a solid door, but a plaster ceiling was a different story. It was well-built, not a flimsy thing of today. Its head would make a good battering ram and its rockers a kind of pick.

I lifted the horse up—it was quite heavy, but I was desperate—and, getting a good grip on it, I began to attack the ceiling. Plaster rained, as well as dust, wads of straw insulation, too, and old mouse droppings, and God only knew what else. I almost choked. And twice got vertigo and fell off the chair, which hurt. But I kept at it. Lathing splintered; I grabbed ends and pulled it down. My fingers and face stung from cuts. I fell a third time, gashing one leg. But bit by bit a sizable hole developed between what I felt were two beams.

And finally a faint light filtered down through cracks between overhead planking.

So very little light but it gave me the final desperate energy to go at the planks with what was left of my poor hobbyhorse. I slammed and battered. I thought my arms couldn't lift my ram even once more. I was crying and I think now I would have given up, except I suddenly realized that the cracks of light were much wider. I managed two more desperate smashes, there was a shriek of rusty nails, and the gray of attic day poured down on me.

I'd been lucky. The end of the planks had been nailed to one of the cross beams I'd uncovered. If I'd attacked the middle of the planks farther along, I never would have freed it. I got down off my chair, pushed the dresser under the hole, climbed up, and in a moment was head and shoulders in the attic, which was lit by two cobweb-covered dormer windows. A final effort, and I stood breathless, exhausted, and drenched with perspiration near the hole I had just made. The gash on my leg looked ugly, my fingers were in ribbons, my face and neck bruised and cut. I could taste blood on my lips.

The attic was large and cluttered with the things one always finds in old country-house attics. There were chairs, bedsteads, stacks of dusty books, trunks, dressmaker forms, an old bicycle, a bird cage, pictures, some old-fashioned skis that looked like dead trees, and a torn kite whose once-bright panels were nearly obscured beneath a thick layer of dust.

And in the shadows, away from the dormers, I saw a high-backed chair in which, for a heart-stopping instant, I thought someone was sitting, until I discovered the "someone" was only a ragged old Pierrot doll.

I went to look out one of the dormers. It had a view of the front driveway down through tree branches. Otis Cramm's big police cruiser was there, but I couldn't see Otis. He had to be skulking about somewhere. Perhaps he'd even come into the house and had heard my frantic batterings and was looking for their source. I didn't care anymore if I ran into him. I think I would have welcomed it.

I left the window. I had only to get out of the house and I'd be safe. Once I could run, I could quickly make my way across the back lawn and through the woods to Essie in her field. It wasn't far. I had only to keep myself under control and suffer the gauntlet of March House for a last time—the upstairs landing, the stairs, the dining room, the butler's pantry, and the kitchen hallway.

I started for a stairwell. *If the door at the bottom is locked,* I thought, *I'll smash it down.* There'd be something in the attic for that. But when I'd reached the foot of the steep dusty little staircase, the door creaked open easily onto the upstairs landing only a few feet away from the darkened guest room, where what seemed centuries ago I had hidden from Arthur Heston.

I stopped there a moment, my hand still on the door handle. I stood still and listened. Except for the titter of sparrows somewhere under the eaves, I heard nothing. I closed the door quietly behind me and moved away from it, feeling as though some awful presence would at any moment come out of hiding in the attic and down the little stairs after me. Simultaneously, I felt a dread of what might lie before me. Would Estelle be lurking with the missing pistol? I'd had enough.

But as I started down the main stairway I began to feel a new dread of something unknown and worse than Estelle. Don't ask me what it was. I couldn't explain it then and can't now. It was something more than awful. It was something akin to sheer horror, and I felt it had to lie beyond the foot of the main hall and the back kitchen door.

I was right. Horror did await me, and I didn't have to go as far as the dining room or the butler's pantry to find it. The horror was just out of sight where the hall narrowed before the dining room's double doors, and as I came out from under the odd-colored light filtering down from the stained glass of the cupola high above the stairwell, I almost fell over it.

The horror was Otis Cramm.

He lay on his back, arms akimbo, his mouth open in surprise and staring up at me from one eye that saw nothing and never would again.

The other eye wasn't there anymore. In its place was an ugly red-edged hole that said only too clearly how he had died.

TWENTY-SIX

There was a great deal of blood. It had spread out across the polished wood of the hall floor in a wide pool that started under Otis's head. I remember thinking how terribly red it was and how very much of it there was. And that awful empty red hole where his eye had been, with the other eye open and staring and looking so alive I expected him to speak at any moment.

I couldn't move. I could only stand there, staring, aware that I should run but unable to. A hunting magazine lay in the blood. On its cover was a photograph of a hunter aiming a rifle directly at the reader, but the hunter's face could not be seen. Blood covered it.

And then I heard a familiar voice calling me. "Margaret! Margaret!" Insistently. It sounded a great distance away.

I looked up slowly from Otis Cramm. Essie stood in the gloom of the dining room beyond. "Margaret, what on earth are you doing here?" She took in my plaster-filled hair, my bloodied face and hands. "Good God! What happened?"

I didn't reply. I couldn't. She started into the hall toward me and then saw Otis and stopped dead. Her breath drew in sharply. "Oh, no. No."

"He's dead," I said stupidly.

She didn't answer. She was staring at me wide-eyed. I remember the shock of realizing she thought I'd killed him. I heard my own voice as though from a great distance, sharp and close to breaking. "It wasn't me. It wasn't."

Her expression slowly softened. "Of course it wasn't." She looked down at Otis again. "God! How horrible! I heard a shot out in my field—at least I thought it was a shot. And then a car leaving Owen's. Very fast. So I came over and saw the back door open."

Dully, I remembered the report I'd heard in the pitch-darkness of the nursery that I'd thought was backfire from Estelle's car.

Essie skirted Otis's body and came to put a protective arm around my shoulders. "Don't look anymore, Margaret. Do you know who did it?"

I nodded. "Estelle. Estelle Perkins."

"Are you sure?"

"She locked me in the nursery." I began to cry like a child. I couldn't help it.

Essie gently steered me into the dining room. "You mustn't try to talk now, Margaret. Let's just get you out of here and patched up. We'll go home, and you can tell me everything. Then we'll decide if we should call the police or let them find him on their own. I don't want them all over you in the state you're in."

I can't remember much after that. It was almost as though someone else left March House, not me, and took the little wooded path back over the stone wall stile to Owen Fuller's. And I'm equally vague today about driving off to Pebbles in Essie's pickup. I was in a bad state of shock. I was frightened, too, but this time not of March House or even Estelle but of the police.

I hadn't taken seriously Essie's admonishment to stay away from murder, and because I hadn't, I was in serious trouble. When I unexpectedly appeared alive, Estelle would surely deny everything I said and could be counted on to come up with every kind of convincing lie at my expense to protect herself. She would probably even have an ironclad alibi for the time I would say she was at March House, with François and all her other friends to lie for her to back up her story. In spite of my minor injuries and the wrecked nursery ceiling, Estelle stood a far better chance of proving herself innocent than I. So far, Fisher had met with no problems where she was concerned, while I, if not already half suspect, was hardly in his good graces. I could expect the Homicide officer to be merciless.

I was going to need a lawyer, I could see that. A good lawyer and Essie to describe how she'd found me and the state I was in. I remember the relief I felt because I could now tell her everything about Boston and what I'd discovered there and what I suspected had happened that night long ago in the Atheneum; about Alice Webb's ending up in the anonymous frigidity of Boston Bay; about Grace murdered and sent back to Martha's Vineyard in Alice's coffin. I wouldn't have to lie to her anymore.

We arrived at Pebbles, and I sank into the deep chair Essie had pulled into the kitchen from her parlor. She busied herself at the stove making strong herbal tea and said, "Tea first, and then we'll look at all those cuts and scratches and get you cleaned up."

The tea tasted vile but magically seemed to bring me to my senses and back to reality. The world around me—Essie, her kitchen, and an ominous new summer storm hanging over the cape across Vineyard Sound— suddenly became clear, as though seen through a just-cleaned window.

Fate is a strange element in our lives that often and inexplicably changes the course of everything. I was looking out the window at the gathering storm, my mind for a moment refusing to think further about March House and what had just happened; Essie was getting out first-aid things to doctor my injuries. Then fate suddenly entered in the form of someone who had nothing whatsoever to do with the March House murders or me, and very little to do even with Essie. Fate, in our case, came in the person of Stevie Hammond, an undistinguished but clean-cut young man in the respectably laundered gray uniform that he wore when reading meters for New England Power and Light.

He drove up in a small company van, and Essie said, "Damn, there's Stevie Hammond," and hurriedly finished the thought she surely would never have expressed if she had not been momentarily distracted.

"The only thing you really have to worry about, Margaret, is whether or not Fisher thinks you went to Boston with Grace way back. Because if he gets it in his head you were there, then he's not going to believe anything you say about all the ghastly business this summer. We'll have to come up with an alibi for you. It shouldn't be hard."

Stevie Hammond rang the front doorbell. Essie called out that she was coming and went to rummage in her battered old fishing creel.

"I keep the meter locked up ever since one Halloween some kids found a way to make it add up twice as fast," she said. She pulled out a key ring and headed for the front door.

I heard her talking to Stevie Hammond. I heard the screen door slam behind her as she went outside, and I heard them both go around to the back of the house.

I heard but I didn't hear. In my mind, there was only room for what she'd said before she left the kitchen. The words echoed over and over. *The only thing you re-*

ally have to worry about, Margaret, is whether or not Fisher thinks you went to Boston with Grace. . . .

Over and over like a tolling bell of doom. So few words, so very few. *Went to Boston with Grace . . .*

But Essie didn't know Grace had gone to Boston, did she? She'd never given any sign she knew. And at the disinterment, everything she said showed she had no idea of it, and certainly not even a thought that Alice or Grace had died there.

Why had she hidden the fact that she knew?

I didn't want to hear the answer. I tried to stop thinking. But I couldn't stop. It was too late. Five years rolled back, and Grace Chadwick was being murdered by someone she knew. Someone Alice probably knew, also. Someone they both trusted. Someone strong and quick who could wear paint-stained jeans and sneakers and park a car at Owen Fuller's and have nobody think twice about it and go right on murdering when things went wrong. Someone who was desperate for money. Desperate enough to kill. A trapped person who'd discovered freedom had a high price. Somebody who could act and put on a wig to hide short dark hair, and gloves to hide garden-worn hands. And powder and rouge to disguise the weather-beaten skin of her elfin face.

Essie? No, not Essie. It couldn't be. It just couldn't.

Except Essie knew Grace had gone to Boston. Knew and had never told me.

Time and her kitchen stood still. My eyes had never left her battered old creel. As though the creel were Essie herself. It was so much her. But I didn't really see it. Not yet. In my mind, I saw something else. Something I didn't want to see, but something that was insistent and that I had to see whether I wanted to or not. I saw Estelle and myself in the darkness of the nursery. I saw Essie in the bedroom beyond, waiting. I saw Estelle come out. I saw the pistol leveled and Essie, unseen by me, kick the door shut and lock it. I saw a shocked-silent Estelle marched down the broad staircase, a hapless Otis Cramm unexpectedly emerging from the dining room.

If someone has killed four people, the fifth must be easy, especially if the killer has a gun. I saw Otis come from the dining room and stop cold with surprise in the hall and then a pistol pointed directly at his head from a foot away. Perhaps there might have been for him a split second's realization before there was nothing. Perhaps not. Otis wasn't one to think quickly. I saw the horror of the shot. I saw Otis fall.

A fast drive then. There was Estelle to be got rid of. But to where? And was Estelle alive or dead? Then, back in all innocence to release me.

Why? Why spare me? Wasn't I a threat, too?

I couldn't answer any more questions. I rebelled. Suddenly. All of me. My imagination was playing tricks. I was overwrought. I hadn't heard her right. Essie was not a murderess. There was a better explanation for everything. I'd ask her and she'd explain. All my thinking was distorted from what had happened. Had to be. I was insane to suspect her, to have the slightest idea she could in any way have even been involved. I was making up things that didn't exist. Could not exist.

My mind said all that. But my eyes were still on the old fishing creel. And on the worn hole in the battered wicker through which Essie always lost things. And my eyes finally forced me to recognize something they'd seen even as Essie left the room—a flat, square, yellow something. And next to it something else, something ugly and dark.

I rose woodenly. I didn't want to go, but I had to. I opened the creel's lid, knowing what was there. And I was right. The yellow object was the diary we had taken from the safe in the nursery. And the dark object beside it, the pistol. They lay, both of them, along with her wallet and handkerchief and comb, on a bed of fresh herbs and flowers she'd picked that morning.

I remember thinking that she hadn't even tried to hide them. But then, that was like Essie. It was like her to be utterly brazen. Or could—a last hope—she have simply taken them from Estelle?

I heard her voice outside, talking to Stevie Hammond. I opened the diary. It was for 1980, the year Grace Chadwick went to Boston. My fingers shook as I turned pages. August, September, October. All those years ago. Jumbled words, small spidery faded writing. The seventeenth of October:

Going to Boston with Alice.

And the next page, the eighteenth of October. Please let Estelle's name be there. Or Rose's.

I read:

Essie Peck in town. Will dine with us.

The words burned. I just stood there, staring, staring.

I heard a motor start up. I couldn't move. The screen door slammed. I heard Essie's footsteps.

And then Essie's voice. "Oh, dear. Oh, dear, Margaret. What have you done?"

TWENTY-SEVEN

I made no effort to stop her from taking the diary out of my hand. I couldn't move. She dropped it back into her creel with the dried herbs and flowers and the pistol and put the creel on the kitchen table.

"Sit down, Margaret." It was said with a smile, but behind the smile there was something else. Robotlike I sat in a kitchen chair. She sighed and said, "I do wish you had done as I asked and stayed away from all this. You've made everything so awkward—and just when I finally had it nearly under control, too. We're going to have to postpone our trip down the Loire—all those beautiful châteaux. For a while at least, anyway."

There was no sense in accusing or even in asking why, although the "why" was obvious. Money, or lack of it, lies behind most of life's tragedies. Besides, I was too shattered. Everything was gone: friendship, faith, self-respect, and, above all, something magical, intimately and trustingly shared.

Now I felt old and tired, devoid of any emotion.

One moment Essie was part of "Margaret and Essie," the miracle of the sky, youth on soft airborne wings, laughter and the whole wide world at our feet. The next she was a complete stranger, a monster, someone who had dug up a moldering body and insanely replaced it with a headless doll; someone who had murdered a feeble old woman, as well as Rose Perkins, Arthur Heston, Owen Fuller, and now probably would kill me, too. The horror of it overwhelmed me.

I found my voice. "What do you plan to do with me?"

She stared blankly a moment. Then she laughed, her voice filled with concern and warm caring. "Do with you? Oh, poor Margaret. Were you frightened? Were you worried I might harm you? Darling, darling Margaret, don't be frightened—not of me." She patted my arm and then said quite matter-of-factly, "Now we must plan. And quickly. When they find that ridiculous Cramm, the police will be everywhere. Likes bees after a queen. They'll look for you, of course, and talk to Heather, and we can't rely on her not to say you went to see Estelle. They'll find your car at The Rookery and Estelle's at Owen's and they'll put two and two together—that you were at March House. Am I not right? Of course I am."

I thought of Estelle. So young and changed, finally, for the better. I hadn't been wrong to trust her.

"Where is Estelle? What have you done with her?"

Essie got that expression she always wore when to answer a question would be to admit she'd done something she knew she shouldn't have. "I've locked her up temporarily, Margaret. She'll be quite safe."

The reply filled me with a fresh wave of terror. I didn't believe her. Estelle, surely, had also to be dead. And then anger suddenly began to surge through me, not so much for Estelle or for Grace or Otis or Arthur or Owen or even Rose. The ultimate crime is to extinguish another's life, but I had never been close to any one of them and in honesty I couldn't really relate to their ghastly murders. My anger was for the total betrayal I'd been subjected to, for the lie Essie was and had been, yes, but more than that it was for the sheer evil of her trying to make first Algar and then Samantha and Estelle appear guilty. She would cheerfully have seen any one of them condemned for her crimes and, where Algar was concerned, his children condemned also to a life of sorrow and misery. I suddenly hated her.

"You planned to buy the house back from Algar, didn't you?" I said.

"Except Rose ruined everything," she said, "thinking she could get it out from under my nose just when Algar was finally ready to surrender and just when after being so broke from ballooning I'd got some money together from selling my field and I planned to sell the old Lincoln, too. It's worth a gold mine these days, that old car, to some collector. She was going to take me to court, Rose said. She said her offer to give me back the property would make my exercising Grace's option to buy it back ridiculous, especially since she was only trying to keep March House in the family. Oh, yes, she'd come blubbering to me about being Grace's daughter long before that. Can you imagine? And now she was going to ask the court to declare me incompetent. Me!" Essie's expression was both indignant and incredulous. "Well," she added, "I didn't think I could handle all that, and she got what she deserved. So don't feel sorry for her, Margaret. Besides, she cost you and me all the freedom we'd ever want."

"And I suppose Arthur did, too?" I asked.

If Essie heard the bitterness in my voice, she didn't show it. She shrugged. "Arthur. Such a fool, that man. The very moment he heard what Rose was up to from a banker down here, he decided to have Grace's Boston trust buy out Algar and gave me a lot of nonsense like Rose did of keeping it in the family. He said there was some cousin someplace, but obviously what Arthur really wanted was a commission on selling the place himself when Grace was finally gone."

Essie paused a moment and looked perplexed. "I don't know why he'd never thought of it before. I'd always worried he might. Just the way I worried about Owen, forever sneaking around."

She laughed, then, as though at a pleasant joke. "I fell, can you imagine? Coming over the stile. And Grace's hat and wig came off. And when I looked up, there he was staring down at me. He'd leaned his fork against a tree."

Her eyes looked somewhere far off but came back to me. "It would have been clear sailing again, Margaret, after Owen. When things calmed down, I could have discreetly bought out Algar, still. Except you went to Boston. Oh, why did you? Now we'll still be desperate for money all the time."

I didn't answer. I could hardly speak. And when I didn't, she sighed and said, "Well, never mind. We all make mistakes. Do come now, dear. Finish your tea and let's go get our balloon ready."

"Balloon?"

"Yes, dear. We can't stay here, can we? So it's out to the barn. We'll bring the first-aid kit and patch you up once we're airborne. I've stocked up the gondola already and got it down; the sleeve, too. Did it right after the exhumation. I felt things might go wrong. There's enough in there to feed us for weeks, and plenty of water. And I've packed some warm clothes into the big blue duffel bag. That's out there, too."

I knew then that she was mad, completely so, that there was a madness there beyond even the awful insanity of murder. Perhaps indeed the murders she'd committed had increased a thousandfold an insanity that had lurked for years but had only manifested itself for the first time at the Atheneum in Boston.

I glanced out the window. The dark line of thunderheads I'd seen over the cape were nearer now. They were bearing down from the north, the harbinger of the same sort of vicious cold-front squall line that had cut short the children's sailing class in the morning. If the winds didn't immediately tear a balloon to pieces, they would take it due south far over the Atlantic.

Consternation must have shown in my face, for Essie laughed and patted my arm again. "Don't worry, Margaret. We'll make it. The greatest flights are often the ones never expected to be successful. We'll run before it and then it will be Europe—or, if the winds are capricious, Ireland or North Africa. It makes no difference which, Margaret. We'll be free."

"I'm not going," I said.

"Not going? Oh, but you must, Margaret. I can't do it all alone, you know that. And besides, it wouldn't be the same without you. So come along. Don't let's argue. We haven't time."

"I'm not going up," I repeated. "Nor are you!"

She stared at me a moment. Something swept across her face then, something so terrifying I shrank back in my chair. There was a look in her eyes that I knew had to be the look Arthur Heston must have seen just before she cranked the window of the old Lincoln shut on his neck. Or the look Owen saw before the cold prongs of the pitchfork seared through his stomach. It was a look of insane and pitiless rage. One of Essie's garden-worn hands shot into her fishing creel and came back out with the pistol.

"Don't be silly. Of course you're coming. Now we must hurry!"

You don't argue with a gun. Not with one that has just killed a man. Not with any gun. If the tense finger on the trigger and the obscene dark round hole of the barrel pointing directly into your face wouldn't stop you from arguing, the mental state of the person holding it would.

I found myself walking to the barn.

Essie had indeed been at work. The big wicker gondola was on its side at the edge of the beach across the short stretch of grass between the beach and the barn itself. The propane tanks were locked into place. The huge nylon sleeve lay folded next to it and needed only to be unfolded along the beach.

"Start unfolding, Margaret, while I hook up the gondola."

Her mood had switched with the speed madness makes possible. From rage to good cheer. She was like the old Essie, and we could have been preparing for last year's flight up Pennsylvania's Brandywine Valley.

I numbly started to roll the big green-yellow-and-blue sleeve out along the beach in the direction of the *Janet B*.

"Margaret!"

I looked up. Essie was smiling. "You won't be foolish and try to run off, will you?"

I didn't answer. Essie's fishing creel was slung over her shoulder, its top hanging open. I was fifty feet away, but I didn't have the nerve to find out how good a shot she was. Privet, bay, and blueberry bushes crowded her property on all sides. There were only two exits, Nashaquitsa Pond or the narrow dirt driveway coming in from South Road. Caught in either, I'd be trapped. I glanced at the sky to the north. It was now darker than ever. Here and there forks of lightning flashed. The air had become deathly still as it does before a storm, and the birds had stopped singing. I tried not to think of what it would be like to be up in it in a balloon. I kept unrolling the sleeve.

"That's good. Come back."

I was down by the *Janet B* now. The incoming tide moaned softly through the after hull. I flipped over a last fold of nylon and desperately looked about for something sharp, perhaps a broken shell, with which to slash a hole in the nylon so it wouldn't inflate. I saw nothing.

Essie called again. She had hooked the big stainless-steel choke ring at the bottom of the sleeve to the two curved steel uprights rising from within the gondola framework. "Come back!" she shouted.

I felt a faint rustle of wind from the water, then stillness again. I went back.

"Essie, we can't. Look out there!"

She paid no attention; she had lit the hot-air burners and they roared. "Won't they be surprised to see a balloon taking off from here!" she cried. There was glee in her voice, a child defying all the rules.

Hot air rushed down the sleeve. In seconds it exploded into a huge beach-length sausage. Another long burst and the sleeve stirred, scraping pebbles. Essie had snubbed the mooring rope of the gondola to an iron ring in an old granite hitching post, and the gondola dragged forward slightly, then was held fast. She heaved the big blue duffel bag into it and ordered me to follow. "Hurry, Margaret, hurry."

I didn't move. I just stood staring at the gondola. What was happening couldn't be happening. I was caught in a nightmare that was getting worse and worse, and there seemed to be no way out. I would step into the gondola, and the balloon would fill. Essie would cast off and we would rise gently up into the gathering storm.

"Margaret!" Her voice was sharp, a whip.

I slowly faced her. She again wore the distorted expression of total madness. Who was this? What terrible creature? This was not the Essie I knew, the gentle, laughing, herb-collecting Essie who so rapturously had one day long ago climbed over the old stone wall and released the little blue butterfly and cried out, "There you are, my darling. Freedom." Not the Essie who, wide-eyed like a child, had looked into the limitless blue sky at the magic of the balloon hanging there and said, "Oh, Margaret, look, look. Do look."

I still didn't move, but when the pistol was pointed

directly at me once more, I obeyed and found myself in the gondola with Essie beside me. She was laughing happily now. "I packed some cold Rhine wine, Margaret. It's in the cooler."

There was another rustle of wind; then the partially inflated sleeve lifted higher.

"Hold tight, Margaret." The burners roared.

"Essie, no!"

"Hold tight!"

The sleeve billowed and slowly and majestically rose from the beach all the way to vertical. The gondola tugged at its mooring line.

"Cast off!" Essie cried. "Hurry!" And when I didn't move, couldn't, she unsnubbed the mooring line herself. Another roar from the burners, and the gondola jerked up. We were airborne.

"We're free, Margaret! Free!" She hugged my shoulders.

The burners roared again. We rose. I looked desperately at the hot-air release, a lanyard leading to an upper-sleeve panel. If pulled, it would spill hot air and cause the balloon to descend. Essie saw my look and smiled. But not with her eyes. In her eyes I saw again that now-familiar madness. I sank down onto the gondola seat, defeated.

What happened then was something I could have predicted if I had not been too terrified to think. The great black squall line bearing down from the north had nearly reached Menemsha, a mile away. Thunderheads draw up air in front of them like giant vacuum cleaners, and a slowly rising wind was momentarily flowing toward the clouds. Instead of being forced south over the narrow neck of land between us and the Atlantic and then out to sea, we began to move over Nashaquitsa Pond into the storm itself.

We were still low over the water, perhaps twenty

or thirty feet. "We need to get up!" cried Essie. "Out from under. So the wind will take us south."

Then many things happened. And very quickly.

She turned her back on me for a moment to activate the burners once more and send the balloon rapidly skyward, and I, looking down desperately, saw the two vehicles coming out of the driveway to Pebbles and pulling up before her little saltbox house. One was my own station wagon, the other a police car. Today, I can only remember thinking that help had come too late.

I stood up and cried out; I can't remember what. Essie turned, and the pistol snapped out of her creel. She must have guessed what I was going to do. I didn't think; I just flipped backward out of the gondola. Both her shots missed.

Forty feet is a long drop, and shallow water isn't the best thing in the world to land in unless you land in it correctly. I had neither time nor the training to do anything but fall free. I hit where it was only four feet deep and smashed down into the sandy bottom hard enough to dislocate my shoulder and break my collarbone, my right arm, and a couple of ribs.

I half stood, half floated, and excruciating pain left me breathless. I went under, came up again, and managed to stand, dimly aware of a swimmer thrashing toward me. I was starting to collapse again, probably to drown, when I was suddenly supported by strong arms.

"You're okay, Margaret, I've got you."

It was Peter.

Lieutenant Fisher was only a yard behind him, fully dressed and looking like a drowned rat. They helped me to shore and then both looked skyward toward the storm.

"She'll be in it in a minute!" Peter cried.

In spite of my pain, I looked, too. The balloon had risen to several hundred feet, and now, a half mile off, was moving rapidly toward the black mass of clouds, its colors brilliant in contrast. I could see Essie in the gondola, a tiny dark figure.

I heard my voice. "Essie. Oh, God, Essie."

Peter tried to lead me away. I held back. "She had a gun. She made me go with her." I was crying.

We waited, with Peter holding me up. The balloon got smaller and smaller very quickly, and then suddenly we couldn't see it anymore, only ugly boiling clouds where it had been, clouds and lightning.

We began to feel the first of the rain.

"Where is Estelle Perkins?" Fisher demanded. He'd suddenly become the cop again. "Do you know?"

"We found her car at Owen's," Peter explained, "after Heather sent me to her house."

I shook my head. I didn't know.

Someone shouted from Essie's house. A state trooper. "She's not here, Lieutenant."

"Think!" Fisher said to me. "Think. She's not at Fuller's. She's got to be here someplace."

I shook my head again. I couldn't think. She could be anywhere.

We were standing by the *Janet B*, and the tidal water moaned in its after hull. Essie had said she'd locked Estelle up; I remembered that. I turned to stare at the darkly ominous old hulk, remembering Essie up on deck cleaning and repairing lobster traps and nodding sternward. "It floods back there every high tide," she'd said. "Anything left behind, the fishes eat."

Fisher said, "In there?"

I couldn't answer.

But Fisher moved then, and with surprising agility. The trooper had come out of the house, and Fisher took a flashlight from him and was up on the *Janet B* in an instant looking into the deckhouse first, then down into the forward hatch. The flashlight probed, he let the hatch cover drop back, went along the rotting deck to the rear hatch, and pulled it open.

He didn't have to use his flashlight. The tidal water had risen nearly to the hatch rim, and they had floated to the surface, face up. Estelle Perkins with a bullet in her chest, but alive and still half conscious. The other was a rotting corpse, long dead. Grace Chadwick.

I was glad I saw neither.

EPILOGUE

Occasionally, I am obliged to drive down Tea Lane past March House. There is a certain sadness in an abandoned house, its driveway, lawns, and flower beds grown up to weeds and brush, its shutters sagging, and its paint beginning to peel.

But some houses succumb to a fate that to me is sadder still. A once-proud family home becomes a country inn or a roadhouse, its walls harboring not the permanent love and care of a single line of people, but simply the fleeting pleasure of endless transients who care for it only briefly and then forget, leaving it to an equally forgotten past.

March House, now called The Inn on Tea Lane—a slightly too precious name for me—is today just such a place, its bedrooms occupied from June through September by strangers, its veranda and front parlor, now dining areas, packed of an evening with visitors from Edgartown and Vineyard Haven come up-island to enjoy its overpriced seafood, blissfully unaware of the horror that occurred there.

Algar Mikele and his family never moved into the old place. Heather refused to live in it, and I don't blame her. "I don't think I could ever look at the barn, let alone walk into it," she said, "without thinking of Arthur Heston. Or, my God, that pond and Rose."

Algar sold out to a syndicate from New York and he and Heather bought a smaller and far more sensible place in West Tisbury. Their money worries came to an end, and Algar transferred all the passion he'd had for March House to the new place.

I spent ten days in the hospital, and I'd hardly been there twenty-four hours when Algar reappeared, having hidden all the time, Heather tearfully confessed, in the attic of my own house on Water Street. I was too exhausted to be seriously angry with her. In fact, I even found humor in the extraordinary deception, and Algar's sincere apology for it helped. Besides, I wasn't the only one who'd been made to look foolish. Lieutenant Fisher, too, suffered that indignity, and, I'm certain, given his policeman's patronizing sense of self-importance, far more than I.

It took time for me to recover from my misadventures. My physical injuries healed quickly enough, although I spent the remainder of the summer with my arm in a cast and my neck in a collar. Emotionally, however, I was absolutely shattered. It wasn't just Essie's betrayal, it was the dream and hope she had smashed with it.

No one likes to grow old. Spring and summer give way very reluctantly to autumn, and I think this especially true where we women are concerned. Essie and ballooning meant youth to me. And I clung to my youth more than most perhaps, accepting my real age in one way by taking my grandchildren every summer, refusing to acknowledge it in another by rejecting out of hand the title of grandmother and deluding myself that I was the children's mother instead. I rode two horses.

Peter, wise for his years, had seen it all in me. "Margaret," he'd said, "why do you have such an age complex? . . . Why not just accept it?" Oh, the cruel realism of those still young.

Lying in my hospital bed, I also had to face the ridiculousness of having a crush on a man less than half my age. But then, fortunately something quite wonderful occurred. After I'd returned home to convalesce, Peter came to see me less and less, and I finally learned he'd fallen in love with Estelle Perkins, and she with him. So much for summer fantasies. But I still have the three lovely shells he gave me on the beach by the Chappaquiddick ferry slip.

I think what helped me recover more than anything was the unexpected kindness and friendship of Samantha Sanderson, who insisted I come to work for the theater in the evenings and who managed to keep me so busy, despite my injuries, right into autumn that I really didn't have time for self-pity.

I have Samantha, too, and Glenn Rothenberg, to thank for what I've always considered the nicest of Christmas presents that year. They came to spend a week with me in New York—Glenn to attend a medical conference, Samantha to take in the latest developments in off-Broadway theater.

Glenn brought one of the senior doctors at University Hospital to dinner, a brain specialist and an extraordinarily brilliant and worldly man of slightly more than sixty who at that point in his life, believe it or not, was single. The next day Samantha reported that he had been completely taken with me.

I must admit I found him seductively attractive in turn. But how much so was only put to test a few weeks later when, after a dinner I gave and when other guests had gone, he produced some photographs of himself taken several years previously in Colorado. He had shot rapids on the Colorado River, had camped out in the mountains, and, of all things, had gone ballooning.

"Have you ever done it?" he asked. "It's the most exhilarating thing ever."

I admitted I had been up once or twice. Clearly, neither Samantha nor Glenn had told him.

"Would you care to try it again with me? I'm going down to a balloon rally in Virginia next weekend."

He waited. I can picture him right now, his gray hair, his sun-bronzed face, his blue, blue eyes, oh, yes. But above all I can picture the eager look he wore of reaching out to embrace life, the wonderful youthful enthusiasm for something new to be discovered.

I studied him for a moment. If I said yes, I knew I might perhaps be committing myself to something more than just ballooning. I had a fleeting memory of a little azure-blue butterfly released into a clear warm summer sky, and then the memory was gone.

"Yes," I said. "Why not? I think I'd like that very much."